Fiction

# A Cottage Called Tranquillity

Bernie Danaher

UPLit✶Press

Copyright © 2025 by Bernie Danaher

All rights reserved.

No portion of this book may be reproduced in any form without written permission from the publisher or author, except as permitted by U.K. copyright law.

# Acknowledgements

Grateful thanks to all the friends and family who have supported and encouraged me down the years. I love you!

This book is dedicated to all the women who are worth more than they believe.

# Chapter 1

The coffee spoons started it.

The old set of coffee spoons that had been in the loft for years – small, innocuous, forgotten, an unlikely landmine awaiting an unwary foot.

Liam and I were in the loft, staring around at the chaos. As we were getting insulation fitted, a clear-out had to happen. *Finally.* Or at least, that was the idea.

Liam had always been a dreadful hoarder. Back home in Donegal, our house had been too small for him to hang on to much stuff, but the move to a bigger one in Dublin had given him his chance. He never threw away anything he thought might come in useful, even utterly useless things.

I used to argue, but it wasn't worth the effort. "It can go in the loft, just in case," was always his response, so "it" always did. As a result, the loft looked like the burial place of a cut-price Egyptian pharaoh, not so much 'King Tut' as 'King Tat'; one who'd gone to meet the gods surrounded by unused multi-purpose blenders, racing car sets that didn't work, and tins containing tubes of glue that had solidified years ago.

Now, stomping around and muttering at the waste of his time, he bumped into a pile of boxes. They went tumbling.

He scowled down at them, swore, and aimed a kick. Something shot across the floor towards me, chinking.

I had to blink at it for a moment before the guilty memory surfaced. An antique shop window, with the light glinting on six silver coffee spoons with cloisonné-inlaid handles, nestled on scarlet satin.

Liam had slipped into the betting shop next door, leaving me unsupervised for a few moments. I'd had some birthday money that Mammy had sent me tucked into my handbag so I could make the furtive, impulsive purchase. The box had to go in there afterwards too, because I knew he'd take the piss out of them – and out of me for buying them.

Over time, I'd become an expert in such small and shameful deceits.

What, in the name of all that's holy, had I ever bought *coffee spoons* for?

Beautiful, like dreams... and as useless.

I used to love poetry. When I was younger, I'd even tried to write some, though I'd have hated to read any of it now. *Proper* poetry, though, written by people who had the gift – that was the stuff of magic. Now I was hit by the appalling realisation that just like that chap in Eliot's poem, I too had doled out my life using coffee spoons.

And where had it got me?

"Are you going to stand there all day?" Liam glared at me. "You're the one that was forever wanting the place cleared out, so let's get on with it. – What's that you got there, anyway?"

"Coffee spoons." With some reluctance, I lifted the case and showed him.

He looked at them with disdain. "They're teaspoons, you eejit. Coffee spoons are smaller. Mammy had a set with the Pope's coat of arms on them. They were half the size of those things.

"Jeez, and you with the education in that posh school! Pity it didn't teach you any common sense. Put them away and make yourself useful for once!"

He moved away, bending so as not to hit his head against the joists. At that moment, I'd have loved to see him bash into one of them and drop dead.

Teaspoons, then. Not coffee. The old fella in the shop all those years ago cannily hadn't contradicted me when I said what they were; he knew an eejit when he saw one.

I silently placed the case to one side, closed on six broken illusions. Something else had been broken too, though I wasn't yet sure what. Somewhere within me there had been a fundamental change.

"Get down the ladder and I'll pass the stuff down to you." Liam picked up one of the bigger boxes. He could carry it easily, having shoulders on him like a bull, but I hoped the tape holding it shut wouldn't give way. That certainly wouldn't improve his temper.

Still. Not being in the same room as him would suit me fine. I nodded and said I'd fetch the bin up, in case we needed it.

Things went well for about ten minutes, while I carried out a stealthy diversion into the dustbin of King Tat's more ridiculous burial goods. The tin of glue tubes went into the bin, and so did – without Liam seeing – a set of headrests from our last-car-but-four. I hated them with a passion, as they'd always reminded me how powerless I was to get rid of *any* of the junk. Then, just as a box of tatty and long-unused Christmas decorations was about to follow them, Liam glanced down through the trapdoor.

"Don't go throwing things out!" he snapped. "Put them in Fergal's room for now. We'll find somewhere for them later."

I could think of somewhere else to put them, but Father Christmas definitely wouldn't have approved. Besides, there'd have been some explaining to do at the hospital. So, I sighed and obeyed like a good little wife, gloomily restoring the disputed items to the rest of the junk. After all, our youngest son was unlikely to want his bedroom again. If Liam wanted it turned into a store for his treasure trove of trash, it wasn't my place to argue about it.

There wasn't a lot it *was* my place to argue about, come to that.

Wondering if there was space in one of the wardrobes to hide any of it, I glanced into the master bedroom. Very apt, that description was. You certainly couldn't describe it as the 'equal' bedroom. My husband took his role as head of the household seriously.

Too much so altogether, if you asked me.

There was a full-length mirror immediately opposite the door, ready to mock me every time I came in. I never looked at my reflection if I could help it, so I got only a glimpse of a tallish, rather overweight woman with long dark hair bound up in a single tight plait.

Someone had said once, long ago, that I had beautiful eyes. Liam had immediately quipped, "Nice eyes, shame about the arse," but that was the sort of thing Liam always said.

The rest of the bedroom wall wasn't much of an improvement. In pride of place, directly opposite the bed, was a framed print saying the marriage of Liam and Frances McEnally had received the Pope's official blessing – though I wasn't sure how that was supposed to improve it. I suspected that hanging where it was it reminded my traditionalist husband of the Church's disapproval of sex; if so, it would explain a lot. His mammy had given us the print for a wedding gift, so I couldn't hide it away in a spare room, however much I wanted to.

'Frances McEnally'. Not a name I'd been keen on, but I hadn't known till long after the wedding that I could have legally kept my maiden name of McKenna if I'd insisted on it. Even if I'd known then, though, I wouldn't have had the nerve. The whole tribe of McEnallys would have descended on me asking why their name wasn't good enough, and there were so many of them you could hardly throw a stone in our town without hitting one.

Bags of outgrown children's clothing came next. Liam had said they'd come in useful for when the boys had children of their own. *No way* would Deirdre or Mairead dress their kids in cast-offs, so I put the bags next to the bin.

"Those can go into Fergal's room too," came the voice from On High.

"'Speak, Lord, thy servant listeneth'," I muttered, dipping into the Old Testament.

"What?"

"Nothing. – Are you *sure* there's any point in hanging on to them?"

"Of course! They're too good to throw out, and we paid bloody good money for them. The grandkids'll be glad of them, someday."

*"All-Holy God."* That was as close as I came to prayer nowadays, except when I went to church of course, but I mumbled it as I carried the bags into their new permanent home. The way things were going, if Fergal ever came home he'd have to sleep in the loft.

Fergal's bedroom, the boxroom. When we first moved in, I'd wondered about using it as a studio – I was a keen amateur artist and had been in the last year of an art degree when I met Liam. The idea of the studio came back to me again when Fergal announced he was moving out, but the idea of what my husband would say put me off.

He'd never cared for my work. The first time I'd shown him one of my fantasy figures, he'd told me he didn't like women to be painting pictures that were 'hardly decent', and said I ought to stick to landscapes. I'd been thinking about asking him to pose for me, as his blond blue-eyed good looks put me in mind of a Viking, but I abandoned that idea on the spot.

After we were married, I discovered his dreadfully old-fashioned notions of what women should and shouldn't do extended to the home and the marriage bed, but by that time, as we were both church-going Catholics, it was too late for me to do anything. For the sake of peace, I soon stopped painting – I wanted my marriage to be an ordinary one like Mammy and Daddy's, not a yelling match like the O'Gradys' up the street. Looking back, it was a big mistake. It had shown him I wasn't prepared to stand up to him, even on things that mattered to me.

Books were next to come down from the loft. Four big, heavy boxes of them, all his, brought up here twenty-odd years ago and never touched since. I'd asked a few times if we could give them to a charity shop, but he said he might want to read them again someday and, of course, I couldn't prove he wouldn't. Now, I didn't bother asking. Struggling to cope with the weight of them, I just tottered into the boxroom and dumped them in their new home.

The next old, dusty box was just about held together with age-yellowed sticky tape. While Liam stomped about and grumbled upstairs, I unfolded the flaps and peeped inside. The ones on top were christening presents for the children, all utterly impractical, and some just plain hideous. They'd have gone into the bin too, if I'd had any choice.

Curiosity drove me to delve deeper. Pity save us, wedding presents, many as useless and ugly as the christening ones. A pair of balloon-shaped brandy glasses and a silver-plated after-dinner mints holder, for God's sake – who in their right mind could have thought they were appropriate? The glasses still gleamed in the presentation packaging, but the mints holder, badly tarnished, was looking very sorry for itself. I remembered thinking as we unwrapped it that it was probably someone else's stupid wedding present, held on to until the opportunity presented itself to pass it on to someone you didn't actually like very much.

Things tarnish, over thirty-four years. And not just silverware.

It hadn't been so bad at first. Even now I wanted to believe if I'd got to know Liam properly when we were courting, I'd have had the sense to back out; but back then, you weren't supposed to have sex before marriage, which ruled out getting to know that aspect of anybody. The stranglehold the Catholic Church still held even then ensured that contraception was next to impossible to get hold of if you weren't married.

Besides, I'd been worried about being left on the shelf. As I'd no opinion of my looks, I'd been glad to find any man paying me attention, and Liam's handsomeness and air of overwhelming self-confidence were almost irresistible. He said firmly that we'd be happy, and why shouldn't we be?

In the early years of the marriage, I was busy learning to be a wife and then a mother and having all the responsibility for a house and family of my own. It took a while before I realised what I'd got wasn't what I'd been hoping for.

We both tried. As staunch Catholics, and soon with a young family to think of, we were stuck with each other. But there's only so long you can go on before the reality shows through, and the reality was that we were totally incompatible. I couldn't give him what he wanted from a wife, and I don't think he ever even wondered what *I* wanted from a husband. With my lack of enthusiasm for playing the part of the domesticated 'little woman', I turned out to be an inadequate replacement for his mother. On the other hand, lacking any sort of romantic imagination, he turned out to be a poor substitute for Roger Moore. So for both of us, the realisation came too late. Resentment soon turned to dull despair on my part and sullen frustration and ill-feeling on his. We put up with the marriage and each other because we had to (his family wouldn't hear of us separating, especially since there were children involved), and would doubtless keep on doing so till death put one of us out of the other's misery.

*Brandy and after-dinner mints, my arse.* I put the stupid thing back in the box, carried the whole thing into Fergal's room and dumped it with the rest of the rubbish.

"Where the feck are you? I'm breaking my back holding this thing up!"

"I'm coming." *Which is more'n she ever does when you're doing your horizontal jogging.*

The second part of this observation, fortunately inaudible to anyone but me, came from the naughty side of me, the side that I thought of as The Tart. She was a wispy, undernourished creature who should have died of neglect decades ago but had somehow clung defiantly on to life and occasionally piped up from her dungeon. She was imprisoned there and perpetually squashed by her opposite number, Saint Frances, an oppressive monument to righteousness that was the voice of my conscience, honed to a razor edge and utter intolerance by an education in a Convent School where the nuns deemed it their life's work to prepare their pupils for higher education followed by lower servitude to whatever man eventually deigned to take them on.

Oh well. At least he'd be away at the football this afternoon, and I'd have some peace.

# A COTTAGE CALLED TRANQUILLITY

'Peace' was an appealing prospect, but His Majesty gave me my instructions before he set off to Croke Park. I wasn't to feck about listening to that 'bloody music' of mine while he was gone. He wanted the house clean for that afternoon.

So, he'd be bringing his mates home after the match, and wanted them to see his house – and wife – were in proper order.

Exactly what kind of order he thought the place was in already, I didn't know. I always kept it spotless. Even more so since I'd lost my little job the previous week and had nothing much else to do now than dust the top of the blinds and hoover under the beds. Sooner or later, I'd start looking for another employer, but right now I was experiencing full-time, forced domesticity in all its utter desolation.

Defiant for once, as soon as he'd gone I switched my CD player on and turned it up loud. Pachelbel's *Canon in D Major*, wistful and haunting, and so lovely that before long my eyes stung. I turned it off. The contrast between the visions it conjured up and reality was unbearable.

How in the world had it come to this?

I'd had dreams, ambitions, possibilities – how had I arrived here? Had there been some moment I should have seized, and hadn't?

*Is this really all there is?*

I sighed. But I had work to do, and fretting wouldn't help.

I went into the kitchen and did the washing up. Liam didn't like crockery being left out to dry, so when I finished I picked up a tea towel – and for a dizzy moment of rebellion, put it down again.

I looked at the wet breakfast things, hating them. Then I dried them, putting them away tidily. *Check.*

The washing was already on the line outside. *Check.* Hopefully, it would dry by midday and I'd get the ironing done before the match ended. *Pending.*

I couldn't remember the last time I'd had the house to myself for any length of time. Though our two older sons Ciarán and Brendan had moved out some time ago, the youngest, Fergal, was always having friends around in the evenings and weekends, making the place noisy; while if he wasn't at work or the football, Liam was a fixture in the armchair in front of the television. True, for the past week there should have been days when I could enjoy the quiet, but the remaining chick was in the throes of moving out of the nest to live with his girlfriend and had the place turned upside down. It still seemed to reverberate with the echoes of furniture thudding on every step of the stairs as he, Brendan and Liam brought it down to the van, and the arguments over who actually owned the X Box that had sat forgotten in a corner since Noah was a lad.

Now, bewildered by both the silence and the sense of freedom, I made myself a cup of coffee and took it into the lounge, where I sat down and sipped at it. In its corner, the television sat sulking. Perhaps we were equally unsettled by Liam's absence.

I blamed that bloody television for the state of my marriage. Liam was so fixated on it that if I dropped dead, the only way he'd notice would be if I fell on the remote control and changed the channel. It wasn't my rival. It had won the battle for his affections decades ago.

I stared at the blank screen. Satisfying images of violence crossed my mind. *You've got no one to protect you, have you? You're all alone. All these years you've been all-powerful: the Square-Eyed God. Now it's just you and me, and thirty-four years' worth of grudges.*

*Be afraid. Be very afraid.*

I wouldn't, of course. The television knew that. It sneered at me in silence. It only had to wait. Liam would be back, and when he returned, it would take over our lives again; for him, it wasn't so much a medium of entertainment as a life-support system. He was easily bored, but creativity was beyond him and despite the boxes of books upstairs, he disliked reading. The television provided him with endless, easy satisfaction.

It could truthfully be said that at least I knew where he was of an evening. The problem was – well, that *was* the problem. Most evenings in our house featured a diet of films featuring killing and screaming, along with documentaries explaining how marvellous various tanks and guns were at dealing out death. He varied things by watching programmes about aeroplane accidents. Porn would have been bad enough, but his fixation with suffering and death drove me up the wall.

He and Fergal often used to play war games on Fergal's PlayStation, when both of them sat grunting and gloating over their 'kills', high-fiving each other when they achieved some bigger-than-usual massacre. At least I'd be spared that now Fergal had gone to live with his girlfriend, though at a guess they'd get back to it at family gatherings. I could see some bright spark suggesting turning it into an all-day tournament, while the womenfolk congregated in the kitchen to produce meals and snacks on demand and talk about babies and housework. Certainly that was all the other women in his family seemed to be interested in. There were times when I wondered whether a couple of them actually realised the century had turned.

Still, at least I'd a husband who didn't go out chasing other women.

He didn't chase me much either. Hadn't for a long time. Maybe after thirty-four years he was bored. Occasionally I'd wondered whether there might actually be another woman, but though I couldn't rule it out, on the whole I thought it unlikely; that kind of deceit takes effort and ingenuity to sustain. I'd heard him grunt approvingly once when one of his mates referred to the tedium of 'parking your car in the same garage for years on end', though presumably nobody ever wondered how the garage felt about having to open up for the same car. I thought I'd have known if he'd found someone else, but I couldn't be sure. We'd drifted so far apart, I could easily have missed the signs.

If the truth be told, I no longer really wanted him to chase me. I liked to think I still had a functioning libido, but an evening of he-man movies and disaster documentaries was anything but my idea of foreplay. Mentioning this would just have led to The Resentful Silence, though, so when it happened, I just shut up and put up.

The lounge carpet was spotless, but I vacuumed it again anyway, in case Liam saw something I hadn't. Because the job was such a mindless one, my mind wandered again.

Was this *it?*

What a shite of a life I'd have to look back on from my deathbed.

'For better or for worse.' No getting past that.

Carpet, clean. *Check.*

Getting low on furniture polish. Make a note on the reminder board in the kitchen. *Check.*

Polishing the furniture was no better at occupying my thoughts than cleaning the carpet had been. Defiantly I refused to clean the television at first, but my nerve broke – civilisation would have come to an end if Liam had spotted a fleck of dust on the Square-Eyed God. The urge to use spray paint on the screen instead of polish was almost irresistible; there was a can at the back of the pantry. I could imagine WORSHIP ME in scarlet, scrawled dripping across the black screen...

But I couldn't do it. Treating the Household God like that would be a blasphemy to end all blasphemies. Instead, I chanted a sarcastic "Accept, O Almighty One, the service offered to thee by thy unworthy and unwilling handmaid," as I polished the screen. *Check.* And *Uncheck,* as regards the spray paint.

The front room – hardly used, except when we had visitors – would only need a general dusting and a scoot around with the vacuum. I was just about to start when I heard the front door opening.

I wasn't expecting anyone, so I craned around into the hall to see Liam back, and behind him was our second son, Brendan, with a face on him like a smacked arse.

My vision of an afternoon's peace shattered like glass.

This was *trouble.*

# Chapter 2

In my heart of hearts, I'd been expecting problems with Brendan sooner or later. A spat between him and his wife Mairead at a recent family gathering had spelled discord. It hadn't altogether surprised me, because he'd picked up his daddy's attitude to women, as well as his habit of thinking wives were there to be talked down to. I'd always put up with it because of 'for better, for worse'– reinforced with the dread of hell-fire, as threatened regularly from the pulpit in my impressionable youth – but the Church's influence had collapsed with all the scandals. Pews that used to be crowded on a Sunday morning stood half-empty now, and the young people in particular saw no point in going, other than to weddings and funerals.

Mairead was one of these. Lasses these days had a lot more respect for themselves and a lot less for the inviolability of the marriage vows. I'd always suspected she would stand for so much and no more.

"Stupid cow!" he exploded almost before he was through the door. "Hasn't she walked out of the fecking house? Over nothing!"

I couldn't help feeling that, far from being stupid, walking out on my son was the first sensible thing Mairead had done since she'd been mad enough to marry him. Though I still saw divorce as a tragedy for all concerned, I thought this one was about the only thing that would shock Brendan out of his belief that he could be as unpleasant as he liked to anyone and suffer no consequences.

The only thing that bothered me was their daughter, Aoife, who'd turned six just over a fortnight ago. Where was she in all this?

"I'm sure the two of you can work it out." Trying to calm the situation, I offered a helpless lie. Then I suggested that perhaps it'd be best for both he and Mairead to have a little time out and cool down.

He stared at me. That was another little habit of his daddy's he'd picked up: looking at me like I was the idiot some village must be missing. "Well, *I* think it'd be best for her to remember she's got a family and a house to look after. Soon as she got that job in Sullivan's, she started getting ideas, and now she's got promoted she thinks she's something else altogether. They want her to sit fecking exams to help her get on even further!" His voice rose as his sense of grievance gathered strength. "She's hardly in the bloody house as it is, now she wants to spend half the day studying shite for them!"

As a matter of fact, Mairead and I talked sometimes on the phone. So I knew she was struggling to cope with the bills, even

# A COTTAGE CALLED TRANQUILLITY

with her job, and her mammy looking after Aoife and taking the child back and forth to nursery and school. When I was working too I'd slipped her a few euro now and again on the quiet to help out, though of course that was over now until I could find somewhere else. She saw the promotion as a lifesaver. But I couldn't say that without betraying her confidence, so I could only conclude Brendan either didn't know what the financial situation was, or resented his wife's step up in the world. It could be either or both – she was increasingly finding it hard to discuss things with him.

However, Bren wanted to be convinced he was in the right and Mairead was in the wrong, so Liam got out the beers and obliged him.

My husband had little time for Ciarán, our eldest, who took after me both in looks and temperament. He got on better with Fergal, the youngest, but he and Brendan not only resembled one another but were the lights of each other's lives – one would never forgive a wrong done against the other. A wet afternoon and evening followed, at the end of which Brendan wove his way out to the taxi I'd called and paid for. I hoped his wife would have the sense to stay at her mother's house and not answer the doorbell if it rang.

By the time Liam and I went to bed, I was very nervous.

I was used to looking out for his moods, and on days like these I monitored him like a seismometer on the San Andreas Fault.

The pints he'd sunk in sympathy with Brendan didn't help, though I'd made sure to serve up an excellent dinner, hoping to sweeten his temper. I hadn't been expecting to feed three, so I gave Brendan mine and said I'd eaten earlier. It was accurate enough, as I'd stealthily gulped down a Pot Noodle while I was cooking.

My husband's every breath as we got into bed told me he was set on a row. I knew from long and bitter experience that I couldn't win. If I kept quiet, I was being sullen. If I argued, I was being provocative. If I meekly agreed with him, I was being sarcastic. He'd have noticed I hadn't joined in the damning of Mairead, guessed I sympathised with her, and added that to the long list of my failings.

I preferred to say nothing at times like this, but this always infuriated Liam, who wanted me to admit I was in the wrong.

There was dead quiet for perhaps two minutes after I switched the light off. I cautiously settled down, hoping I might have misread the signs.

I hadn't.

"Will you tell me why you'd not a word to say to your own son tonight?" The words came flying at me like stones, and my heart sank again.

"I said my piece when he came in," I replied, keeping my voice level, while in the back of my mind, the words *Pity it didn't teach you any common sense* repeated themselves endlessly. "I think he already knows what I think."

"And how *do* you feel about it, eh?"

My only hope of a peaceful night was to say Mairead was completely in the wrong. A few decades ago, Brendan could have summoned the parish priest to tell her to respect and obey her husband. Those days were long over, thank God, but I suspected Liam looked back on them as a golden age.

I meant to say what he wanted me to say. There was no sense in arguing, and my suggestion that both of them take time out and think it over clearly hadn't been outraged enough, so there was no point in repeating it. I was tired, and I hadn't the energy. I was used to caving in, just to keep the peace and get some sleep.

Once I'd submitted, Liam usually left it at that. However, in my mind the despised coffee spoons glinted for a moment, and the words *Pity it didn't teach you any common sense* suddenly twisted about and fell out of my mouth, too quickly and too loudly for me to stop them. "If she'd any common sense, she'd have done it years ago."

That did it. I hadn't just handed him the gun, I'd loaded it with bullets and taken the safety catch off.

"For the love of God, they're both as miserable as sin!" I added desperately, into the now electric silence. "He wants a domestic servant, and she wants a career. It doesn't mean either of them is wrong, it just means they want different things out of life. If they can't find any middle ground, isn't it better if they stop making each other unhappy?"

Liam had never been physically violent, but as he surged towards me, I thought this was going to be it. I scrambled backwards, trying to pull the pillow across to protect myself.

I have no idea whether the movement or the small sound I made jerked him away from the edge or whether I'd misread him. But though he didn't hit me, he had a tongue on him that could cut like a chainsaw, and he used it. I lay with my arms wrapped around my head, trying to block out his voice.

Sex between us had never been frequent, and over the last few years, it had become something that happened when he felt like it – usually when he'd been out drinking and came home blearily determined to prove to himself that we were happily married. Tonight he'd certainly been drinking, but the first warning I had that anything else was on his mind was when I suddenly felt his hand jerking at the hem of my nightdress.

"Unless that's something else you'd rather not do?" he hissed at me. "You won't stick up for your own flesh and blood and now you're too fecking hoity-toity to open your legs for your husband?"

By this time, I was beyond any thought of resistance. I rolled onto my back and parted my knees silently.

Usually, there was at least enough time for me to get ready. Now, however, he was determined I was going to be shown what was what. Fury on Brendan's behalf fuelled his lust, and the drink drowned his self-control.

I shrank from his anger, his roughness, the smell of the ale on his breath. Some of me wanted frantically to struggle, but if I did, he might become violent. Though my submissiveness down the years had ensured I rarely provoked him to more than contempt, the fear I now had of what he might be capable of was strangling me. Best, on all counts, to simply let him do what he wanted.

My dryness earned me a muttered "Frigid cow!" But though he must have felt the convulsion of pain as he thrust into me, he wouldn't stop because of that, and I lay as still as I could and let him get on with it, showing no sign of how much he was hurting me. I was damned if I'd give him the satisfaction. I clenched my teeth and kept silent, my fists gripping the sheet beside me, while tears of pain and rage trickled down the sides of my face.

Eventually, he finished. He pulled away from my shocked body as though the touch of it soiled him.

"From now on, start acting like a proper fecking mother," he snarled as he thumped over onto his other side. "Brendan's upset enough without you taking that bitch's side against him.

"Now, goodnight."

"Night," I whispered. 'Good' didn't come into it, but there'd be more ructions if I didn't reply.

I waited till his snores told me he was well away. Then I crept from the bed and tiptoed across the room to the door, freezing every time a break in the rhythm suggested he might have woken and found me missing.

Careful not to make a sound, I put on my dressing gown, opened the door and slipped along the corridor to the bathroom. I had to use the toilet, stifling my whimpers in a towel as the hot urine stung my sore flesh. In the medicine cabinet there was an old tube of some cream or other for 'soreness and itching', which I usually dabbed on as a lubricant beforehand, but tonight I hadn't had the chance. I used it gingerly now, mopping up my tears with the towel as I did so, and gradually the stinging subsided.

When I was done, I crept down the stairs, stepping over the eleventh tread because it squeaked.

I sat down on the seventh. The dressing gown hung off my shoulders, but I couldn't feel the cold.

I should have known better, especially when he'd already been in a rage. Why had I provoked him?

For a long time, I sat there crying – silently, as I'd long ago learned to do because he hated it when I disturbed his sleep. The tears surprised me. It had been years since I'd cried so hard; I'd thought I hadn't that much feeling left in me.

*For better, for worse.*

I just hadn't expected it to be this much worse.

# Chapter 3

The atmosphere in the house the next morning was dreadful.

Liam could usually handle his drink fairly well, but the previous day he must have overdone it. I heard him fumbling in the medicine cupboard, looking for a hangover remedy. Usually, he'd get me to find it for him, but I guessed he was wary of asking me for anything right now. There wasn't even any complaint when I served him a breakfast roll containing bacon with the fat still attached.

He watched sullenly as I sat down with my breakfast and got out my laptop, a castoff of Brendan's. I mostly used it to keep in touch with my friend Bridie and a few pals from Uni, but lately I'd thought about trying digital art. Unfortunately, even if I found a decent program, I'd have to use a stylus and touchpad, thus showing Liam I was up to my old tricks again, despite his disapproval.

No digital art, then.

Oh well, at least I'd started looking for a new job, and I'd already sent out a couple of applications. If I'd nothing more to look forward to than dusting and vacuuming this bloody house till I fell into the grave, I'd not be responsible for my actions.

Sore in body and resentful in mind, I opened my mail inbox.

There were no replies to my job applications, but there was something interesting there, all the same: a letter from Bridie Byrne.

I'd met Bridie (her real name was Brigid, but nobody called her that) in a warehouse I'd worked in for a while some years ago, when Liam was made redundant. She was slightly older than me, but we'd hit it off from the start and had a lot of laughs.

From things she'd said, I suspected Bridie had guessed a lot about my home life. She'd meant to be helpful, of course, but 'marriage was for life', so I'd always steered the conversation away again. When she finally retired to the Yorkshire Dales in England with her husband Paul, I'd missed her so much I hadn't resisted when Liam found another job and, being the family breadwinner again, ordered me to quit the warehouse and 'start making our house look decent like it ought to.' In those days, it was possible to run a house in Dublin on one wage, and as a wedding present Liam's father had given him a sum to put down as a deposit that left us with a very modest mortgage.

Bridie and I kept in touch via e-mail, keeping the phone bills low and the privacy high. She had a daughter, Marianne, who'd emigrated to Australia and was getting married next week. Bridie and Paul were flying over for the wedding and staying for six weeks, leaving their cottage empty and their German Shepherd in kennels. I'd been sorry to hear about the dog, because when they'd visited us once on the way to a family wedding in Naas, they'd brought him along. Liam hadn't been pleased, but Sharp was sweet-natured and I adored him.

I couldn't have offered to have him here, because bringing him over on the ferry and collecting him again would have cost way more than the kennel fees. And besides, Liam would've given out yards at the bare idea.

Their son Peter would have looked after Sharp if it was only for a few days, but his work commitments were so heavy he couldn't even get time off to go to the wedding, and he might have to travel elsewhere in the country at short notice. She was rather worried about leaving the cottage, too, but when your only daughter got married, you had to go, didn't you? And if you were going all that way, you might as well go sightseeing too.

The e-mail was full of news about it all. The thought of the empty cottage crept into my mind as I read it. So did the thought of Sharp in kennels. Bridie wasn't happy about that, the one shadow on the trip of a lifetime.

There were also all the things she'd said and written over the years (especially after meeting Liam) that I'd ignored. She'd kept mentioning the spare room in the cottage, always there for a friend in need, no questions asked. I knew she meant well, but marriage was for life, blah, blah. However miserable I was, I'd promised in a church: For better, for worse.

I no longer took the demands of my faith quite as seriously as I used to. Attendance at Mass on Holy Days, for instance, had quietly slipped off the agenda, though every time the dates appeared on the calendar Saint Frances muttered to herself about Hellfire. I wasn't quite as naïve as I used to be, and the

Catholic Church no longer had the stranglehold on me that it had done, but even now I was an easy prey to guilt. Though I never went so far as to ask exactly what the consequences would be if I simply ignored the Church's teaching, the anxious feeling persisted that Something Bad Would Happen. Saint Frances always insisted the consequences would be dire, especially when my attendance at Sunday Mass started to slip as well.

On this particular issue, however, religious teaching chimed fairly accurately with my own views on the sacredness of the given word, even on fairly minor matters. I disapproved of running out on a marriage just because it wasn't perfect, and I took my vows extremely seriously – I'd *always* kept my promises, and promises made before God were extra special. When the first of many marital problems arose, I told myself 'I. DO. NOT. QUIT.' And I stuck with that.

This morning, however, 'I. Do. Not. Quit' failed to galvanise me. I felt again the sense that something had changed – that last night's rape had merely poured petrol over the barely acknowledged resentment that had simmered inside me since the day I'd packed my art equipment into dustbin bags and left it out to be collected with the trash.

Over the years, I'd got into the habit of letting my occasional bouts of anger and resentment wash through me until I could 'talk myself down' out of it and into what I preferred to think of as a more sensible state of mind. Now, despite the horror of what had happened the previous night, the old habit dragged at me. I started to make excuses for the dreadful situation we were in.

We'd become parents less than a year after we became man and wife. Maybe if we *both* tried – for God's sake, he surely couldn't think this was as good as life could get? Surely seeing Brendan's marriage on the rocks would shock him into thinking about improving ours? Surely he hadn't meant last night to go the way it did, and regretted it? Maybe we could go to counselling. There must be *something*...

We could try again. We could take it back to basics. There were self-help books. I'd go to the library. This was the rest of our lives we were talking about: thirty, forty years perhaps. Maybe we could turn things around. Maybe we could get close.

I ignored the little voice that whispered in my mind, *Are you sure that's what you actually want?* Because of course it was.

He was my husband.
*To have and to hold.*
*For better, for worse.*

I reminded myself resolutely, yet again, that I had a lot to be grateful for. And I *was* grateful, especially for the good health and prosperity of our three sons. Ciarán owned a successful estate agency but was currently on holiday in America with his wife Deirdre and their sons Aidan and Connor; Brendan was a manager with a letting company; Fergal was in the last year of a technical training course, at the end of which he planned to go back to Donegal to start work in my father-in-law's very successful engineering firm. I had a lovely house (a semi in the Dublin suburbs), and up till last week a job in an art gallery – my degree had finally come in useful, and Liam had grudgingly admitted a second income would too, as long as the house didn't go to ruin. I'd loved the sense of independence being employed again gave me, but redevelopment plans for that part of the City Centre meant the shop had to close, and the proprietor was still deciding whether and where she planned to reopen it.

Bridie had sent me loads of pictures of the cottage in the Dales and raved about the delights of the place. I wondered what it would be like to stay there for six weeks with no one but myself to please all day long. I'd enough saved up from my wages at the gallery to do it – I'd set them aside in a separate 'Rainy-Day' account for emergencies, though running away to England certainly hadn't been an emergency I'd imagined when I opened the account. My boss Clare had given me a parting gift which had made a nice little topper-up to it.

Ah, what was the point? Liam would never agree to my going.

*Does Liam have to know?*

The serpentine whisper of temptation from The Tart made my heart judder.

I couldn't do it.

I just couldn't.

You'd have to be... *brave*, as well as selfish and irresponsible, to do something like that. I wasn't brave at all, and I hoped I wasn't selfish or irresponsible. If I'd had the courage I was born with, I'd have flattened Himself years ago, stuck the TV remote up his rear end and marched out. But I'd taken the path to doormat-hood at the start, and I'd been a doormat for too long to change now.

I couldn't *possibly* do anything so bold as to walk out.

The whole thing was ridiculous. I'd have to ask Bridie to change her plans, the booking with the kennels and everything. And how would I get to the cottage? I'd never been there, though I knew roughly where it was. But catching the ferry to England, and driving all that way, on my own? And staying there, all on my own?

... All on my own...

... with no television...

... no screaming...

... no gunfire...

... no plane crashes...

... no PlayStation massacres...

... and no real-life massacres pored over in gory detail on the News...

... with Sharp, laughing up at me, because he hadn't had to be locked up in the kennels till Bridie and Paul came home...

... and that view to wake up to every morning, and the peace up on the shoulder of the hill...

... and being able to do *what* I liked, *when* I liked...

No. That would be far too much like giving up, which I wasn't going to. Because I'd promised. And I. DO. NOT. QUIT.

I sighed. There would definitely be advantages, if only I was braver and less bloody responsible. When I came home, I could go to the library and find one of those books about How To Save Your Marriage. Liam might even read it with me – six weeks' absence would surely make him miss me. It might be the spur we needed.

I sighed again. *In your dreams!* My husband might have heard about modern feminism, but if he had, he certainly didn't believe it should apply to me. The dizzy advantages of Women's Liberation had been slow to penetrate our community in the

West of Ireland, and his family had been cast-iron traditionalists, like most of their generation. In his mind, just as it had been in his father's, a wife's duties were fixed as solidly as a rock. I had to be in his house to look after it. If I wasn't, who'd do the cleaning and the dusting and the shopping, and have his meals ready for him when he came home? He'd only agreed to me getting a job as long as it didn't interfere with my responsibilities as a housewife, and he'd hated it when I got home late and he had to wait for his tea. The only way a 'How To Save Your Marriage' book would have an impact on him would be if I hit him on the cock with it.

Pity.

Liam finished eating. "I'm away to Fergal's," he said, getting up. "We'll go down to Brendan's. If Mairead isn't back, we'll go to the pub or come back here and play 'Call of Duty'."

'Call of Duty'. That damned game again! Never had one been more ironically named; wasn't it the call of duty that kept me here day after day?

"Make sure the place looks nice," he added. As he passed, he leaned over to kiss me.

Without even thinking, I jerked my face away.

The slap he gave me in reflex made my ears ring.

We stared at each other. I knew that in his clumsy way he'd been trying to apologise for the night before, but all I felt was a flood of scalding rage. I sat perfectly still and silent, waiting for his next move.

I think he realised there was *nothing* he could say now that would do any good. He was probably expecting tears, but if I'd had any left, they'd have been coming out of my ears as steam boiling off my fury.

With a curse, he turned away and stormed out of the house, slamming the front door behind him.

# Chapter 4

His contemptuous words about the coffee spoons rang through my ears again, mocking my education in a 'posh school'. "Pity it didn't teach you any common sense."

*'Pity it didn't teach you any common sense.'*

'PITY IT DIDN'T TEACH YOU ANY COMMON SENSE!'

For a couple of minutes, I sat completely still. There were so many emotions churning around inside me it felt as if my brain might burst with the force of them. I couldn't pick out anything as a guide to what I should do now, though all the years of propitiating that man as if he were some angry god who must be appeased at all costs rose up in a blazing tide of fury at how my service had been rewarded.

How dared he! HOW FECKING DARED HE!

I could not, I simply *could not*, endure this without retaliation.

It was fortunate for him that he'd driven away in his car, though the temptation was there to ring the *gardaí* and report him for a drunk driver – I very much doubted whether he was sober enough after last night's shenanigans to be legal to get behind the wheel, though that had never stopped him before. If it had still been on the drive, I might well have keyed it from end to end on my way out.

Out? Saint Frances was aghast.

Yes. *Out! Out!* The Tart was dancing about behind the dungeon door, rattling its steel bars in her frenzy.

There was no other option. *OUT.* And stay out.

I had no way of knowing how large the window of opportunity would be; it depended on whether Fergal and Brendan were at home and what they wanted to do if Liam got together with them. I ran upstairs and dragged a suitcase from under the bed, tipped out the spare bedding usually stored in there and threw into it everything I'd need, from a clean nightdress and a handful of knickers to my best pendant and my 'Rainy-Day' passbook. Then I flew downstairs, snatched up my laptop, and got our joint savings account book out of the sideboard drawer too. I'd need money, and some of it could come out of that. It wasn't stealing; I'd put into it whenever I'd been able. I could have dipped into my Rainy-Day account straight away, but why should I? It was Liam who'd driven me to this.

Now I had to let Liam know what was going on, so he wouldn't call the gardaí and set them looking for me. There was a pad and pen by the phone. I could put down Bridie's landline number in case there was an emergency.

*They can trace phone numbers*, said a warning voice in my head.

That might be over-dramatising things, but at that moment I wasn't in the mood to take risks. If anyone wanted me, they had my mobile number. If I got away, I'd decide for myself when I wanted to be contactable and look for a signal if there wasn't one at the cottage. I wouldn't call anyone on the landline, just in case.

I glared at the paper. Then I wrote, so fiercely the point almost went through it:

GONE AWAY

SOMEWHERE SAFE

WHERE I WON'T GET RAPED OR SLAPPED

As an afterthought,

I'LL BE BACK

EVENTUALLY

I put it on Liam's chair, with the TV remote on top of it. He'd most likely be the one to find it, and if he did, he'd hide it bloody fast. If one of the others did – well, what if they did? He could explain himself to *them*.

As thrilled as I was horrified by what I was doing, I ran back upstairs and grabbed the suitcase. I was going to go to hell for my sins, but first I was going to Yorkshire. In the back of my mind Saint Frances was wailing like a banshee about what the family would think, but I ignored her. For once, I was going to put *me* first.

Liam might have changed his mind and come back while I was packing. He might be coming up the path *now*, might catch me in the act as I opened the front door with a suitcase in my hand.

I hurried into the front room, crept to the bay window curtains, and peered out.

Nothing.

But he might have parked down the road – he hated the bother of manoeuvring his car alongside mine on the drive.

There wouldn't be any neighbours around at this hour. Nobody to see as he got his wayward wife back under control. Nobody he'd have to worry about seeing him drag me back into the house. I could almost feel his iron grip closing on my wrist, grinding the bones together. He'd never hit me till this morning, but if he caught me trying to run out on him, he'd be livid.

The warehouse I'd worked in with Bridie had a big notice-board. In one corner of it, there'd been a poster. Though it was years old and faded, the printing was big and bold, and still caught the eye.

**DOMESTIC VIOLENCE.**
**ONCE IT'S STARTED, IT'S NOT FINISHED.**

I'd congratulated myself it would never apply to me.

I made my mind up. If I ran, I might make it. I had to try, even at the risk of getting caught. I wouldn't be able to live with myself if I chickened out now.

As I ran back out through the lounge, I caught the television glaring at me. *'You'll be back,'* it seemed to sneer. *'And if you think you've had it bad up till now, you wait and see!'*

There was a bloody hideous cut-glass vase on the sideboard. We had to keep it prominently on display as Liam's sister had given it to us as a wedding present. It came into my hands almost as if it had jumped into them. At this distance, even I couldn't miss.

The smash was apocalyptic.

I stood staring at the wreckage, breathing hard. *That's wiped the sneer off your face, hasn't it, you fecker?* Then I turned and walked out.

There was no one outside. As if traumatised into obedience by the television's fate, the suitcase followed me docilely. I got into the car, feeling as though all this was happening to someone else entirely.

The pub down the road had Wi-Fi. The car park was around the back, and I'd be safe enough inside. Liam had fallen out with the landlord six months ago and had sworn never to go there again.

I bought a glass of lemonade to justify sitting there while I used it, feeling like a criminal on the run. There was a sailing at half-past two, which would get me to Holyhead in a few hours. I'd have to wait on the docks till then, but there was no help for that.

Bridie would know the rest. I had her number in my phone contacts, and pressed it with a shaking finger.

I could have cried with frustration when I heard the familiar, perplexing message on the answering machine: "This is me answering and if it's not, I'm away doing something, so leave a message, willya?"

I moaned softly. She *had* to be there; she *had* to tell me I could come over. Where else could I go if she didn't?

Her address was on my laptop. I'd look it up when I got to Holyhead. The cottage actually belonged to Peter. He'd been mad about racehorses almost from the cradle and having served his apprenticeship at one of the big Irish stables, he'd moved to one in Yorkshire – Middle-something... Middleton? He'd been successful enough to afford to buy an old barn a few miles down the road and have it converted, but although he'd bought it as an investment, he'd pressed his parents for years to come and live there. So there they were, my only hope of sanctuary. Without them, I'd be lost. My savings weren't nearly enough for me to stay away for more than a week even if I could find somewhere at such short notice, not in High Season.

What if they'd gone to London a day or two early, to visit friends or something, before heading to the airport? What if they'd already locked the cottage up, and put Sharp in kennels?

"For the love of God, Bridie, answer the bloody *phone*," I breathed, dialling the number again.

The answering machine again. I cut the call.

Time was passing. There'd be a deadline for buying the tickets.

I logged onto the website.

Single or return?

'One-way ticket' sounded horribly final...

I could just pack up and go home while there was still time to fix things. Liam shouldn't be back yet. I could clean up the wreckage and pretend I'd tripped over the vacuum cleaner cable and knocked the TV off its stand. There'd be no end of a row, but at least he wouldn't know I'd been running off and leaving him – I'd sneak the suitcase back in when he was having a shower or something. As for the vase, I'd say I'd been so upset over the telly that I'd dropped it by accident when I was cleaning it. However unlikely it was, it'd be an awful lot easier to forgive than me smashing his beloved telly with it.

'Fix things'? From her dungeon, The Tart brayed derision. It was a nice way of saying, 'Go back and wait for him to slap the other side of your face whenever he feels like it.' He wasn't usually violent, but if he came home with the drink on him and found his television destroyed, I'd probably get a hiding.

I clicked on 'Book Ticket' before I could think better of it. I wouldn't need a return ticket till I knew when I'd be coming back. If the worst came to the worst, I'd stay a night in a hotel somewhere and drive back to Holyhead the next day. One night without me might put the shockers on them all.

Nothing about this was funny, but I was filled with the hysterical urge to laugh. I was running away to England, I didn't know when I'd be coming back, and I didn't even know if the sanctuary I was running to was available.

It was the sort of thing I'd have scoffed at if I'd seen it on the telly. Who, in the *real* world, would do anything so bloody lunatic?

I got back into the car and headed for the ferry.

At one point, the sight of a building society logo reminded me Liam might think about blocking my finances. He could claim my debit card and our savings book were missing – or stolen even! – so he could put a stop on the accounts. I wouldn't put it past him to try getting my Rainy-Day account blocked too, pretending someone had stolen that passbook as well. I doubted if he *could*, but I was pretty sure he'd try – and what if he got lucky? If he succeeded, I'd be stranded and penniless in a foreign country. It might pay me to ring the bank to warn them he might try it.

It was a Sunday, so none of the banks would be open, but I'd paid for the ferry ticket on our current account's debit card, and I could also use it at a cashpoint to withdraw the allowed maximum. A machine in Wales would give me Sterling. I'd also heard petrol was cheaper in the UK than in Ireland, so I'd fill up the car when I got over there.

Liam probably wouldn't act *straight away*, but he'd do it fast enough when he realised I wasn't coming home any time soon. I'd better not rely on the debit card being any use to me for very long, though I'd make withdrawals daily until he blocked it. If he blocked our joint savings too, I could access my Bank of Ireland account through the Post Office, so I was still financially viable.

I hadn't a road atlas for the UK. Ciarán had bought me a sat-nav for Christmas, but it was still in the boot – I'd never needed it. When I was at the port, I'd get it out and see if I could get it working. Surely there'd be UK maps on it? If not, I'd buy a map somewhere. I was going to England, not the bloody Sahara Desert!

I'd no idea how far Yorkshire was from Holyhead, either, but if I had the names and the general directions, I'd muddle my way through. If I got lost, all I'd have to do was find out where I was and ring Bridie, and Paul would tell me how to get back on the right track. Paul was steady and quiet, unlike Bridie, who flitted about like a dragonfly. He'd patiently give me instructions.

I took a deep breath and fixed my concentration on the road. I had the ticket booked. I was going. I'd never driven into the ferry terminal itself, but I'd seen the signposts in the City.

My calmness surprised me. The only thing different was that I disobeyed everything my driving instructor had told me about watching traffic to my rear. I only checked my mirrors once, when I had to make a right turn. I overtook no one, never left the inside lane no matter how slow the vehicle in front of me was. The ribbon of tarmac now felt like a rope bridge across a gorge, and I clung to it tightly. What was behind me was so terrible I didn't even want to think about it, but if I kept my eyes forward, everything would be all right.

I had nowhere else to go.

# Chapter 5

This close, the ferry looked *huge*.

The sight of the big ships ploughing back and forth from Wales wasn't a novelty. When the children were little, sometimes we walked out along the South Wall to watch them.

This time it was different. This time it had come *for me*.

My car was in the first lane of waiting cars. It was the only one with a single driver. I felt conspicuous and vulnerable.

*Still* nothing from Bridie. What could the woman be doing?

God forbid, was she in London already, with her phone buried in her handbag so she couldn't hear the ringtone?

At that moment, my phone rang.

I snatched it up. If it was Liam–

*Bridie.*

"Jesus, about time," I croaked.

"Glory to God, *alannah*, what's wrong? Fourteen missed calls! Have you murdered that bloody husband of yours at last?"

It was a joke, of course. I'd always felt disloyal talking about my troubled marriage. Nevertheless, it hadn't taken her long to sum Liam up when she and Paul visited. After that it had been easier to be more forthcoming now and then.

My heart was thudding. "Bridie, you know you've always – you know, when you said if I needed somewhere–"

"God almighty, you *have* murdered him! Hallelujah, I thought I'd never see the day!"

I was halfway between crying and laughing now, but I somehow explained the situation.

"Mother of God! – Paul! Young Fran's finally come to her senses!" She put the phone back to her mouth. "Where are you?"

"The ferry port. We're loading any minute. Bridie, I don't know if I'm– I need somewhere to stay, just for a little while–"

"Get yourself on to that bloody ferry, and don't you dare talk yourself out of it!" she barked. "I'll get Paul to send you the directions, and if you're not here by midnight, so help me I'll come over there and drag you out of that bloody house by your ear!"

I might have argued, even then, but a dock supervisor was waving the first car to start. "I've got to go – they're calling us on!" I squealed.

"Then put the phone down and *get going!* Give us another ring when you get to Holyhead!"

I could pretend the engine wouldn't start. The people behind me would think *women drivers* and swerve past me. Then I could creep to the terminal, get a refund and go home. Maybe Liam wouldn't have got home yet. I could just rip the note up and start clearing the mess. Nobody would ever be the wiser.

The picture of the television exploding into pieces around the shattering vase replayed in my mind. So did the image of what Liam's reaction was likely to be.

**DOMESTIC VIOLENCE.
ONCE IT'S STARTED, IT'S NOT FINISHED.**

# Chapter 6

The ship docked on time, but it took me more than four hours to get from Holyhead to the Dales. Paul had sent me the instructions via text, and I'd copied them onto a piece of paper and clipped it to the dashboard, but the country was new to me. I drove slowly, studying the unfamiliar road signs anxiously as I went and fretting because the speed limits were in miles per hour. The equivalent figures were there on my speedometer if you looked hard, but they were small and faded. You couldn't be forever peering at them *and* concentrating on the road ahead.

I turned off the M6 at what I was moderately sure was the right junction, but as the sun sank, I worried I'd missed a turning somewhere and was now lost among those green fields and rolling hills and villages with strange-sounding names. When at long last I reached the village of West Witton and came to the signpost saying 'Melmerby' that Paul had told me to look out for, I was hugely relieved. Even finding the lane I now had to follow included a steeply rising narrow Z bend didn't bother me unduly, though I could have done without tackling it at the end of a long drive in an unknown country. A mile or so across the high moor, a couple of turns among a small group of grey stone houses which presumably constituted Melmerby, and there – thank God! – was the cottage. Bridie had draped a green and gold Leinster flag over the hedge as a welcome.

The tyres stopped on the gravel with a soft crunch, and the engine note died with a little sigh, as though relieved its labours were done.

My echoing sigh was one of relief, because it had been a long, trying journey.

The surrounding landscape hadn't probably changed significantly in the last how-many centuries and didn't seem likely to change in how-many more. The phrase 'Eternal Hills' didn't just apply to Rome; compared to the average human lifespan, these graceful, powerful folds of rock were pretty damned eternal, too. Now I was finally sitting among them, the things that had loomed so huge and terrifying ... somehow *shrank*.

With the car's engine off, I could hear the quiet. A vast, living, velvety quiet, broken only by the hoot of a distant early owl and the last cawing of rooks settling for the night.

The gate standing open in welcome for me bore a wooden nameplate. I got stiffly out of the car and took a few steps back to look at it. Night had practically fallen by now, but a lantern beside the front door cast enough light for me to confirm what I already knew it said. Made by Peter in woodwork class for his mammy and daddy, it had hung above Bridie's door back home in Ireland.

*'Suaimhneas'*. 'Tranquillity'. Oh, how much I needed tranquillity!

Bridie's photos had done the cottage justice: a converted old barn, quite modest, a two-storey building with a sunroom tacked on the back to take advantage of the glorious view. I knew there was a patio on the far side of the entrance hall, though I couldn't see it from here. At the opposite side of the gravelled parking area, behind the Škoda Paul had moved over to leave room for me to drive in, a couple of steps led up to the cottage itself.

I locked the car door, feeling suddenly weary and very glad not to be driving any more. At that moment there was a torrent of deep barking from the other side of the house, and I heard Bridie's voice saying, "Yes, she's here at last. Let's go bring her in!" And there was Sharp, leaping around the side of the house in the lamplight with his claws slipping on the paving in his eagerness. His black mask was laughing at me as he jumped up and put his paws on my shoulders and licked my face so hard I had to lean back against the car to save myself from falling over. I wasn't afraid of him at all, but I'd forgotten he was so *big*.

"Now, you know better than jumping up on people!" scolded Bridie, striding up and giving him a cuff across the shoulders he probably hardly felt. He fell obediently back to all fours, though, his tail still waving with joy. "Ah, Fran, I thought you'd never get here. Now come and give us a hug!"

She didn't wait for the hug, but enveloped me in one of her own. She was small and wiry and redoubtable, with a pageboy cut of perfectly white hair, and a general appearance of neatness that didn't quite go with the pair of violently pink bunny slippers on her feet.

"Ah, I know!" she laughed, seeing me stare disbelievingly at the latter. "But who cares! Now, leave your things for a minute and come indoors. Paul's just putting the tea on. You must be starved, driving all the way up here. I sent the cavalry out to get some macaroons, specially!"

I couldn't speak. Bridie must have realised this, because instead of waiting for an answer she steered me towards the house, reminiscing aloud about how we'd always had coconut macaroons in the warehouse on Friday afternoons, making a little celebration of it because we finished early that day. "I always mention you when we have macaroons – don't I, Paul?" she cried, as the two of us entered the kitchen, with Sharp laughing in our wake.

"That you do." Paul was warming the teapot, but he gave me a slow, welcoming smile. Unlike his wife, he was tall and broad. All his movements had an air of deliberation about them – a combination that had earned him his nickname of Panda at his office, where he'd been a legal advisor. His hair was still thick, though its clusters were the colour of iron; the blue eyes under their heavy brows were quick with intelligence.

I sat down at the stout pine kitchen table and grabbed a few tissues from the box Bridie pushed towards me. There was probably some non-verbal communication going on above my head, but I was too exhausted for embarrassment. A cup of strong, sweet tea materialised on the chequered yellow tablecloth in front of me, so I picked it up and sipped at it. Moments later, a two-tier cake plate appeared beside it, with iced home-made fairy cakes on the bottom layer and macaroons on the top.

"Thought so." I managed an effortful smile, picking up a fairy cake to reveal the ivy pattern.

"I knew you'd recognise it!" Bridie chortled. "I saw it on a market stall a couple of months ago, and I couldn't resist!"

The retailer we used to work for had sold various designs of this series of cake plate. Ivy had been popular, and I'd always intended to buy one, but it had been one of those things you mean to do and never quite get around to. When they were discontinued, I'd been regretful.

After I'd drunk the tea and eaten a couple of macaroons and a fairy cake, I went out to bring in my things and secure the car for the night. Somehow, the kitchen already felt like home as I stepped back into it, except for having an air of contentment *my* home completely lacked. It was neat and clean, with slate flooring, pine fittings and an Aga range. An enormous bunch of lavender sat in a brass vase on the deeply recessed windowsill behind the sink; I sniffed appreciatively at the scent of it. Sharp's basket was in a cosy corner by the Aga, out of the way.

Bridie told me which room upstairs was mine and ordered me to go make myself comfortable and have a rest if I needed to. "Or if you want a bath, that's the door right next to yours. You do whatever you like while you're here."

The pine stairs were steep and spiral like a unicorn's horn. I wasn't very keen on open-plan stairs, but I kept my eyes upward and avoided looking at the spaces between the steps. Probably seeing my anxious expression, Bridie made Paul bring my suitcase up for me. "That damned staircase is a death-trap, so it is.

It's got grippers, but don't be trying to come down it with your feet wet!"

The landing was small but bright. Three doors opened off it. I needed the loo, so I timidly opened the door to the bathroom.

The room was *much* nicer than ours, tiled in soft green, with green scalloped curtains on the window. And – oh! The size of the bath, standing all by itself on claw feet, with a shower head on a hose attached in between the taps on the back. There was a shower curtain on a square track overhead, but right now it was neatly draped away at the back, held by a bow of green ribbon over a brass hook on the wall.

Our bathroom at home only had a shower cubicle. This bath was deep and inviting-looking, with a row of coloured jars on the shelf behind it, and a basket full of soaps. Visions of long, luxurious soaks floated into my head.

When I'd done what I needed to, I went into my room. All in peach shades, stylishly co-ordinated, with furniture as old-fashioned as it was beautiful. There was a double bed, with a mink-coloured fur throw folded across the top of it; a wardrobe and chest of drawers; an old-fashioned kidney-shaped dressing table in one corner with a triptych mirror on top, a floral cover and a posy of lavender in a cut-glass vase; and finally, a small but comfortable easy chair, placed to take advantage of the view through another deeply recessed window framed by heavy peach curtains and containing another vase of lavender. The many-paned window stood ajar, letting in the breeze.

*Gorgeous.*

Saint Frances, of course, was livid with me. She was shouting at me I should go downstairs, admit I'd made a colossal mistake and go back home. I'd deserve whatever Liam would say after that disgraceful loss of control.

*Disgraceful loss of control?* The Tart bawled back at her. *Who lost control first? What started all this?*

I took my mobile out and looked at it. Fifteen missed calls. All from Liam. I'd felt the vibration as I was driving, but I'd ignored it, telling myself it was on safety grounds. There'd been one while I was in a motorway service station too, so I could have answered that one, but I just ... hadn't.

Fifteen. I could imagine him, standing in the lounge, staring at the wrecked television, the note crumpled in his hand and our sons standing beside him, dumbfounded.

*No Call of Duty for you lot.*

I switched it off in case it rang again and I answered it out of habit. Just for a while, I wanted to pretend I was safe.

I'd always believed my husband wouldn't ever raise a hand to me no matter how angry he became, but the lurch of my heart at the thought of how he'd react when he came home and found the television smashed to smithereens had shaken my belief. The slap this morning had been purely impulsive and had hardly any genuine force behind it – I'd reacted more out of shock and anger than actual hurt, though he damn-well shouldn't have hit me at all! The question now was what I could expect when I eventually went home, and whether it would be worse or better for being delayed. There was no question of me not going home at all; where else *could* I go?

I'd done the utterly unforgivable. The television was quite new, and it had been expensive. I was indescribably thankful I hadn't stayed to confess what I'd done. Coming home to find his life-support machine destroyed with a family wedding present – it'd have been a miracle if he hadn't had a heart attack on the spot. Having Brendan and possibly Fergal witnessing it would have put the tin lid on it altogether.

*He'll have to find out how the vacuum cleaner works now, won't he?* The Tart, irrepressible, piped up gleefully. *And amuse himself for the whole bloody evening with no telly!*

He'd be like a caged lion, pacing up and down and snarling occasionally.

*It was absolutely disgusting, you doing that*, Saint Frances lectured me. *It'll serve you right if he DOES give you a good beating when we go home. You're not **thick**. You went to a decent Catholic school. You ought to know better!*

*Yeah, so*, I replied bitterly. A fat lot of good it had done me, too – I'd ended not even knowing a coffee spoon from a teaspoon. It could also have warned its pupils against making themselves a doormat for some bullying bastard to wipe his feet on for the rest of their lives, but that subject hadn't come up either.

*It's not being a doormat*, the Saint insisted. *The man has to be the head of the household. That's just the way it is. It says so in the Bible.*

*Yeah. It also says they should stone rebellious teenagers to death, and gay people are an abomination and deserve the death penalty.*

For all the presence of that damned picture of the Pope blessing our marriage (ha!) and another of the Sacred Heart, our household wasn't a strongly religious one – unless of course you counted the worship of the tyrannical Square-Eyed God in the lounge. Liam and the two younger boys rarely went to church these days except for funerals and weddings, and my own reluctant attendances were starting to feel more and more meaningless. The last time, listening to a sermon that seemed completely irrelevant, I'd thought sadly that the priest and I believed in different Gods. He had the weight of the Church behind him, but...

I started putting my things away. Considering the frenzy in which I'd packed, I hadn't done too badly, though I'd forgotten a few minor things, which I could replace when I found the nearest village shop. The last town I'd come through, Hawes, was some distance away. I'd spotted a supermarket there, but by then I was just so frantic to get to Bridie's house I hadn't wanted to stop for anything.

But now I *was* here, and everything was all right, and I could do whatever I liked, and nobody would be angry with me about anything. At that realisation, I flopped down onto the bed and cried again, utterly overwhelmed.

When I was fit to face the world again, I went downstairs again and had a brief conversation with Bridie, which ended up with her threatening to 'put that damned money in the Aga if you keep trying to give it to me!' This was embarrassing, but fairly predictable, and I resolved to buy her a really nice present instead.

"I'll explain what's happened– when I've calmed down a bit–" I began, wiping away fresh tears, but her hand on my shoulder stopped me.

"You don't have to explain anything, *alannah*, not till you want to and you feel up to it. We're just glad you knew you could come to us. You can stay here as long as you need to because we've got the room free and you won't be any trouble at all. I know Sharpie here'll be glad of the company, won't you, boy?"

The dog immediately rolled onto his back to have his tummy rubbed. I couldn't resist, and his blissful expression drew a watery chuckle out of me.

"You've got a job for life there," Paul rumbled, amused. "We weren't happy about leaving him in the kennels. He'll be far better off here at home. You're providing us with a free dog minder, not to mention keeping an eye on the cottage for us. Peter would have called over now and then, but there's nothing like letting people see someone's living here."

It was kind of him to say so. The idea of my being able to look after Sharp for them had emerged somewhere in the middle of my attempt to explain my arrival, along with trying to give Bridget money for my keep. It meant I had to stay here until their return, but so what? I hadn't a job to go back to, and after six weeks without me to wait on him, Liam might even be glad to have me home again, even if I *had* smashed his bloody telly. It was true I was doing them a favour by looking after their property in their absence, so that made me feel a little better about being here.

Shortly afterwards, I found myself in the sunroom with an interesting book, another cup of tea, a pretty china plate with three more macaroons on it, and Sharp for company.

Looking out across the darkened dale, lit only by a few farmhouse lights, I felt as though finally, after everything that had happened to me, I could start to unwind.

# Chapter 7

I waved until the taxi was out of sight. As the sound of it faded, quietness swept back in, reclaiming the valley as tangibly as the sunlight that trailed after a sweeping cloud on this morning of changing weather.

"You'll be *fine*," Bridie had said, hugging me before they left. The previous night, she'd given me a list of people to ring if I needed help, and instructions for stuff like the boiler, which was sometimes temperamental.

Paul had added gently that I wouldn't need any of them. "You're just going to relax and enjoy yourself. When we come back, we won't recognise you."

That was as likely as it sounded, but I liked the idea. "Just you and me now, Sharp!"

He looked up and wagged his tail, apparently unworried.

Now what? Being able to do whatever I liked was so new to me it was alarming. More alarming still was the thought that if I'd walked out on Liam today instead of yesterday, Bridie and Paul would have been on their way to London by the time I rang them, and I'd have been driving around Wales alone, a foreigner with very limited resources, looking for somewhere to stay.

Routine rescuing me, I went inside and washed the breakfast things. Sunshine through the window behind the sink played on the bubbles, painting them with iridescence; a chore I resented at home was suddenly a joy. I tilted the last plate, watching the way the reflected light danced on the shadowy ceiling before I put it to dry.

The vacuum cleaner in the pantry had a message taped to it. '*Not to be used except in case of Dire Emergency. By Order of the Management.*'

A duplicate of this was on the tin of spray polish, stored with the rest of the cleaning stuff on the shelf above.

No cleaning to do. It felt positively *sinful*.

Right.

Feeling slightly dazed, I went upstairs and started running myself a hot bath, the most outrageously luxurious activity I could imagine. There was a jar of rose-scented bath salts on the windowsill, and it was already open, so I put two handfuls into the water, sniffing appreciatively.

A book? There was the one I'd been reading in the sunroom yesterday. It wasn't *Lord of the Rings*, but the plot was decent.

... A drink?

The powdered chocolate which Bridie had casually said was too rich for her and she wished someone would use?

This wasn't luxury. This was *Decadence*.

The bathroom seemed to encourage my recklessness. There was a wicker chair for my clothes and my book. The mug could go on the shelf behind. I lowered myself, wincing, into the hot, scented water. The bath was so deep the water came up almost to my shoulders when I was finally reclining in it, and so long I could put my legs out straight. I couldn't remember being able to do that in a bath since I was little.

A bath made, in fact, for two...

I grimaced. Even if we'd had one at home, Liam would never have shared it with me. He'd have loathed sitting in 'dirty' bathwater, particularly if half the 'dirt' was somebody else's.

*Who cares what that miserable old **diabhal** thinks?* The thought took me by surprise; I shrank a little in the water, shocked by my disloyalty. Then I snorted defiance. I'd come here to relax. Why the hell should I worry about Liam?

I picked the book up, found my place, and began reading.

Of course, the steam soon started getting at the pages.

It wasn't my property, so with a sigh I put it back on the chair. Then, after adding a little more hot water into the bath, I slid down until the bubbles brushed my chin, enjoying the sheer bliss of everything.

It was more sensuous than I'd expected. Lifting one leg idly out of the water and pointing its foot at the ceiling, I watched the clots of bubbles slide down my bare skin and thought quite unsuitable thoughts about what might transpire if I *was* sharing the bath with A N Other. A N Other who found the sight of that naked, elevated leg intriguing, and who wanted to investigate further...

*Dream on!* sneered Saint Frances, so savagely that I withdrew the leg as though the air had suddenly become icy cold, slamming it back into the water with a splash. *Like anybody's going to fancy you! How many pathetically desperate men d'you think there ARE in Yorkshire?*

She sounded so remarkably like Liam that my feelings of sensuality curdled, and tears pricked at my eyes.

Was it such a sin to want to be wanted? Wanting to be *desired*; wanting to snatch just one moment of gold out of the dross of my existence? Were the sporadic, joyless instances of my husband's lust all I was ever to know? Was I doomed forever to just lie waiting to be used, out of habit, out of routine, because I was *there*? The same position, the same place, the same lack of any sort of foreplay, and opening my legs on demand?

Twice during our marriage, I'd hinted about introducing a little variety into our so-called love life. Liam had been *outraged*. On the second occasion, he'd torn up the discreet publications I'd found in a charity shop, accusing me of bringing pornography into the house when there were children in it. There'd been no 'love life' at all for months afterwards, and it seemed he was now convinced I was a whore at heart – after that second incident it was ages before he allowed me out of the house on my own, presumably in case I started leaping on anything in trousers.

They'd told us in school we had to be especially careful to resist the sins of the flesh because Woman was Eve and subject to lust. It was our duty to save ourselves for our husbands, and submit to them in this as in everything else. Fleshly desires were the devil tempting us to sin. Only in marriage, in attending to our husbands' needs, would we find the fulfilment intended by God.

Fulfilment! I could have hooted at the very idea. If what I'd found in my marriage bed was God's idea of 'fulfilment', He clearly knew nothing about women. The newer generation of priests might be less likely to preach that sort of thing, and Father Kelly seemed a kind and understanding young man on the rare occasions when I went to Confession. Possibly he'd have given me a sympathetic hearing if I'd confided in him, but I never had. There wasn't any point. He couldn't save me from Liam.

Only I could do that.

*What was I doing?* I sat upright in alarm. God could send me to Hell for thinking things like this – or so the nuns would have said. Marriage vows are sacred. 'What God has joined together, let no man put asunder.' Jesus Himself had said so, and that was that.

I whimpered, wrapping my arms tightly around my knees. Tears stung my eyes. *I. DO. NOT. QUIT.* Where had these terrible thoughts come from? I'd been a faithful wife for over thirty years. How could I throw away everything I'd devoted my life to?

*Take what you want, says God. And pay for it.*

I'd been an excellent student at school, passed my Leaving Certificate and then got my degree, leaving the path open for an art career. But Daddy became ill; Mammy needed support and accused me of selfishness for thinking about leaving. There was no chance of a career in art in the small town where we lived. Resigning myself, I came home again and got a job that was supposed to be temporary.

The company I joined was owned by Liam's father. Liam's interest dazzled me, along with the prospect of having a home and family of my own. Even Mammy couldn't expect me to pass up an opportunity to marry and produce grandchildren, especially when the bridegroom was from such a respectable family, known in the church. And I'd still be living locally, available if required.

Liam had not been a passionate suitor. He'd been content to wait for sex till we were married. Though I was relieved not to be put under pressure, at the same time I was faintly disappointed. I smothered my unease at his lack of eagerness and daydreamed about what it would be like when we were finally married.

Remembering, I gave another crack of bitter laughter. When we entered the honeymoon suite on our wedding night, the first thing Liam did was check the television worked so he wouldn't have to miss the football that evening.

My hopes were shattered. Even the sex, when it finally happened, had felt ... dutiful. Not bad; in fairness, he'd done his best not to hurt me more than necessary. But lovemaking wasn't anything like as enjoyable as I'd hoped. Even I wasn't naïve enough to think it would be wonderful at the first attempt, but surely there should have been something better than this: this oddly unemotional business of opening my body to seal a binding contract with the near-stranger on top of me who fumbled with the unfamiliar territory for a moment or two before finally, thankfully, doing the deed that would allow him to roll off and go to sleep with the air of duty done.

The whole thing had been a resounding disappointment, and the rest of the honeymoon hadn't improved matters. Instead of spending all day in bed, making up for lost time, he'd been more interested in meals and sightseeing. Sex, it seemed, was something that could wait till last thing at night, when I was so tired all I wanted to do was roll over and go to sleep. At least when I was asleep, I could forget being anything but irresistible.

It had been the same ever since. Lovemaking was just another thing he did occasionally, simply because I was there. And my dreams had died, slowly and painfully, one by one – dreams of being wanted, of feeling desired and special and sexy. I turned to chocolate for comfort. The pounds gradually crept on, the children arrived, and the woman I might have been disappeared slowly into the grey oblivion of despair.

I remembered reading something somewhere, years ago, that had struck a chord: something about how couples' attempts at a happy marriage fail, but they just stumble on together, both as miserable as sin, while their dreams shrivel and die.

I'd had dreams too, of being a happy artist if not necessarily a successful one; of being a happy wife and mother.

*Jesus Christ.* I let go of my knees and pressed my hands to my face, feeling the tears course through my fingers. Where had it all gone?

A whine startled me. Sharp was sitting by the side of the bath, watching me anxiously.

"It's all right, Bab." I pulled myself together and wiped away the tears before putting out a hand to pat his head. "I'm just feeling sorry for myself. – It wasn't all bad, you know. We had the boys." I told him about them, with justifiable pride, because they were making something of themselves. "Wonder if they've told Ciarán yet," I added dismally, hoping they wouldn't have because it would ruin the last few days of his holiday – especially if anyone other than Liam had read that note.

I ought to have rung home last night – my husband would certainly have been expecting me to. No use doing it now; he'd be at work, with his mates listening. I hadn't even switched my phone on, and the boys might have been trying to contact me too.

*How selfish can you get!* said the judgmental voice in my head. *Fooling about and leaving them to worry! And ESPECIALLY putting that private stuff out for the boys to see! If you'd controlled yourself, none of this would have happened. And you wouldn't have worked yourself into this stupid state, 'thinking'!*

"Oh, shut up!" I slid back down into the bath and dunked my hair under the water. It floated around me like dark seaweed; longer than most women's of my age – almost waist-length – but I liked it, despite it being a pain to dry. There was grey in it now, but in bright sunlight it sparked here and there with auburn as bright as a fox's pelt – my grandmother had been a blazing redhead. When loose, it had permanent waves from being kept in a single long plait down my back, where Liam couldn't complain about it looking a mess.

"I should have done this years ago." My voice sounded odd now my ears were underwater. "Instead of waiting hand and foot on that *amadán* of a husband of mine."

I might drive over just for a look at nearby Middleham Castle later. If I felt like it, of course.

This was *freedom*.

This was what I'd *come for*.
So I was bloody well going to *enjoy it*.

# Chapter 8

"I don't suppose they'll allow dogs in the castle, Bab, so we'll find somewhere you can have a run first and we'll just have a look at the place afterwards."

I was talking to Sharp as we bowled along the road to Middleham in my car. I was feeling more at ease, and the prospect of an expedition – a short one, anyway – appealed to me.

I suspected we were nearly there, and if I wanted to give him a chance to run off some of his energy, there was a suitable place along this road. A short distance further on, I could see some flat ground on the left, just as Paul had said, with a pond beside it. The turf had tyre indentations here and there, but it didn't look boggy.

I drove warily onto it in case it was softer than it looked, but the ground remained firm. I pulled up and turned off the engine. The silence flowed back in, broken only by Sharp's excited snuffling.

"Want a run?" Wasn't that a daft question, now. His tail was waving like mad.

I put the choke chain around his neck before I unfastened him from the seatbelt clip. I'd look around the place carefully with him under control before I let him loose, just in case there was any livestock around. At a click of my tongue – delivered with as much assurance as I could manage, as Paul had taught me – he whisked into position at my heel. He stayed there as I walked away from the car to survey the landscape.

It was beautiful. Even with dabs of cloud blocking the sunshine every so often, the scenery was marvellous. Not awe-inspiring, the way places like the Derryveagh Mountains are, but gentle and welcoming. Something in me that was desperately tired reached out to it and found rest.

"Heaven must be like this. If there is one," I told Sharp. "Do you know, somebody actually went to the trouble of giving all the different clouds Latin names? It wasn't enough for him just to admire them, he had to trap them and pin them down by categorising them. So there you have it: not a collection of enchanted heavenly islands, just a sky full of–" My memory let me down, and I went on, less confidently, "Cu Hum – I know that's the abbreviation for *one* of them, but I think it was the big white fluffy ones. Or was it the little white fluffy ones? Ah, whatever. What was the full name, you're asking? I'm sure it ended in '-us'. They all did. What was it, now?"

*Cunnilingus Humongous? I wouldn't mind a sky full of that.*

This came from The Tart rather than Sharp. I usually hushed her up, but today I felt free to let the poor soul have her say. After all, there was nobody here to disapprove of either of us, though Saint Frances grunted.

"Um." Picturing a sky full of Cunnilingus Humongous, I felt inclined to agree. It wasn't something Liam had ever tried, since he regarded oral sex as 'dirty', but it had a guilty fascination for me. While admiring certain handsome male actors on television, I'd sometimes wondered if they might be more willing than my husband to 'duck and dive', as Bridie had once put it in one of the warehouse's many unrestrained moments. I could still remember the women roaring with laughter at the expression...

To distract myself from the vision, I spoke to Sharp again, with a slightly unnatural brightness.

"Let's check the place out. I'll let you go when we know there's no trouble for you to get into." I strolled towards the pond, intending to see if the path there led right around it and to ensure there were no animals in sight. The hillside at the back seemed to offer good grazing but was as empty as the surrounding land. Within a fold of it, I could see what looked like a shallow crag.

"Ok. I'll let you off the lead, but behave yourself. And mind, when I blow this –" the whistle was on its ribbon around my neck – "you come straight back. And no going into that muddy bit over there, or you'll stink the car out and you'll have to go in the boot regardless. Right?"

The dog looked up at me, his eyes bright with anticipation, his tail waving. I dropped my hand to the catch on the leash, ready to snap it off the choke collar.

At that moment, there came a distant shout with an unmistakable note of fear in it.

I thought my imagination was playing tricks, but the dark ears against my wrist twitched, listening. Sharp's jaw snapped shut and he gazed intently towards the crag.

"Oh, God. You heard it too," I muttered, straightening up and staring uneasily in the same direction. "It's probably just some gossoons larking about…"

It probably was. But if it wasn't, who else was around to help? And it hadn't sounded like a lad's voice.

I didn't dare release Sharp now. Not until I'd checked.

I fetched my First Aid kit from the car and then scrambled up the track. Fortunately, I'd my phone in my pocket, and even in areas where ordinary signal strength wasn't good, you could usually make an emergency call. I didn't know where the nearest hospital was, but they could easily land an air ambulance by the pond.

The way was wide and clear, with two deep ruts; perhaps this had been a quarry once. As I got close, I saw the height of the wall of stone facing me. If anyone had fallen from the top of that – and the bit of fencing I could see up there wasn't stout – they were extremely badly hurt. Possibly dead.

I was breathless from hurrying, and my heart was thudding in dreadful anticipation as I stared back and forth along the foot of the vertical face. There was no sign of any kids. Nor of a body, thank God. There was a hearth in the middle of the open space, but no fire.

"Hello?" The call emerged thinly because of my nervousness, not to mention my being short of breath.

I almost missed the faint moan away over to my right.

I panted around into the bay formed by the curve of the crag. Over to one side lay the tumbled figure of a man – not broken by a fall from high above, I realised with a lurch of relief, but hurt by a nasty slip down the steep, grassy path down the side of the bay. Marks on it showed where he'd slid, and there was a chunk of rock in the middle that wouldn't have done him any good. If it had only been an embarrassing slip down on his arse, he'd be up on his feet by now, not lying still, covered in mud. Even from here I could see blood. If he'd hit his head on that rock hard enough on the way down–!

I took out my mobile with a trembling hand, ready to dial 999.

*Find out what you have to report first, you daft old biddy! If he **has** cracked his skull, you check the damage, control the bleeding and call an ambulance, and tell them to get a bloody move on.*

Even if he *hadn't* cracked his skull, he could easily have broken a bone somewhere, perhaps even a leg. In that case, he'd need experts to get him out of here and into hospital; no way would *I* be able to help him back to the car. I'd better find out fast what an ambulance crew would need to know.

I'd done a First Aid course years ago and could remember bits of it. I might be *some* use – I was the only help available, anyway.

I hurried up to the casualty.

At a swift glance, I thought he was about ten years younger than me – average height and build, and wearing a sensible heavy jacket for hiking around the countryside, as well as sensible boots. He was lying awkwardly on his back, immobile, though by the state of him, he'd rolled at least once. The angle of his legs didn't immediately suggest either was broken, but he must have fallen hard enough. His face was filthy, like the rest of him. Blood was spilling through the mud on his forehead, streaming down the side of his temple and into his dark hair. More oozed through his torn jeans at his left hip.

A middle-aged walker who'd come to grief, perhaps. Whoever he was, he needed help, and that made him my responsibility.

"Hello?" My voice was quavering with fright as I bent down. "Are you all right?" It was a daft question, but more tactful than 'What the hell were you playing at, going up there at your age?'

He turned his head. His eyes were closed under the smears of mud, but as I spoke, they flicked open and stared up at me. Against the surrounding of black earth, their grey irises were startlingly luminous.

I gulped with relief. He wasn't unconscious. He mightn't even be seriously injured. He was bloody lucky; he could have smashed his brains out against that rock if he'd hit it hard enough. Well, he still *might* be hurt; 'anything from concussion to skull fracture', my training reminded me. I peered anxiously at his ears but saw nothing leaking from them.

The next step was to find out if he'd broken any bones. Then see about stopping the bleeding (not life-threatening) while we waited for the ambulance if one had to be called. And keep him warm – there was a picnic-blanket in the car. I could get it easily enough.

I gave Sharp the order to sit and stay, and he obeyed immediately.

"Don't move." I crouched beside the casualty. "Where does it hurt?"

"More like – where doesn't it?" He was English, and to my inexperienced ear he sounded well-educated, though his voice was tight with pain.

"Can you move your legs at all?" That seemed a good place to start. Skull injuries were a specialist's job. *First, check for fractures.* "If it hurts, stop straight away!"

Slowly and with difficulty, he straightened his legs. "Left ankle. I caught it in something. Hurts like hell. Don't – think it's broken, though. I can move my toes."

"That's something, anyway."

I asked about his arms. One of them was OK, the other trapped between his hip and a rock. With wincing care, he drew the trapped one free. As he lifted it, he saw the blood on it that had leaked down from the jagged tear on the side of his upper left thigh. He bit his lip. "Shit."

"I don't think it's as bad as it looks." I fished a clean handkerchief from my pocket, folded it with its previously inner surface now on the outside, and placed it firmly on the wound. With my other hand, I helped him press on it.

The ring finger had no wedding band, though I thought I could see the faint indentation where one had lain. *Mind your own business, you nosy old biddy.*

The arm itself seeming OK, I asked him how many fingers I was holding up.

He glanced blearily. "Three."

"You sure your vision's OK? You've walloped your head."

"I'm fine. I just feel bloody stupid."

Now we'd got concussion ruled out, and it seemed his life was in no immediate danger, I had to treat the injuries that were within my competence. I told him I was going to have a look at the wound on his head and if he'd no objections, I'd bandage it up. Pity knows why anyone should want it *not* bandaged up, but that was the spiel.

The blood had come from a cut to the scalp just above the hairline. A rather inexpertly-wound bandage secured a dressing in place on it, but the bleeding was already sluggish. The deep cleft between his brows suggested he certainly had a grand headache – either that or he was getting impatient with this daft fat stranger who was pretending to be competent.

With his gruff permission, I checked his ribs. He said he'd no pain anywhere below his waistline; I suspected he'd have had to fall from a much greater height to have fractured his pelvis, anyway. I pressed gently around the top of his abdomen, noting as I did so that he'd a flat belly that felt very solid compared to the beer gut Liam had been getting on him lately.

From his terse replies, he thought all this was completely unnecessary, but our First Aid trainer had impressed on us it was far better to be too thorough than not thorough enough.

So, that left the *really* scary bit – moving him. If he'd spinal damage, it could leave him paralysed, or even kill him outright. That came firmly under the heading of Things Amateurs Should Not Try, 'unless it's a choice between moving the casualty or leaving him in a potentially dangerous situation.'

He didn't seem to be in any immediate danger. Best for him to stay where he was until a professional could assess the situation; even if his back *was* OK, walking on a broken ankle over ground like this was out of the question.

"I'd best call an ambulance." He seemed to have got off lightly: a couple of fairly shallow cuts (though a blow to the head was always risky), a left ankle that might or might not be broken, and undoubtedly an interesting selection of bruises.

"No!" His reaction was so swift and sharp I almost dropped my phone in a puddle.

"Janey Mack!" Rattled, I glared down at him. "I did a course in First Aid, *acushla*, and one thing they were big on was knowing when you've reached your limits. I'm not spending the rest of my life knowing it's *my* fault you're in a wheelchair, thank you very much."

"I'll be fine. Honestly. For God's sake, I don't need an ambulance. I just took a tumble and got a few knocks on the way. Just give me a hand up, please. If you wouldn't mind."

I eyed the outstretched hand distrustfully. After a blow to the head, his judgement was hardly likely to be reliable.

"Fine. I'll do it myself." He tried to wedge the handkerchief into the tear in his jeans, evidently under the mistaken impression that that would keep it secure against the wound underneath.

"That you won't." If he was that determined, I'd help him – but if I had to, I'd call an ambulance, regardless.

I took a wrist-to-wrist grip before bracing myself to take his weight. "Take it slowly, and if it hurts, stop."

"Yes, I *realise* that."

"If your leg falls off, I'll use it to kick your arse, talking to me like that." To keep myself steady, I was treating him like one of my sons back when they were boys. If I let myself think too hard, I'd get panicky, and right now we couldn't afford that. Besides,

I thought, bolstering myself, if he got himself all over attitude I'd just threaten to walk off and leave him to it, and see what he made of *that*.

To do him credit, though, he didn't seem angry. A flush went through what I could see of his face behind the mud – probably quite a good-looking face if it'd been cleaner. He glanced up at me and muttered, "I'm so sorry. That was churlish of me. I'm – I'm just a little shaken."

"It's all good."

I took up the strain with extreme care while he braced his other arm for extra leverage. If he could just get into a sitting position unhurt, we could work on the possibility of getting him standing.

The muddy earth seemed reluctant to part with him. However, as I pulled and he pushed, it loosed its grip, and he sat up.

"Right. This is the dodgy bit." He paused to catch his breath. "Perhaps if I turn onto my knees and get up that way…"

"Using the ankle you think isn't broken?"

"If I'd broken it, I wouldn't be suggesting using it!" He glared back at me for a second before again dropping his head guiltily. I'd seen enough wounded male pride in my sons to know it when I saw it.

"I still think we ought to call an ambulance. You need to be checked at the hospital, anyway."

"I'm not going to the hospital. I don't need to."

I surveyed him, my hands on my hips. "So, you're on your own, out in the middle of nowhere, with an ankle you can barely stand on, and you're not planning on going to hospital. Where *are* you planning on going, and how're you planning on getting there?"

He pulled his phone out of his pocket and switched it on, doubtless intending to demonstrate his male resourcefulness by Googling the local taxi. How he thought a taxi would get up here, I was waiting to find out. Did he think a 4x4 would turn up?

As I could have predicted, there was no signal.

He stared around, looking helpless. "I'm staying in Middleham. If I can get back there, I… I'll manage somehow."

"You're a tourist?"

The crooked smile was oddly endearing, even if it was a bit obscured by mud. "Yes." He hesitated. "You don't sound like you're a local yourself."

"I'm not." My reply was on the short side, so I added less gruffly that I was just staying here for a few weeks. Then, sighing, I bent down to try helping him get to his knees. "Right then, if you're sure you're up for it. But if you end up in a wheelchair, don't come running after me complaining!"

He turned over slowly and with difficulty, rolling onto his uninjured right side and pushing himself up to his knees.

Even with my help, it was clear he knew standing would be bad. He put his left foot to the ground with great care and hissed through his gritted teeth. I kept his left arm around my shoulder, and he leaned on me heavily, if reluctantly.

When we were side by side, I found he was rather shorter and slighter than Liam, though his body was firm and compact.

"Thank you." He settled his arm awkwardly around my shoulders. "I'll just try…" With a deep breath, he inched his hurt foot forward and tried again to put some weight on it. There was no mistaking the spasm of pain through his body, and I heard him swallow and stifle a 'Fuck!' He hated to admit it in front of a woman he didn't know from Eve, but that *hurt*.

Saint Frances said *Just give him a lift to Middleham, keep your mouth shut, walk away and leave him to it.*

The Tart said *Never mind Thursday, it's your birthday!*

All my life I'd been Respectable Frances. Do-The-Right-Thing Frances. Don't-Take-Risks Frances. The Frances who would never have bought a box of 'coffee spoons' glimpsed in an antique shop's window. On the day of *that* purchase, my common sense must have had a Spasm.

I took a deep breath and spoke firmly, as if talking to a child. "It's up to you, of course, but if you've any sense, you'll let me take you to a hospital. You don't know what you've done to that ankle, and if you try walking around on it, you could make it worse. What d'you say?"

He asked where the nearest hospital was, and I had to admit I'd no idea. "But I've a sat-nav in the car. Would you know how to use it?"

"Don't you?" He said it without thinking and apologised.

"I've not needed to." I'd no intention of telling him my husband thought I was too stupid to operate it.

There was a pause while he considered his options. "I don't like to impose on your kindness."

"Well, it's that or an ambulance, isn't it?" I blushed a bit at my daring, but a rueful grin dawned behind the mud.

"Honestly, I don't need an ambulance." He tried the ankle again and grimaced. "It hurts, but I'm sure it's not broken. I broke my wrist once, and it's nothing like as bad. I think if I strap it up, and rest it for a while, I'll be fine. If it gets any worse … Do you know if there's a doctor's surgery around here, just in case?"

"There'll be a vet, but if we took you there and you *have* broken your ankle, they'd put you down." That went down like a lead balloon, so I hurried onto safer ground, suggesting I drive him back to the cottage, where I could get the number of the surgery and see what they recommended. I'd have to drop Sharp home, anyway, as I couldn't take a dog into the surgery if they said to come in.

He nodded, thanked me and said I was very kind. I suspected he'd avoided adding 'even if you have got a misplaced sense of humour.'

*Very kind or very stupid,* I thought to myself as we started the slow journey down to the car, Sharp walking docilely at heel.

By the time we got back to the car, I reckoned my new companion was in more pain than he wanted to admit. He'd tried not to rest more of his weight on my shoulder than he could help, but he was hobbling badly. I worried whether I was doing the right thing in taking him home instead of to a doctor or a hospital, no matter what he said. Still, if the pain didn't ease off, he'd have to go whether he liked it or not.

He worried about his muddy clothes making a mess of my car.

"Ah, it's only mud. It'll brush off when it dries." *And feck what Liam would say if I couldn't get all the marks off it.*

"Anyone can have an accident, so," I added awkwardly, as I fastened Sharp in the back seat. "It's just one of them things."

Somewhat dazed by the way an outing had turned into a rescue mission, I started the car. Mindful of his hurts, I drove as slowly and carefully as I could back over the turf, praying harder than ever that the tyres wouldn't find a soggy patch and get bogged down.

Luck was with me. They didn't.

# Chapter 9

As I drove back to the cottage, it occurred to me that the man beside me could be an opportunist criminal. He could be lulling me into doing exactly what I *was* doing – driving him to somewhere he could attack me at his leisure.

My experiences with men so far hadn't given me much reason to trust them. I'd been downtrodden for years by my husband and I was only here because he'd raped and then hit me. So if I'd a functioning brain, I'd have done better to think about my own safety before making ridiculous offers to another one, whom I didn't know from Adam.

*Ah, stop thinking before you overheat*, I told myself, bolstering my wavering courage with a snort. The Good Samaritan in the Bible hadn't dithered around worrying before he acted, and nor should I, beyond a basic regard for my safety. Besides, the chap beside me would likely be feeling too battered to think about getting up to any mischief. After you turn forty, you don't bounce like you used to.

Getting back to the cottage took about fifteen minutes. My tongue-tied and embarrassed-looking companion seemed resigned to his fate, only speaking up to thank me several times.

It was rather late to wonder whether Sharp would object to him coming into the house, but I thought the dog would only react if he thought I was frightened. I thought it best to mention this, and our guest nodded. "He's got nothing to worry about from me," he added, with a speaking sort of glance to say I hadn't either.

I believed him on both counts, but as Liam had remarked more than once, naïve was my middle name.

I let Sharp out first. "Don't get in the way when..." I floundered to a halt. I'd brought a stranger here in my car and I hadn't even asked what his name was.

"Mark. Mark Reeves." He'd opened the door already and now dropped a hand quietly for the dog to smell, presenting it turned downwards with the fingers safely folded inward. "He's beautiful. Your German Shepherd."

It all seemed unnecessarily complicated to explain about him not actually being mine, so I just nodded distractedly because my mind was already rambling onto the worry of how far away the nearest hospital might be, and said his name was Sharp.

I thought it best to get Mark sitting down in the kitchen to have a rest, and a good cup of tea would probably steady him down a bit after his tumble. While he leaned by the door, I helped him get his muddy jacket off, and once he'd got his belongings out of the pockets, I dropped it into the washing machine. A short wash should get it clean, and it shouldn't take much drying. Resolutely, I told myself that no, I *didn't* have any ambitions on taking the rest of his things off as well while I was about it.

*If he wouldn't mind, why should you?* The Tart piped up daringly. *HE's not that shite you're married to.*

*Oh, shut up. He's hurt.* I rounded on her. *And I came over here for a break, not to go whoring.*

*You could offer to kiss his bumps better. A bit of that 'cunnilingus humongous' wouldn't be a bad idea, either.*

*Will you be QUIET!*

Regardless of her opinions, now I had to concentrate on getting through this mess safely. I'd been stupid enough to get involved, so best keep it short and safe. Having been raped once, I was in no hurry to risk experiencing it again. Liam was right, at least about my tendency to act before I thought – I really *was* an eejit.

We got him into a chair at the kitchen table – I whisked the pad off it first so he wouldn't have time to worry about getting it dirty. Underneath the hiking jacket, he'd been wearing a thinner pale grey one, which I draped on another chair, and beneath that a grey Ralph Lauren T-shirt to go with his black denim jeans. The latter were ruined, but as he'd nothing else to put on till he got back to his B&B, presumably the nurse at the surgery or the hospital would just help him take them off until they'd treated the wound underneath.

His boots were still rather muddy, but this was farming country – they were probably used to muddy boots. I brought over a cushion and put it on the chair opposite him, and he lifted his injured leg to rest it on it. A couple of pieces of kitchen towel under his heel kept everything clean, and I knew that injured limbs need to be elevated.

I asked if he'd like a drink.

"Yes, please. It's been a … trying morning." He sighed. "But I really would like to wash my face too, please, if I could trouble you? I must look as if I've plunged head-first into a bog."

He had a point. His face *was* still filthy. He'd tried to wipe off some of the drying mud, without success.

I boiled the kettle and set out two mugs. I preferred coffee but he asked for tea – black, one sugar. He'd probably also need painkillers, so I fetched the biscuit barrel; I only had Paracetamol in the house, and he shouldn't take them on an empty stomach.

When I carried the tea over to him, he was looking rather embarrassed and asked if he could use the toilet first.

This was rather awkward. Struggling up those stairs would do his ankle no good at all. But he only needed to pee, and the garden shed yielded an old jug that would do, so I handed it to him with a paper handkerchief and then tactfully went out to check if the washing on the line was dry.

His quiet call a minute or two later told me something I hadn't realised: I knew his name, but I hadn't bloody told him mine!

*God, he must think I've the social skills of a baboon.*

I went back and took the jug matter-of-factly. As I emptied it into the toilet upstairs, Saint Frances approved of the fact that I was finally behaving in a suitably sexless manner. *He probably sees you as the equivalent of a fat old cousin – one from the common side of the family, too.*

Blinking back a few angry tears, I rinsed the jug thoroughly, took it downstairs and left it outside the back door, just in case. That done, I marched back to the table, where I announced, more loudly than I'd intended to, "My name's Frances. Frances McKenna. I'm sorry. I should have said." The Saint demanded loudly where *McKenna* had come from when for the past thirty-odd years it'd been *McEnally*. I ignored her.

He eyed me cautiously. "I didn't like to ask."

"I'm not normally this much of an idiot. Well, I am, but that's neither here nor there. Let's get you fit to travel."

While he sipped the hot tea and nibbled a biscuit, I half-filled the washing-up bowl with warm water and fetched him the rest of the necessaries. "Will you need anything else?" I asked.

He said no, adding politely that he'd take his T-shirt off to save it from getting wet.

"Feel free." Determined to act all blasé, I sat down opposite him and picked up the biscuit barrel to help myself to one while he smartened himself up. I'd a husband and three sons. It wasn't like I was going to see anything I hadn't seen before, though as an artist I'd be interested in seeing him from that perspective.

*Oooooh...!*

"Nice!" I thought to myself, as, carefully trying to keep it clear of his muddy face, he pulled the T-shirt up. Too late, I realised my mouth had still been in gear. Worse still, it hadn't been just the artist who'd spoken.

Fear squeezed my heart suddenly. How could I have been so careless? *Oh Mother of God, now what do I do?*

"Pardon?" He looked slightly puzzled. Fortunately, he'd still been pulling the fabric off over his head as I spoke, and so hadn't actually caught me staring.

For a split second, I thought about explaining I was an artist. In the same second, I realised that even back in the day, artists weren't supposed to ogle their sitters, let alone make potentially offensive comments. Any way I tried to play that one, it was doomed to disaster.

"Biscuits. I knew I'd forgotten something when I went to the shop this morning, and it was 'Nice' biscuits! This thing's hardly got anything in it!" Desperately I improvised, brandishing the biscuit barrel at him. "I just remembered. I was going to get digestives too, and didn't I go and forget both of them? I've only got Rich Tea in the house!"

"Ah. I see." He looked at me a bit doubtfully but let me get away with it. He probably had me down as one of those old biddies who go weird living on their own.

*Look at THOSE!* screamed The Tart. Her attention was still riveted on him, though after that *faux pas,* I gave up interest altogether in biscuits. I ducked my face to my coffee mug and kept it there, staring fixedly at the tablecloth. Still, my memory didn't have an 'erase' function. He *did* have a toned chest, and all the rest to go with it.

I'd sketched real-life models regularly when I was studying for my degree, and I'd seen male torsos close up often enough. Both Brendan and Ciarán had some hefty muscles on them, and when Liam was younger, he'd been fit. But even in spite of my recent unpleasant experiences, I was completely unprepared for the jolt of admiration that shot through me when I found myself opposite a muscular male torso to whose owner I was neither married nor related. It seemed even decades of a dreary marriage hadn't extinguished my libido entirely, though whether I could ever endure Liam putting his hand on me again was a different matter.

"The soap may be a bit... girly," I babbled, trying desperately to change the subject. The Tart fancied leaping on him with the bar of soap and lathering him within an inch of his life, but I ignored her; I was in enough of a lather myself without listening to *her* suggestions. "There's some shower gel, but that's probably the same."

"I have two options. Mud or," he inspected the packet, "'Freesia and Jasmine'. I think the 'Freesia and Jasmine' is the lesser of two evils, don't you?"

"Marginally." Trying to pull myself together, I went to the kettle and refilled it for no particular reason, but all that masculine musculature kept demanding my attention. Fortunately, he'd put the washing-up bowl directly in front of him and seemed to be too busy scooping water to notice me doing a starving-tiger-eyeing-a-steak impersonation.

Saint Frances reminded me I was a middle-aged married woman, and that 'forsaking all others' meant I shouldn't be thinking things like *that*.

I listened with half an ear. Out of the corner of my eye, I was watching the water trickling down his torso while imagining that it was sweat, and I was causing it. The Tart suggested various exotic ways in which this might be possible. It seemed she'd picked up a certain amount of information from those sex-guides, even if Liam hadn't, and I'd only glanced through the pages.

While his face was safely hidden in the towel, I was free to admire the intriguing way in which the well-defined muscles in his shoulders and arms slid smoothly under the skin, but as he emerged again, I hurriedly transferred my gaze up again.

The Tart thought dazedly that 'birthday' actually didn't come anywhere near it. Any number of birthdays with Christmases thrown in wouldn't have sufficed.

He was slightly older than I'd originally thought – probably about fifty – but the mud had made it difficult to have a proper guess. What I'd been able to see of his face had suggested he was quite good-looking. Without the covering of mud, he was... was...

*... bloody gorgeous.*

Below the black hair, winged with grey, he had level eyebrows and those grey eyes; also a straight nose, well-defined cheekbones and a mouth that was an artist's dream, though at present this last was compressed, undoubtedly with pain. I bit down on a gasp, with some difficulty.

"Would you like another cup of tea?" The Tart wanted me to add *and would you like it hot and strong*, and there'd been a time when if he'd said 'yes' to that question, he wouldn't know what had hit him.

*In your dreams,* said The Saint, bitchily. She, too, knew that years had passed.

She most likely held me responsible for what Liam had done, too, and sent me a queasy reminder of what a man's violence felt like. Would I like a repeat of it?

"No, thank you. I haven't quite finished this one." He wrapped the towel around his neck and ran his hands through his rumpled hair to tidy it a little. The gesture made him look oddly boyish for a moment, though there was emphatically nothing boyish about his body. He looked down at his ankle, clearly testing it, then winced and asked apologetically if I'd any painkillers in the house.

It was the work of a moment to fetch the Paracetamol. "I can drive down to the village if you need something stronger...?"

"These will be fine. Thank you." He swallowed two and, switching helplessly into Mammy mode, I said he shouldn't take them without food.

He obediently ate another biscuit.

"I don't think one or two will put much of a lining on your stomach. Go on, I'm getting some more tomorrow." Even as I spoke, I groaned to myself. God, wasn't I nagging him like I was his mother!

*It was never like this in the movies*, The Tart agreed gloomily. Sitting opposite a half-naked hunk and all I could find to talk about was my shopping plans and the lining of his stomach.

Feck!

*Situation normal, Frances McEnally. Situation bloody normal.*

# Chapter 10

The people at the surgery thought from the description it was probably just a sprain, so they recommended he visit a local pharmacy. I didn't know where that was, but Mark's iPhone was obliging, so I drove him to Leyburn. In the chemist's there, the pharmacist agreed the injury was a sprain, and gave us advice on how to treat it. We got more dressings and some ointment for the gash on his thigh – the cut on his head had already closed up, but though gently cleaning and treating it wouldn't hurt, it was better to leave it uncovered to heal. Some stronger painkillers and a stout support bandage for his ankle completed the repair kit. He'd have to keep his foot strapped up tightly and elevated for a couple of days, and then start exercising the joint carefully as soon as the easing pain allowed him to. In the meantime, if the pain worsened significantly or he developed a fever, he was to go straight to A&E to get an X-ray.

He looked relieved as he limped out beside me, using a hiking pole we'd found at the cottage to help support his weight, but I knew he was worried, too. He'd already told me he was on a few days' hiking tour and had booked bed-and-breakfast places so he could walk from one to the next. Getting a sprained ankle would definitely have put the tin lid on *that*.

"Not broken, so," I remarked as we walked slowly back towards the car.

"No. I can walk on it. It's not feeling as bad as it was, and those tablets are helping, but it's still uncomfortable." He shifted his grip experimentally on the hiking pole. "I don't suppose you know of a shop around here that sells parrots, so I can complete my impersonation of a pirate?"

"Sorry, I don't think the supermarkets around here would stock them." I glanced at him with a bit of a grin. "Order one on Amazon. They should have plenty of them there. And don't forget the cutlass and the hat while you're about it."

He grinned back, getting the pun, but sniffed that he was probably rather old for cutlasses and pirate hats.

"Jeez, listen to you talking like you're decrepit. I've seen 'Pirates of the Caribbean'. You could be an understudy for yer man any day of the week."

He looked surprised and flattered. "Jack Sparrow?"

"I was thinking Davy Jones, actually."

Given I'd hardly known him for an hour, teasing him like this was a risk, but it paid off. He made a pretend swipe at me with the hiking pole, laughing, but I dodged away. "Ah no, maybe you're not *quite* old enough. But it'd definitely spare the make-up department half the job."

"I should chase you from here to Richmond!"

"Ah, but you won't be chasing anyone for a few days, willya, me old sea-dog? Not with that ankle."

He glowered. "Kicking a man when he's down?"

"Is there a safer time?"

But the sudden uprush of joy from finding someone to laugh with had made me daring. I went on driving the needle in. "I don't see you going far as a pirate, anyway," I continued. "'Peg Leg Pete' has credibility. 'Mild Sprain Mark', now, *that* won't put the fear of God into anybody."

"It doesn't *feel* like a 'mild sprain'," he retorted, trying with difficulty to get on his dignity while he was hobbling across the pedestrian crossing. "I'll have you know, it feels like a very nasty sprain. And believe you me, if I had a plank, *you*'d be walking it."

We reached the car a couple of minutes later. I opened the passenger door and held the hiking pole while he got himself inside.

"Back to Middleham, Cap'n?" I asked, still grinning as I dropped into the driver's seat and dropped the pole across the back seat.

"Please." He fastened his seatbelt, but he was looking worried and awkward again.

Immediately I felt anxious. What if I'd misread the situation and offended him? "What's wrong? I didn't mean…"

"No, no, it's nothing to do with you, honestly." He sighed and explained that he was only booked into his bed and breakfast place for one night. He was supposed to move on to another place every day, but that was obviously no longer going to be possible.

"I don't see how I can rest effectively if I'm going to be shuttling from one place to the next, and it's a bit damned pointless anyway if I can't even enjoy the scenery. I'm going to have to cancel the whole thing and take a taxi back to Darlington tomorrow morning. I can get a taxi at Euston. I'll have to do my recuperating at my hotel."

"Is there no one could look after you at home?" The words were out of my mouth before I could think better of them. Mortified, I apologised immediately.

He looked out of the window. "I don't have a home, as such. I ... I split up with my ... my partner recently. She–." He stopped talking for a couple of moments, obviously very upset. Then he said shortly that when he went back to London, he'd have to start looking for somewhere to live. "It may take a while to find somewhere, but if it does, it does."

Silence fell and lasted until we got back to Middleham. The guest-house owner became genuinely motherly as soon as she saw he'd had an accident, and insisted he should spend the rest of the day recuperating in the guest lounge. He didn't even have to move on next morning, as his room would be free for the second night if he needed to rest up a little longer. With that sorted, all he had to do now was cancel the other reservations.

I'd come in to see he was all right. I told him I'd drop his jacket off the next day, when it was dry, and asked if he could manage without the hiking pole now he was indoors. He thanked me for my kindness, said he was sure he'd be fine, and said he hoped my husband appreciated the wonderful wife he had.

"I hope he does too." He probably heard the ironic note in my voice. But, "I'm glad it's all worked out for you, so," I continued, thrusting my hands awkwardly into my pockets in case he might try to shake one of them. "And mind how you go with the ankle, right?"

"No more rock climbing," he agreed with a rather hollow smile. "Thanks again. Goodbye."

"'Bye." I went out of the front door and down the path. At the front gate, I looked back once and smiled, patting my shoulder to remind him to order the parrot from Amazon. *Who's a pretty boy, then?* suggested The Tart, but I wasn't in the mood.

I left him to it.

# Chapter 11

Nothing had changed at the cottage. The trees were loud with birdsong, and the lavender-heads in the border bowed again and again under the attentions of dozens of bees. Sharp came to the door to meet me, wagging his tail. I slipped his collar and leash on again. I owed him a walk, and I didn't feel like taking him back to Middleham.

Well so, I'd had a bit of an adventure and done a good deed, and I was glad Mark hadn't broken his ankle, though it was sad to think he'd be going back to London earlier than he'd expected when he'd so little to look forward to. His jacket was clean, so I pegged it out on the line. It'd dry in no time with that brisk wind lifting it.

The moors weren't far away. If there were no sheep up there, the dog could run around a bit. If there were and he couldn't, we could have a good long walk. Maybe that would soothe the wild restlessness I felt.

The bowl and washing stuff were still on the table, with the cups and the biscuit barrel. 'Nice', for God's sake. What the hell had got into me, blurting that out?

Ah, I'd put them away when I got back. After all, I had nobody to please but myself. I could do whatever I wanted ... but...

I gave myself a mental shake. I could draw! Now, what was wrong with that?

The place was an artist's paradise. I could spend hours at the patio table outside. There was nobody to stop me, nobody to scowl at the waste of time when there was a house to keep clean and meals to cook at the proper times. I could reconnect with a part of my soul that had been withering away for years.

The thought cheered me as Sharp and I strode out up the road, heading towards the moors.

The next morning, I returned to Middleham.

There was space to park opposite the guest house, but I drove past it and parked further down, giving myself a walk back past the convenience shop.

He wouldn't be in there, so why was I peering in as if expecting him to leap out at me? He'd be in the guest lounge up the road, resting his foot, and at some point tomorrow he'd be gone.

I knocked on the guest house door. The landlady answered it and I thrust the jacket at her like it was contraband and the gardaí were after me, and asked her to give it to him.

I could ask if I could pop in and see how his ankle was…

*Get a hold of yourself, you bloody eejit!* I thanked her, turned on my heel and walked away.

They sold stationery in the shop. Pencils – yes, only HBs, but I could manage. Also a pencil sharpener, a tray of watercolours with a paintbrush in it, and an eraser the size of Roscommon. Lastly, a sketch pad, which the assistant found 'in the back'.

I'd got everything I'd come for. And while I was in there, I bought a couple of packets of biscuits as well. Digestives and Nice.

I made my purchases and drove home in triumph, carefully ignoring the guest house as I passed it again. He wasn't my business any more. A couple of hours spent sketching in the sunshine, and I'd forget all about him.

Well, that was the big idea.

It had turned breezy that morning, but not cold. I wouldn't let it stop me. I hunted for things to anchor the paper, choosing a green glass paperweight with bubbles inside it, a brass unicorn, and a book that claimed to contain a history of everything.

The paperweight offered possibilities as a subject. Its transparency made it challenging, but I knew how to tackle it, though without proper pencils I'd have to sacrifice a huge amount of subtlety. It would be good, it would be *beyond* good, to create again.

An hour later I stared down at a travesty of a sketch. Even with decades' lack of practice for an excuse, it was awful. It was bloody *terrible.* A ten-year-old could have done better – a ten-year-old with neither talent nor interest, let alone training.

"Feck it!" I tore out the page, screwed it up and hurled it towards the dustbins. A gust of wind immediately blew it off course. I swore again.

In a temper, I retrieved the paper and binned it, then threw everything back into the carrier bag. I could have cried with frustration and disappointment. What would be the use of me spending hours out here working if that kind of shite was all I was going to come up with?

I dumped the carrier bag on the table and stormed back indoors to find something else to do.

God Above. It was almost enough to make you put the telly on.

Almost.

## Chapter 12

The sound of the doorbell at about ten o'clock next morning startled me half out of my wits.

I'd taken a look inside the book about the History of Everything – if it was no use as a paperweight, it might be useful as a distraction – and found it unexpectedly enthralling. So much so that I'd been late going to bed, and after breakfast I'd made myself comfortable on the sofa and started reading it again. Drawing could wait till I'd got over the vexation.

Of course, the first thing that sprang to my mind was that somehow, by some evil miracle, Liam had tracked me down. Comforted by the way Sharp flew at the door, barking – there was no way my husband would try to force an entry with him here – I crept to the window and peered out.

A huge bouquet of flowers made it hard at first to tell who was standing there, but it definitely wasn't Liam. As I realised it was Mark, my heart momentarily stopped and then started dancing about behind my ribs like it was doing the bloody polka. I hadn't even the wits to keep the great big smile off my face as I opened the door. "Aw, you shouldn't!"

He handed over the bouquet and I buried my nose in the nearest lily, inhaling blissfully.

"I absolutely should have." Fending off Sharp's welcome, he handed over a great big box of chocolates too. "The flowers are from me, and the parrot sends these with his regards."

Then he coughed. "Wipe your nose," he added tactfully. "Pollen."

Bloody hell, didn't I just know how to make a grand impression? I put the gifts down on the table, darted to a wall mirror, and saw the state of my nose. There was a box of tissues on the small table underneath, so I pulled one out and used it. Still sporting a suggestion of fluorescent yellow, but too giddy with excitement to worry about it, I hurried back and invited him in.

"You'll have a cup of tea, won't you?" I demanded. "But how's your ankle? Could you do with the pole again?"

"I'd love a cup. Thanks. And my ankle's still not great..."

I'd left the hiking pole propped beside the door, so I snatched it up and handed it to him. Then I pointed him to an armchair in the lounge area.

He limped over to it and sat down, trying not to make it obvious he was glad to take the weight off his ankle, which would still be sporting that support bandage. Sharp pranced beside him, asking for a pat. "I'm afraid I can't stay very long. I've got a taxi waiting for me."

I'd shaken my brain back into motion and walked over to take two mugs out of the cupboard, but at the last words I froze. "A taxi waiting?"

"I said I'd be a few minutes. I hoped you'd be in." He gave me a rueful look. "I'm going back to London, but I hoped I could say goodbye before I go – and thank you properly. Last time seemed rushed."

"You're cutting your holiday short, then." I thawed back into movement, but I was operating on auto-pilot.

"Yes. There really wasn't any alternative."

I sat down opposite him. There was a slightly awkward silence while we sipped our drinks. "I really was grateful for your kindness," he told me. "Few people would have done what you did."

I could feel myself blushing. Hurriedly I disclaimed, saying I was just sorry he was going to lose the rest of his holiday. "'Specially when you're... well, when you're going back to what you're going back to."

By the way he sighed, he clearly wasn't looking forward to it. Still, he tried to sound philosophical, saying we all have to do things we don't want to do.

An idea had flashed into my mind, so crazy that at first I shoved it straight out again. But I found myself opening my mouth regardless, and then somehow the words tumbled out. "This is going to sound crazy, and it probably is, but... if you'd like to finish your holiday, you could always kip on the sofa here." I was staring at the cup in my hands now, knowing my face was ablaze with embarrassment. "Except it's not my place really, it's a long story, and ... Look, I'm not coming on to you or anything, you haven't to worry about that." I swallowed. "Just till you'd have gone home anyway."

It was plain he didn't know what to say. His silence and the realisation of my own insane recklessness rattled me, so I put the cup down on the table with suddenly shaking hands. "Sorry, sorry, sorry. I don't know what got into me, asking. It was just an idea."

"It was a very kind idea. But shouldn't you ask your husband's opinion first?" He was looking at the gold band on my left hand.

"No." My voice was flat. "He's not here, and I don't care what he thinks."

His brows rose. "You're here on your own … and you're asking a total stranger to stay with you?"

"Crazy, isn't it?" I could either laugh or cry. "You probably think I've escaped from an Institution. Maybe I have, at that."

He waited till I looked back at him. When I did, his face was very serious. "I think you're very unusual. And very kind, of course – especially to make an offer like that." Then he paused. My suggestion had surprised both of us, and even if I'd taken leave of my bloody senses, he most likely thought *one* of us should think the thing over. There were potential pitfalls. Even if *he* was as straight as a die (and let's face it, what reason did I have to think he was?), *I* could have any kind of psychological issues. The last thing he needed was to be saddled with was an accusation of assault or robbery or worse by some delusional woman he'd mistaken for a Good Samaritan.

Oh, I knew very well why he was hesitating. I looked back at him with a kind of dogged defiance, waiting for him to refuse.

The words of that polite refusal were already forming. I would accept them with equal politeness, and that would be the

# A COTTAGE CALLED TRANQUILLITY

end. I'd walk him to the door and watch him to the taxi, and maybe wave as it took him out of the gate. He'd go to Darlington and catch the London train, and there'd be no more jokes about Mild Sprain Mark or buying a parrot from Amazon.

Instead, I heard him saying that if I was serious about letting him stay, he'd promise me I wouldn't regret it.

It was just as well I'd put down my cup of coffee, because if I hadn't, I'd have dropped it. "You'll stay at the cottage? With me?"

He grinned suddenly. "I'd like that very much, if you're sure. I'll pay you, of course."

"Ah, I'm not bothered about money." I smiled hesitantly back.

We looked at each other for a moment longer, probably both wondering what we'd let ourselves in for. Then I nodded. "Let's go get your things in from the taxi, shall we?"

# Chapter 13

Saint Frances was absolutely beside herself. *What in the name of Almighty God have you done?!*

I'd no idea. The invitation must have formed in my loins and popped out of my mouth, bypassing my brain altogether. Even the pause hadn't been long enough to allow me to think better of it.

I couldn't blame him for hesitating. This wasn't supposed to happen. But then *he* shouldn't have been dancing around on the top of a steep wet muddy path the other day. Without that, the situation would never have arisen. Still, it wasn't as if I was young and attractive, or anything. He couldn't possibly think I might have any ulterior motives.

*It really IS your birthday!* crowed a voice from the dungeon. The Tart evidently *did* think so.

I wasn't so sure. Although I'd done my best to ignore the fact, since I left Mark at the guest-house it had seemed almost as though one of the colours had disappeared from the spectrum. There was no ignoring the way my heart – not to mention other areas – had leaped into life when I looked out of the window and saw him. But it was utterly unlike me to be this impetuous, though to be fair I'd rarely had the chance.

What had got into me? I didn't know this fella from Adam, and I'd invited him to stay here. In a house where there was no one within earshot. He could be a rapist or anything.

He could be other unpleasant things too, and I'd invited him into a house I didn't own. He could be a thief. I could wake up tomorrow morning to find the house cleared of its valuables, Sharp stolen, my purse empty and my car gone.

I hated myself for being so suspicious these days, but Ireland wasn't what it used to be. Even in decent enough areas of Dublin, like Blackrock where we lived, you always took your car keys and money with you when you went to bed. Probably England was much the same. with its fair share of charming rogues.

Still. I'd asked him now. Done was done.

*So be it,* I thought, finishing my coffee while my unexpected new guest sat opposite me, rubbing Sharp's tummy and playing with his ears. *Here goes on the **second** stupidest thing I ever did in all my life.*

If he was to stay here, we'd have to get him comfortable. The sofa could accommodate him easily, and with care he could now take both of his boots off. We managed it, but he said he'd have to just wear socks indoors.

He wanted a change of clothes. I put his rucksack beside him, and he took out dark blue jogging pants and a matching T-shirt. He'd been unable to get his jeans off past his hiking boot for the past two days and was painfully aware of not having been able to shower, but that was simple enough to solve – I'd a shower upstairs he could use. He'd have to go carefully with those steep stairs, but if he wanted to keep the bandages mostly dry, he could rest his foot on the side of the bath, using the grab rail to keep his balance, and rest a towel across the bandage on his thigh. If he was careful about where he aimed the shower head, it might not keep off all the water from that and his strapped-up ankle, but it should keep off the worst of it. The cut on his head should be healed enough by now to be washed, as long as he didn't rub it too hard – and he was hardly likely to do that.

I told him where the bathroom was and watched narrowly as he walked towards the foot of the stairs. He was still nowhere near right, but though he left the hiking-pole leaning at the foot he was steady enough on his legs without it. I thought about offering to help him upstairs, but it'd probably offend his daft masculine pride. Either that or he'd accept my help and thank me again, and though I thought his mammy would have been as proud as Punch of the polite fella she'd brought up, the flowers and chocolates he'd bought me were enough thanks for anything I'd done and might do. If he kept thanking me every couple of minutes, I could see the two of us having what Granny had used to call an Argufication.

The flowers! I'd better put them in some water before they started drooping. God above knew where I'd find a vase big enough; they'd need something the size of a milking pail.

Leaving Mark to make his halting way upstairs on his own, I started searching the cupboards. There were a few vases of varying sizes, but as I pulled out the first, the memory shot into my head of that ghastly one at home, now consigned to the dustbin of history in several million pieces.

The strange thing was that Liam still bought me flowers now and then, when he thought about it. Usually something from the supermarket petrol station, with the price tag still attached. But as dutiful as I always was in putting them in water, making that terrible old vase work for its keep, the contrast now was like switching on the telly and seeing a colour picture when all you've ever seen before was black and white.

And, now having seen colour for the first time, could I go back to watching monochrome?

Eventually, I found a big glass vase that would hold the flowers the way they were – the arrangement was beautiful, and it would have been a pity to split them up. I put them in pride of place in the middle of the hearth.

The front of the card said, in neat handwriting, 'With grateful thanks, from Davy Jones and the parrot.' On impulse I put it away in my purse, hidden behind my debit card.

I was plumping the cushions when I heard the bathroom door opening. Remembering what Bridie had said about the stairs, I shouted to Mark to be careful coming down them if he'd wet feet.

He thanked me for the warning.

I shut my eyes. More thanks! That Argufication was coming any minute now.

"Now, doesn't that feel better?" I said encouragingly as he reached the bottom, praying he'd have the sense to just nod.

Self-preservation was clearly not his thing. "Very much, thank you."

*Janey Mack.* If I'd had a cushion in my hand, I'd have hurled it at him.

Still, it seemed harsh to cushion somebody for being too polite, so I kept my encouraging smile pinned on my face and pointed to the sofa, inviting him to make himself comfy.

He hesitated. "If you're really sure you don't mind me staying..."

While he was upstairs, I'd thought some more about the risk I'd taken; my experiences with men so far hadn't been good. I'd believed I knew where Liam's limits were, and I'd been proven wrong. I could be making another terrible mistake, with God knows what consequences.

Mark's hesitation was reassuring, despite Saint Frances hissing he was faking it.

I said I could put up with him, as long as he behaved himself. I tried to sound nonchalant, but I suspected my nervousness showed. "One toe out of line and I'll set Sharp on you," I added.

He smiled back at me, gently, as though he understood. "Consider me suitably terrified." Far from standing impressively beside me to protect me from all comers, my faithful minder had rushed into the garden, scattering the birds off the lawn. A fat lot of use *he'd* be in an emergency, I thought sourly, unless Mark started impersonating a sparrow.

Oh, well. Maybe he just knew I wouldn't need him.

It was too early for lunch, but after I'd put my guest's dirty clothes in to be washed with the rest of the waiting laundry, I made us another drink and got out the biscuits. Fortunately, I'd emptied the Nice ones into the barrel last, so they were conspicuous on top.

Feeling I owed him some explanation of my situation, I explained about Bridie and Paul, and how I was 'house-and-dog sitting' while they were in Australia. Ending the story, I sipped at my coffee, sighed, and admitted I couldn't believe I was sitting here telling all this to a perfect stranger. Though I'd always been a bit of an eejit, I must finally have gone stark, raving mad.

"Join the club! – though being sensible all the while is enough to drive you mad." He smiled.

"I ought to be all right then. I've been insane off and on for decades. Quietly, of course." I couldn't keep an undercurrent of bitterness from the last three words as examples of my lunacy came to my mind – chief among them, saying *I will* to Liam McEnally for no better reason than the fear of ending up alone and unwanted; wasn't *that* bloody ironic? I pushed the thought away, unwilling to remember either my naïveté or my husband.

"And you're living here all on your own?" he asked.

"Yes, thank God," I said promptly. It wasn't the most sensible admission to make, but he'd find out soon enough. Anyway, if he tried any funny business, I knew about his bad ankle. One solid kick on that, and I'd probably put him in hospital.

*Pity,* said The Tart regretfully. *He's no good to you there.*

*I've told you to shut up.*

His silence had a questioning quality, so I mumbled that while I was here, I had some thinking to do. I was thankful he didn't pursue the issue, merely remarking I'd come to the right place.

"I hope so." A pause. "Look, if my mobile phone rings – I don't have it on a lot, but if I'm not around and you hear it, please don't answer it."

He was taking a sip of tea. Both eyebrows rose.

Almighty God, those eyes; I'd never seen any the colour of them. Storm clouds, with the sun behind them. "I wouldn't answer someone's phone anyway, unless they told me to. If it rings, it can go on ringing."

That was a relief – I couldn't imagine what Liam would say if he rang my phone and a man answered it. As though there was any chance of *me* having a fancy man! I rammed a Digestive into my mouth and chomped on it as though its taste could mask the bitter taste of reality. *I'm fat and ugly. He wouldn't fancy me anyway.*

With an effort, I turned my thoughts to practicality. I needed to go shopping. That meant leaving him here.

*Trusting* him. With a house that didn't belong to me.

He looked comfy enough on the sofa, with his bad leg propped up on a footstool. I'd brought my quilt down and draped it over him, in case he felt like having a lie-down or got chilly.

I explained I had to go to the shop, and asked if he'd be OK on his own for an hour.

"Absolutely." I'd left *A Brief History of Everything* on the coffee table. He asked if I minded him reading it.

"Of course I mind," I said, checking I had my keys. "I'll charge you for it, too. Ten euro a page."

He'd already opened the book, but he looked up and grinned. I grinned back at him, but his smile faded, leaving him looking at me with an unexpected intensity.

"Thank you," he said in a low voice. "But there's one thing you *could* do for me, if you would: stop insulting yourself, you don't deserve it. You strike me as being kind and decent; you're not any kind of idiot."

"This is hardly 'sensible', is it?" I waved my arms to encompass the entire ridiculous situation. "I meet a stranger who's had an accident and has injuries a medical professional should check out, so I prove I'm as daft as he is by *not* calling the medical professional, and try to help him compound a possible broken back. The next time I see him, I invite him into a house that isn't mine, make him tea, put him on the sofa, and tell him I'm living in it on my own. *Now* I'm going to drive into town, leaving him free to ransack the house, steal the dog and make a getaway in a taxi, which I know he's already got a number for. Though just in case he hasn't, there's a card pinned up over the telephone over there."

"I can't ransack the house and make a getaway until my other clothes are out of the washing machine," he pointed out, straight-faced. "Not unless I disconnect it and take it along with everything else. If I did, I wouldn't give much for my chances of making a getaway. It wouldn't take Hercule Poirot to spot a limping felon trying to manhandle a large dog, a bag of swag and a washing machine out of a taxi and onto a train. We'd stand out a mile."

My tension broke in laughter. "There is that, I suppose. I'll just have to make sure I get back before the washing machine gets to the end of the cycle – good job it's on a long wash. Enjoy your read and have a nap if you feel like it. I'll be back in an hour."

# Chapter 14

Saint Frances had been insisting I ought to tell somebody in my family what I was doing. I'd been away for over forty-eight hours now, and it wasn't just Liam who'd be worried sick in case anything had happened to me. Driving towards Leyburn, I finally admitted she was right. As soon as I'd parked, I'd do it. Before I lost my nerve.

It was the wrong time for ringing Liam, who'd be at work. Ciarán was still in America, and if he hadn't already heard the news I didn't want to risk spoiling his holiday with news of a family spat. Fergal was probably studying, and if he was in a lecture, he'd have his mobile switched off.

Brendan was my best bet. Most likely he'd be in his office, but if he was in his car, he could take the call on his hands-free. Besides, he was the one Liam would most likely have turned to.

I switched the phone on, connected to the Internet, and watched guiltily as a stack of notifications arrived. I could read them later.

Brendan's mobile rang out. I held my breath.

"*Ma!* Where the feck are you? We've all been worried sick!"

*Mustn't tell him where I am. He'll tell Liam.* I reminded myself wildly that I wasn't at the cottage, so even if the call was traced, I was safe enough. "I'm OK," I said, hearing my voice quaver – the accusation in his tone tore at me. "I said on the note I left I would be! I've ... I've just come away to be on my own for a while."

He breathed out, hard, and told me Liam had been on the phone to everyone in the family, asking if they'd seen me or heard from me. He was even talking about calling the gardaí.

Jesus, he must have been mortified, ringing round telling everyone I'd done a runner. And they'd told Ciarán too. So much for his holiday!

Anger rapidly succeeded guilt. "Did he want them to arrest me for trashing his bloody telly?"

"That's not fair, Ma. Of course he was upset about the telly, but he was worried like the rest of us." He swallowed. "We've hardly dared watch the news in case your– We were thinking you... that something had happened to you! And the kids have been worried sick!"

I'd scared the grandkids. Jesus, how selfish did that make me?

That said, what in the name of Blessed Mary had any of them *told* the little ones for? It wasn't as if I was incapable of looking after myself, or had disappeared into thin air without a word!

If any of them had had the sense to keep their gobs shut, the kiddies wouldn't even have had to know I was AWOL. Did anyone actually believe I'd stay away indefinitely and not contact *anyone* to say I was still in the land of the living? "Did none of you read the bloody *note?*" I hissed.

"Daddy told us what it said. What the fecking hell were we supposed to make out of you saying you were going away somewhere safe?"

*Daddy told us what it said.* He'd got to it first, then. Doubtless he'd given them a censored version, so they didn't know what else it said. I didn't know whether to be glad or sorry.

With that in play, it was hardly surprising he'd got no further than 'talking about' contacting the gardaí. They'd have wanted to see the note for themselves, unless he warned the kids not to mention it, and either would have set off all sorts of questions he wouldn't want asked. No, he'd sit tight and await developments for as long as he could.

"Look, I'm sorry. I just had to … get away." I shut my eyes. In hindsight, it seemed to me everything I'd done that morning had been inevitable. The eruption had been sudden, but the pressure under the volcano had been growing for years. It only needed the right combination of events to set it off.

"Mammy, what the hell got into you?" Now his tone was aggrieved. They'd had a scare, but now it would be Business As Usual and it was Mammy who was at fault, Mammy who had to do all the patching up. "Perhaps it's not perfect at home, Daddy's not a saint I know, but any marriage can go through a bad patch and…"

An explosion of bitterness and fury in my brain blocked out the rest. Did he actually *hear* himself, lecturing *me* about the sanctity of marriage?

I'd had reasons for my actions. Liam would have known that, if no one else did. Even if he didn't actually admit to what he'd done, and I very much doubted if he would, he could at least have admitted we'd had a row and I'd most likely just gone off somewhere to cool down. He could have taken over my job for once – been the peacemaker, the one whose task it was to calm the situation. Clearly, he hadn't, leaving everyone else to whip themselves into a panic because for once in my damned life I'd thought of *me* first.

I was a grown woman – why did they all assume the worst when I'd *told* them I was going somewhere safe and would come back? I'd looked after the whole bloody boiling of them for years, couldn't they even trust me to look after myself for forty-eight hours? Why the bejeezus had they had to take a single scene and make a three-act play out of it?

I couldn't tell him now what Liam had done to me – those things were between husband and wife, and we'd deal with them somehow when I went back. But what *could* I say? *We were cleaning out the loft and found something special I'd bought – I thought they were coffee spoons, but your daddy said they were only teaspoons and I'd been taken for a fool*? How – without mentioning the fact I'd been raped and hit – could I explain the loneliness and misery that had all at once become unbearable, the sense of time passing and life being wasted?

'A bad patch', my arse! The bad patch had started on my wedding day and it was still bloody going.

It pained me to admit that though Brendan was my son, he was a self-centred little shite. He'd seen me as 'Mammy' all these years, and that was the way he wanted things to stay. Even now, it hadn't dawned on him that there might be a person behind the functions – a person with hopes and dreams that were slowly suffocating as the years ticked by.

I'd wanted to escape for a while, to find a brief respite from the dreariness of my life. Chance had swept me away to the Yorkshire Dales; to a cottage, a dog, and a man lying on the sofa – a man with eyes like sunlit thunderclouds and a body like mortal sin.

*I haven't touched him!* I pleaded as the gravity of my situation flooded over me. *Only when I had to, to help him. I said 'Nice', but that was an accident. It's not like he'd fancy me anyway. I couldn't help looking, could I? Liam looks when those programmes have naked women in them.*

Saint Frances was ready for that. *That's just on the television! The man in that house is real, and you're panting after him like a whore. What did Jesus say? 'Anyone who looks at a woman lustfully has already committed adultery with her in his heart...'*

So if you're an unwanted husband or a despised wife, just forget all the immense, astonishing potential you have for loving and being loved, because *it isn't going to happen.*

Bitterness at the injustice of it all exploded again. *Well, if I'm damned for committing adultery with him in my heart, why the feck shouldn't I do it in my bed as well, then?*

"Ma?"

I jumped. Brendan's diatribe had finished, and he was waiting for a response.

"I'm sorry," I muttered. It wasn't entirely his fault he was a self-centred eejit; who'd made him that way? "I just... I needed to get away for a while. I should have rung before, but... I was just... I didn't."

I listened to him getting his temper under control. He didn't want to risk making me run any further amok by telling me what he *really* thought. "As long as you're OK, I suppose, and you'll be coming back," he said, begrudging. "You'll be ringing Daddy, won't you?"

If Brendan reacted like this, how would Liam behave?

He wouldn't cry, unless he was drunk – now and again I'd seen him drink enough to get maudlin. When he'd cooled down he'd undoubtedly been ashamed of what he'd done, both on the morning I left and the night before it. But he'd go on and on at me for my wickedness in wrecking our television, and my selfishness in deserting our home and worrying the whole family. He'd reduce me to a state of miserable guilt, scold me into making an abject return home, and then spend the rest of my life making me suffer for what I'd done.

As for him reading some bloody book on improving things in our marriage! I must have been delirious even thinking of it.

"I ... I will. But not yet," I prevaricated. "If you could do it ... and tell Fergal as well. And Ciarán..."

"It might be best if *you* speak to *him*." His grim tone suggested he'd no wish to contact his older brother; the two of them rarely saw eye to eye. "The fecker said if he'd known what you were going to do, he'd have sent you the petrol money."

Well now, that would have gone down a bomb with his father. The two of them had never got on either. Ciarán was far too much like me, but he had a core of steel I lacked. Though maybe up till now, mine had manifested itself in endurance rather than resistance. *I. DO. NOT. QUIT*, I thought proudly.

Or maybe just doggedly.

"I'll ring them anyway. Though how I'm supposed to explain why you're acting like a crazy woman, I don't know!" He breathed heavily for a moment. "Where the feck *are* you? Are you sure you can cope on your own?"

I smiled sourly. Mothers – especially your own – are incapable of operating outside the home. They do not possess sex drives. They can't possibly be suspected of having secret lovers with whom they might be indulging in illicit passions. *Especially* mothers who've eaten far too many chocolate bars and are nobody's idea of a MILF.

"I'll be fine," I said soothingly, squashing an urge to tell him I was in Manchester providing sexual services for both of their football teams and the reserve squads as well. "I'm in a lovely place in the country, and I'm absolutely grand. You've no need to worry about me."

"Of course we're going to worry about you." He sounded ungracious about it, as if he resented my putting them all to the trouble.

"Well, you needn't. Now I've got to go get some shopping. I'll ring you again in a day or two."

"And Da. You ought to ring him, Ma." His tone was emphatic. "He's your husband, remember that. He has a right to know what's going on and how soon you're coming home."

Fear squirmed again, and the dragon of anger snarled. It wasn't only husbands who had rights – didn't wives have them too? There'd been little 'loving and cherishing' when Liam had grabbed at the hem of my nightdress and pulled it up, or when he'd slapped me for turning my face away from him the morning after. But I said I would. In a day or two.

I wasn't sure about ringing Ciarán in America, but I could send him a text reassuring him I was all grand. In hindsight, I should have done that straight away, then he wouldn't have been caught on the hop when the eejits at home rang up squawking like a flock of panicking hens. Though to be honest, I was pretty sure he trusted me enough to be sure that whatever I'd done, I'd enough of a head on my shoulders to keep myself safe; his comment about sending me the petrol money suggested that. And Deirdre would probably have persuaded him not to say anything to their children before they came home to Ireland, at least not unless there was definite news. She'd a head on her shoulders, that one.

After today, of course, his confidence might well prove misplaced. But was I *always* to be the sensible one? Was I never to take the risk of having an adventure?

Brendan sighed loudly. There was no reasoning with females. "Well, look after yourself, and don't do anything stupid, wherever the feck you've hidden yourself." He hesitated, and then added, turning the thumbscrews of duty, that he loved me. That they all did.

It took a superhuman effort not to ask, 'Then why don't any of you fecking *show* me you do, now and then?' But I was used to not complaining, so I just mumbled "I love you all too," and cut the connection.

I loved them, yes. But none of them could save me, even if they wanted to.

*The only one who could save me was me.*

# Chapter 15

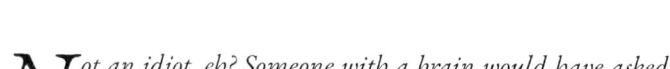

*Not an idiot, eh? Someone with a brain would have asked what he ate **before** they went shopping to feed him.*

I put several more packets of Nice biscuits into the basket, to bolster my feeble excuse. 'Nice', indeed! Thank God I hadn't said 'Cor', or 'Wow', either of which would have been impossible to explain away. Bridie would have come out with something like 'Well, cop an eyeful of *you*!' and got away with it.

She'd told me the supermarket in Leyburn was larger if I needed more choice. I had a lot more options now for meals.

*You can't beat a nice thick sausage*, said The Tart helpfully. Probably not meaning the sort you fry.

I was still smiling as I reached the car. Of course it wouldn't happen, but it was nice to pretend it might – and that if some handsome stranger said 'Please', I'd say 'Yes'.

You can always dream.

What were we to do this evening? I'd be quite happy with my book, but it seemed rude to curl up with it and ignore him. He had the 'Brief History' book, but perhaps he'd get bored with it.

There was a television in the lounge. I'd vowed never to switch it on, but if he wanted to watch something, it would be rude to refuse. I could make an excuse, go into the sunroom and read there.

*Doesn't matter how rude he thinks you are,* Saint Frances interrupted. *He shouldn't be there at all. I bet he thinks you're gagging for it. Next thing you know, you'll be raped. Don't come crying to me when it happens.*

Raped *again*, I reminded her sharply, and flinched; I didn't want to think about that. Besides, 'rape' is when you don't want it, I thought, remembering the way Mark's muscles had moved under that smooth skin. Almost without intending to, I imagined having him slowly peel me out of my clothes and press me back down onto the bed...

I should be so lucky.

Not that I would, of course, because I was a married woman and *forsaking all others*.

And who'd fancy me, anyway?

Well, whatever, it *was* rude to invite someone into your house and then neglect them. What else could I offer him as entertainment rather than the telly? I ignored several lurid suggestions from The Tart; she'd clearly got far more out of those naughty magazines than I had, by the sound of it. Most of her ideas would be bad for his ankle. Others were likely to end up with someone straining something; I suspected she was unclear on the difference between 'rapture' and 'rupture'.

I spotted a charity shop nearby. Inspiration struck. People donated games. Maybe I could find a jigsaw puzzle which we could do companionably if he didn't want to read. He didn't seem the sort of person who'd want to watch the telly *all the time*.

There was a section inside where you could buy four books for a pound, so I couldn't resist having a look in case there might be any that looked interesting.

I was flipping through them when my eye was caught by one whose red and black cover demanded 'ARE YOU IN AN ABUSIVE RELATIONSHIP?'

My hand stole out of its own accord.

There was a list of boxes you were supposed to tick if the statement applied to you. The book's previous owner must have been out of her mind to get married in the first place – she'd ticked every one of them. I hoped she'd taken the hint and skedaddled.

*Or perhaps you aren't the only daft mare who Does Not Quit,* came a mutter from The Tart.

I ignored this, but I couldn't stop reading.

Tick.

Tick.

Tick.

Tick.

... *Dear God in Heaven.* I was ticking all the boxes too.

I shoved the book back onto the shelf and stepped backwards. I'd come in here for entertainment for Mark, not for bloody books!

Jigsaw puzzles! I surveyed them with a mixture of relief and despondency. Absolutely, perfectly moral and safe. No possible occasions of sin in *them*.

*That pinkish piece with the knobble fits in THERE!* supplied The Tart, just to prove me wrong. She could find occasions at the drop of a hat.

I bet Joan of Arc had never had problems like that with *her* voices.

# Chapter 16

It was probably a Divine Warning that a scatter of raindrops fell on the windscreen as I pulled up on the cottage car-park and applied the handbrake.

As I switched off the ignition, my phone rang.

I was half-expecting to hear from Ciarán, so I pulled it out of my pocket.

*Liam.*

Well, I'd have to speak to him sooner or later. I swallowed, wiped my suddenly damp palms down my thighs, and pressed the 'Accept' icon.

The first few sentences were almost unintelligible, he was in such a fury. I caught a few words, but none I couldn't have done without hearing.

The sound of him raging at me jerked me back to that bed, and his looming threat. The breath caught in my throat, tears stung my eyes, and regardless of the rain I clawed at the window control as if opening it could give me more air in my lungs.

What little courage I'd managed to gather with the width of the Irish Sea between us simply collapsed. If I couldn't get a grip, I'd start hyperventilating. As I held the phone at arm's length, trying to distance myself from the tirade by any means I could, I told myself to just press the 'End' icon, but my thumb wouldn't move.

"I'm sorry. I'm so sorry." By the time he finally paused for a reply, I was almost whimpering.

'*...stupid fecking bitch...*'

"I know. I shouldn't have done it. I'm sorry."

'*...trying to turn our kids against me...*'

"I was just upset."

'*...lost your fecking marbles...*'

"I know."

'*...nothing to bloody do with them...*'

"I'm sorry. I know."

'*...if you don't get your fat arse back here...*'

"Soon. I can't...."

'*...if you weren't sodding frigid...*'

"I'm s–"

By this time I was crying, my fist rammed against my mouth. The enormity of the grudge I'd handed him was starting to dawn on me. And I had to go home to this.

But by some miracle, the word 'frigid' struck the one scrap of self-respect that hadn't been swept away. I gripped it, feeling the hot roar of rage starting up, dispelling the miasma of dread that had been simply waiting for the reckoning.

The 'good old days' of men having all the power were gone. There were laws in place now to protect women, and if he chose to drive me hard enough, I was willing to fight back with any weapons I had. I was sorry for the damage and upset it would cause to the family, but I'd suffered long enough!

"No. Actually, I'm not bloody sorry. Any more than I'm bloody frigid, if I'm treated like a human being instead of a cow in a field! I left because of *what you did*, and there's no excuses for that, and you know it. I bet you made damn sure the kids never saw that note, didn't you?" I snatched a tissue out of my pocket and wiped my eyes. "I'm sorry I scared them, for what it's worth, but all you have to tell them is that I've been asked to house-sit for a friend for a few weeks, and I'm doing it. What *else* you want to tell them is up to you, but I want a break from you, Liam. That's what I came here for. And I'm going to take it."

I don't think he expected that. There was a startled pause before he demanded where the hell I was, and how long I proposed to stay away.

"Where I am is my own business, and as for how long, it's a few weeks." Why should I make his life easier by knowing the details? Then, feeling that his slightly more moderate tone deserved something, I added, "I'm sorry about your television."

Almost before the words were out of my mouth, I realised I'd made a mistake. I'd rocked him back on his heels by standing up to him for once, but apologising had given him back the high ground. So before he could take advantage of it, I took a deep breath. "Actually, I'm *not* sorry about your fecking television either! I should have done it years ago. And I hated that bloody vase, too!"

His precious television was a sore point, it seemed. He screeched that if I'd had a problem, why didn't I *say* something instead of going off the deep end?

"Say something?" I yelled back. "Because you wouldn't have bloody listened to a word I had to say! All you ever cared about was that fecking box in the corner! Well, there's no television here, just peace and quiet. And when I come home, *if* I come home, I'm going to get a life of my own. I'm not wearing myself to a bloody shadow any more worrying what you think. I'm going to paint again, and I don't give a shite if you don't like it. If you want a skivvy, you can bloody well go out and find one. 'Cause *my* days as one are over!"

He had plenty to say to that. I let him rave for a bit.

"You'll *have* to manage," I hissed when he finally ran out of breath. "There's food in the house. You can cook it like I do every bloody night, or you can live off bloody takeaways. I'll be back when I'm good and ready.

"Yes, I *do* remember I'm your wife. I remember every word I said, including *honour and cherish*. You said those words too, but you bloody well forgot them fast enough.

"So there." I hit 'End' and switched the phone off. He could yell and scream at a dead line till his teeth fell out.

The past few minutes had been so traumatic I was trembling. I had a bottle of water jammed into the side panel of the passenger door, so I leaned over, hooked it out and started gulping from it.

Gradually my pulse slowed. My hands stopped shaking.

I wasn't sure what the consequences would be of what I'd said, but as fearful as I was when I thought of what it might bring, I couldn't regret it. Other than crawling home to lick my husband's boots till he considered I'd grovelled enough to be forgiven, what else could I have possibly done? I'd finally found some self-respect the day I did a runner. If it wasn't all to be so much wasted effort and anguish, I had to keep going somehow.

I had a lot to think about. When I'd put the shopping away, I'd check on Mark and then take Sharp for a walk. Obviously I'd have to do that on my own, which would afford me time to do a lot of thinking.

And I had an *awful* lot of thinking to do.

# Chapter 17

*You've bloody gone and done it this time.*

I stood in the middle of the narrow wooden footbridge, leaned against one of its outward-sloping sides, and looked down into the river. I'd broken off a small branch from a bush, and now I nipped the leaves from it, one by one, and let them spiral down to the ripples below, to be carried away out of sight. So many helpless leaves, floating on the tide of events, torn off from their anchorage and borne away to who knows where.

They'd had no choice about their fate. That was my doing, the doing of an indifferent and omnipotent goddess who was as careless of them as the official one – that one Up There – was of His sparrows. He might observe the fall of every tiny bird, but he wouldn't bloody well put out a finger to save even one of them from falling off a twig into the snow, frozen to death in a hard winter.

But I'd been the architect of my own disaster. I'd had a safe, stable life – maybe it wasn't a very happy life, but it was familiar and secure: 'Fifty Shades of Dull', if you wanted to find a title for it. In that moment of madness, I'd detonated a bomb under it. For all my brave words to Liam at nearly five hundred kilometres' safe distance, there was no saying what – if anything – I'd be able to salvage from the wreckage afterwards.

The words *abusive relationship* crept back into my mind. I thrust them away. My marriage was unhappy, yes, but it couldn't possibly be *abusive*. I was just depressed, that was all, otherwise I'd never have done something so bloody stupid. It would have caused ructions in even the most blissful relationship. Mentally stable people don't go around chucking vases through expensive televisions and fleeing the country just because their husband gives them a one-off little clout. It wasn't like Liam was anything like Michael O'Grady back home, who was forever giving Sarah a bruise or a black eye that she told the neighbours she'd got falling downstairs or having a tin fall out of a cupboard and hit her face.

Had I been justified in smashing the Square-Eyed God? At the time, it had felt not only right, but *glorious*. Perhaps that was how Kamikaze pilots had felt, aiming their explosive-filled planes at American shipping, proud to die for the Emperor and take as many of the enemy with them as possible. But shortly after experiencing that feeling, they were *dead*.

Some holiday this was turning out to be! Restlessly, I turned and followed Sharp, who'd wandered happily onto the opposite bank when I unclipped the leash from his choke chain. I was supposed to be relaxing, and now I'd put myself into a situation where relaxing was pretty damned impossible.

Still, the peace of the riverside woodland made it hard to worry for long, or at least at my usual intensity. It might be morbid to feel comforted because this beautiful place had been here long before I was born and would still be here long after I was dead, but somehow the sense of its continuity was consoling.

When the idyll ended and I returned to Ireland, the storm would break. Liam in the flesh would be a completely different prospect to Liam safely at the other end of a phone call, and I'd have to change the habits of decades if our marriage was to survive. His habits as well as mine – especially that of regarding me as a domestic servant whose wants and needs he could ignore.

Could it be done?

We wandered on companionably for a while. Paul had mentioned a tiny, ruined church hereabouts. Clouds had drifted along by this time. The odd patter of rain swept through the wood, but it wasn't cold and I didn't mind getting damp. In Ireland, we'd call this a 'soft' morning; not at all disagreeable to walk in, if you were properly dressed for it and had a warm fire to go back to.

"Am I just getting carried away here?" I asked aloud. "Can things change? Can *I* change? Do I *want* to change? Do I want to change *enough?*"

Yes, possibly. Changing Liam would be the problem.

Long ago, I'd read somewhere that even if you can't change situations, you can change how you react to them.

Could I use this... revolt?... as a pivot, or was it merely a brief pause in the long, slow grind of annihilation?

Preoccupied, I nearly missed the church. As ruins go, it wasn't impressive. Even when it was intact, it would have been a tiny building, hardly the size of a garage by today's standards. Only one wall remained, though the bases of the others were there, smothered by the undergrowth. A tree was growing inside.

A plaque on a post stated that the church had originally been dedicated to Saint Simon. There were a few details of its history. For part of its life, it had functioned as an alehouse.

Paul had also mentioned the hermitage, almost directly opposite it. Shaped stones lined a small hollow in a shallow crag, enclosing what looked like a fireplace. Surely it wasn't the only shelter the hermit had had; it wouldn't have kept off a heavy shower, let alone the snows of winter. At a guess, some kind of wooden structure had enclosed the front of it to offer extra protection. Now, however, only the stone remained. The green silence of the woodland had long ago swallowed any holiness the place had possessed.

I walked over slowly towards it, trying to imagine the utter simplicity of such a life. If you wanted to be free from distractions, this was your place. A priest would probably visit once or twice a week to say Mass. Other than that it would be peaceful, apart from the odd visit from locals asking for prayers.

Peaceful, yes. Though I'd read these mystics could get themselves so wound up about temptation that The Tart's pipings-up paled by comparison. At least *I* never visualised devils taking on the form of succubae and tempting me to damnation while I slept, with the proffer of sexual delights beyond imagining.

"More's the pity," I muttered. There had been nights – far too many – when any incubus brave enough to suggest rendering me unspeakable sexual services would have limped away hours later, nursing its overworked willy.

Though my Catholic upbringing had made my teenage years hell after learning that masturbation was a mortal sin, I'd grown into a more balanced and humane attitude towards that, too. I no longer believed in a God who bothered with such trivia. But even now (I could have said *especially* now, after the events of the last couple of days), the idea of having a demon sidle around the corner and make me an offer I couldn't refuse had undeniable appeal.

I'd studied art at school, working to prepare for my degree, and gone through a period of dabbling in fantasy art, loving the freedom of imagination the genre offered. Fortunately, art was one of the few classes in St. Clare's that weren't run by a nun, or they'd have marched me up to the Head. It had always annoyed me that while classical artists showed female demons as voluptuous beauties, they portrayed male demons as revolting – horned, horrible and usually downright ugly. The suggestion was that women weren't interested in anything above waist level, so demons didn't have to bother making themselves look handsome.

But surely the opposite was true? Women valued beauty as much as any man. So wouldn't a handsome demon stand a far better chance of success? Anyone would turn away an ugly-looking thing with horns and fangs, out of sheer self-preservation. But if the demon were handsome – if, by any chance, he had a fit, toned body, and a firm, sensuous mouth, and–

*Stop right there!* bawled Saint Frances, while The Tart sniggered knowingly in the background. But the canvas was already unrolling in my mind. I could see every detail, as though it had been there all the time and someone had swept aside a curtain to reveal it. For the first time in years, my fingers ached to paint – to *really* paint, not just dabble with sketching and kiddies' watercolours. To reproduce what I could now see so clearly in my mind's eye; to create not so much an image of Mark as of what he represented. To work – however long it took me to become good enough – towards the picture of a Lucifer whom a woman would find irresistible.

Despite Liam's dislike of my painting, I'd tried to carry on with it at first. It was too important to me to just give up, and I'd hoped he'd give over moaning, even if he could moan for Ireland when he was minded.

But the opposite happened. Far from tolerating it because it made me happy, he became more and more resentful of it. He'd never have admitted it, but I suspected it was because his mother spent every spare hour in the kitchen, cooking and baking, and he thought I should do the same. There were times when I thought his mammy might as well have been in the bloody house with us, because he parroted her views like a ventriloquist's dummy. Until the day she died, I dreaded her visits – she haunted the kitchen even when I wasn't in the house, rearranging everything, and telling me when I *was* there how to cook every dish the way Liam liked it; and Himself thought he was in seventh heaven, especially as she too disapproved of my paintings.

Eventually, of course, I'd caved in. My painting stuff went in the bin. It wasn't worth the strain on our marriage, and by then I had Ciarán as well. Mother-in-Law had wanted him christened Conall after her father, but it so happened I was the one to go to the Registry Office, so she was out of luck. She didn't speak to me for weeks afterwards.

When, I wondered now, with growing fury, had I become such a bloody *wimp?* Why the hell had I given up something I valued so much, to placate a selfish eejit who couldn't draw a straight line with a ruler, and his mammy who was a bully and a shrew?

Peace. I'd wanted peace, and I'd been willing to sell anything for it, not realising that in the process I was selling myself. No wonder I'd slowly become this dreary thing everyone took for granted; even the kids, the youngest two in particular, saw me as a set of functions under the heading of 'Mammy'. *Janey Mack.* I felt like kicking myself when I realised how much I'd given up and how little I'd got in return.

Well. When I went home, *that* was going to change. I'd get myself another job so I could buy proper painting materials. It didn't matter what work I did, as long as it financed my dream. I'd strip out one of the boys' bedrooms and turn it into a studio, and if Liam didn't like it, he could do the other bloody thing. No TV would be allowed in it, but I'd have my music player there.

I wasn't waiting till I got home, either. Tomorrow I'd see if I could find a shop selling decent pencils and good sketching paper rather than the stuff I'd bought in the convenience store. Damn the expense! I'd survive on toast till I went home if I had to. After all, I had something to hand that would come in mighty useful for a few preliminary sketches, the basis of what would one day be my masterwork.

The original model.

# Chapter 18

Mark was awake when we got home, and there was no evidence of the place being ransacked in my absence. I made drinks and set about the preparations for dinner.

Although he was as pleasant as ever, and even shocked me by asking several times whether there was anything he could do to help, I got the distinct feeling there was something he wanted to say. So I wasn't entirely surprised when he suddenly leaned forward and laid his wallet on the coffee table, pushed it towards me and asked me to look after it for him.

I wasn't quite sure how to take that. "You think someone's going to break in and steal it?" He was hardly calling *my* trustworthiness into question, considering he was giving it to me. Or – a darker thought – was he testing me, to see if I'd help myself to one of his credit cards and go on a spending spree?

"Of course not." He was looking at me steadily. "It's occurred to me you don't know the first thing about me, and you've asked me to stay here."

"Nope. Still not getting it."

"My cards, my driving licence, my contact details, everything I have on me is in that. If you wanted to report me to the police, that would be all you'd need."

"And what makes you think I'd be wanting to report you to anybody?"

"Well, in my clumsy way, I was trying to make you feel a little more secure. You don't know me from Adam. I'm sure I'm flattered you think I'm obviously trustworthy, but I felt having it until I leave might make you feel more comfortable."

It was just as well that I'd had long practice in the art of thinking before I reacted; the first retort that sprang to mind was that the cottage wasn't a bar, that he had to put a credit card behind the till to guarantee his welcome. I put down the spoon I'd just picked up, because I was tempted to throw it at his head.

He was right, of course. I didn't know the first thing about him, other than that he'd been in a relationship that had come to a bad end – and there could be all sorts of reasons why that had happened. Insofar as I'd thought about it at all, I'd hoped he might talk a little about himself when he felt more comfortable with me, but that was up to him to decide. My offer of sanctuary wasn't dependent on me knowing the first damned thing about him other than that he was a decent-seeming chap who needed help.

*And good-looking doesn't come into it, of course,* sneered Saint Frances.

The Tart elbowed her to shut her up.

Decent-*seeming*, of course, was no guarantee whatsoever. I could point out a score of people we were on first-name terms with in our church who'd be ready to swear on the Bible that

Liam would never raise his hand to me. Maybe that wallet wasn't such a bad idea.

I eyed it and him for a moment, then turned around and picked up the spoon. "Put that thing away again."

After a moment, I heard the slight sounds of him doing so.

"I hope I didn't offend you by that," he said quietly. "I'd understand if you were feeling a little anxious about me by now, but I couldn't imagine any other way to offer you reassurance that you can trust me not to abuse your kindness."

"I appreciate that," I said with a nod. "But the fact is, I'm probably not as dim as you might think. If I wasn't as sure as I can be that I could trust you, I'd have taken you to your guest house and left you to it."

"Then I'm glad you were. And I assure you, you won't have any cause to regret it."

Conversation lapsed then, but it was a comfortable quiet. He asked if I minded him reading, and I said go ahead.

It didn't take long before dinner was ready. As I was setting out cutlery on the two waiting trays, I asked if he could switch on the media player on the shelf behind him. "I like a bit of music while I'm eating. I hope you've no objection?"

"None whatsoever. Actually, I'd be delighted." He twisted around and flicked the switch; it was already plugged in at the wall, and Paul had connected it to my phone by Bluetooth before he left. "That was one of the things my– my girlfriend and I didn't see eye to eye on. One of many things, now I come to look back on it, but you don't see that at the time."

"Ah." I shrugged. "Sometimes it's easier to be blind than to admit you've been an eejit. I should know that well enough, God knows."

We exchanged covert glances, both having volunteered sensitive information.

Dinner was nothing special, but from the way he praised it you'd have thought it was Cordon Bleu. He'd have made the effort to wash up afterwards, too, in spite of his ankle, but the fact that we had a dishwasher made that idea redundant.

When this was loaded and switched on, and everything else was tidied up and put away, I made drinks for us. As I sat down, I remarked how grand it was to find someone else who enjoyed music. The player was still on in the background, low but audible.

"Górecki, Symphony No. 3, second movement," he said, pointing at it. "I can't hear it well enough to be sure, but I'd guess it's the Zinman version, with Dawn Upshaw. Brilliant."

I'd never got into it enough to know one version from another, but finding he liked one of my favourite composers was as if he'd dropped diamonds in my lap. "You like Górecki?"

"Very much," he replied warmly. "I've some of his stuff on my iPad. Perhaps we can see if I've got anything you haven't heard – and the other way around."

And so far, he hadn't even mentioned the telly.

The rest of the day passed without event. Both of us read quietly. At one point in the evening, I nodded off, and when I woke up there was a certain pleasure in finding that he'd drawn the curtains and switched on the table lamp, creating a cosy pool of light in the dimness that had swallowed the cottage.

"Good, you're awake." He looked across with a smile. "My turn to make the drinks, I think."

"As long as you're not doing that ankle of yours any mischief."

"They said I should exercise it in moderation." He limped over to the kitchen area.

"You know, this is one of the stupidest things I've ever done in my life," I told him, "and yet it's probably one of the best. I'm so bloody sick and tired of being sane and sensible."

He actually beamed. "Do you know, so am I! Isn't ordinary life *boring?*"

I said no more until he'd brought the drinks. Then, "Now, that surprises me."

"That I think life is boring?" he said, obviously startled.

"Not so much. I'd think most people would find their lives are boring, if they ever stopped to think about them. But you – I'd you down as the sort of fella who likes their lives to be organised. And too much organisation's the mother of boredom."

He frowned slightly, and explained that in his job as a construction manager, he had to be *extremely* organised, or a hell of a lot of things could go wrong that could cost the company dear. Not to mention – in the worst case – costing him his job.

I leaned forward. "You keep your clothes in a wardrobe, yeah?"

"Doesn't everyone?"

"Then I'll bet you fifty euro it's all colour co-ordinated." I sat back again, grinning, but almost at once I realised with dismay that rather than grinning back, he looked rather upset.

"Perhaps you have a point."

"I'll give you a bit of advice," I said. "Find some way to be crazy, because otherwise, if you keep yourself shut up in a box like everyone else expects, someday the box will burst and all hell'll break loose."

"I never *set out* to be boring, you know. Who does? Somewhere along the way, it just happened." And then he began talking, explaining how he'd ended up falling on his arse down the side of the old quarry.

Inevitably, it involved a woman – Rebecca, some years his junior – who without any warning had dumped him like an outworn suitcase the previous week, leaving him not only homeless but mentally and emotionally battered. He'd taken annual leave from his job and fled the scene of the crime, most likely hoping to find some opportunity for recovery while he hiked around the lanes of the Yorkshire Dales. There, he'd come across the quarry and, smarting from the new fear that he was 'old and boring', decided to climb the path to the top. All had been going well until he was on his way down, when the eruption of some bird or other from the undergrowth had startled him so badly he lost his footing.

"So I was already trying to do something just a *little* silly," he ended ruefully. "I certainly didn't intend to slip and fall, but that silly crow or whatever it was had other ideas."

There was no way I was going to make any comment about Rebecca, though I had my own opinions about any woman who could treat her lover so callously. Instead, I nodded and said good on him for doing something different. Even if it didn't turn out quite the way he'd intended it to.

"I know it's not what you were hoping for," I continued, "but I'll be honest, it's nice having someone here. And if you want to stay a few days, you're welcome."

Steeling myself against the embarrassment, I told him once again that I wasn't coming on to him, and that I'd not got ambitions to be one of them cougars you read about in the paper. With a figure like mine, I wouldn't stand a cat's chance if I did, but that wasn't what I was asking for.

"I'm so bloody lonely at home," I ended. "It's different here, but it's grand to have someone I can listen to music with. And laugh with. I'd like that too, because I'm sick and weary of not being able to. That's all."

He smiled. "That sounds like something both of us could enjoy."

Bedtime came.

I suspected both of us were glad I'd set out fairly what the position was regarding my reasons for having him here. Both of us were battered; both of us needed to draw breath. There were no silly expectations.

(*Pity*, muttered The Tart.)

He hobbled upstairs to use the bathroom while I let Sharp out for a last run around the garden. Then, when I was sure everything was tidied up and locked up, I waited while Mark got himself settled down again on the sofa.

It would be dark, out here in the country, for a lad born and bred in the City. I told him so, and asked if he'd prefer the curtains opened. He thought this was a good idea.

There was a moon out there, almost at the full, and as I swept the heavy damask back, the moonlight streamed in, casting the elongated shadow of the vase on the windowsill across the tabletop.

Staring out through the panes, I felt a sudden desperate longing for my own country – not Dublin, but for the green and blue Northwest where I'd been born. For a moment I was nearly sick with it. It had been so long since I'd been back.

"You come from the country, then?" he asked.

"Not now," I said briefly.

"I'm sorry." He hesitated. "I wasn't prying. If I've upset you, I apologise – that was the last thing I wanted to do."

"None of it's your fault." I sighed, letting my shoulders sag. "For what it's worth, I've done a runner from my husband. I've lived with him nearly thirty-four years and he'd have treated me better if I'd been a bloody dog – and he doesn't even *like* dogs."

The window pane was chilly against my forehead. It was somehow easier to talk looking out across the almost featureless dark landscape; like the anonymity of a confessional. "We met when I worked in his daddy's company in Donegal, but we moved to Dublin because that was where the proper chances were back in them days. We made a go of it, but I was so homesick. I used to dream I was back home and wake up crying, but there was nobody I could talk to about it. It'd have broken my parents' hearts to know I was so unhappy, and Liam was just fixated on the money he could make."

"That must have been terrible for you," he said gently.

I nodded. "I bloody hated the place, and I still do. It's dirty and it's crowded and it's soulless, and you can't hear yourself think. It's worse now than it's ever been. And now the kids are finally all grown up and gone, I'm going to be on my own. Totally, completely on my own, even with him there.

"But the weird thing is, I've been less lonely on my own here than in that bloody house of ours with the whole damn crew in it. I wish I *lived* here. I wish I could look out every day at that view. Even if it was raining buckets or there was a fog down so thick you couldn't actually *see* the fecking thing, you'd know it was there. It feels like a friend." I straightened up and glanced around at him. "And why I've told you any of this, I do not know."

"Perhaps because I feel like a friend too? I hope so."

It was too early to call it on that, but I felt as if at least there was a possibility it might be true. The night to come – the night with no locked doors in between us and no possibility of help reaching me in time if I'd made the most horrible mistake – would go a long way to confirm it, but somehow I felt at peace.

I switched on the light over the stairwell and then walked to switch off the table lamp. As I came back again, my hand rested for a moment on the back of the couch. "You're sure you'll be all right now? There's nothing more you need before I go up?"

I don't think he'd realised I was so close. He jumped. And then, as if it was the most natural thing in the world, he picked up my hand and kissed it. "Nothing at all. Thank you for everything."

I withdrew my hand gently. "You're welcome."

The silence between us that had been comfortable now seemed very loud as I pulled the spare quilt over to make sure it wouldn't slip off him easily, and pushed the broad, padded footstool a few inches closer so he'd have wider support for his knees.

Finally, everything was sorted.

"The jug's by the back door if you don't feel up to struggling up them stairs in the night. If you wake up and need anything, don't go doing anything stupid and hurting yourself." Carefully I refrained from looking at him. "I'll leave my door open. Just give me a shout."

"Goodnight." His voice was soft.

"Sleep well. I hope your foot's better in the morning."

# Chapter 19

It seemed the weather sympathised with me.

When the sound of a gale flinging fistfuls of heavy rain against the window woke me in the early hours, I got out of bed and went to see. The water was streaming down the glass.

I stood peering out into the dark turmoil outside, feeling suddenly as though the house was a cage. My whole *life* was a cage, and I couldn't break out of it.

In 'the movies', of course, my next course of action was clear. I'd tiptoe downstairs, open the back door and run out into the rain. There I'd be overtaken by the dashing hero, who'd snatch me into his arms and declare his unconquerable passion for me – and then, with any luck, shag me senseless on the lawn in the deluge, complete with the appropriate soundtrack.

But I wasn't *in* 'the movies'. The dashing hero with the sprained ankle was fast asleep downstairs, and about as likely to pursue me outside and shag me senseless on the lawn as I was to paint like Leonardo da Vinci.

Various other equally improbable romantic scenarios flitted through my mind. But even if I somehow managed to creep downstairs without setting Sharp barking his head off, and succeeded in sneaking myself under the quilt with my hapless guest (after all, I wouldn't be intending to disturb his ankle), well … what if he hadn't read *that* script either?

The embarrassment for both of us would be unimaginable.

But it was still easier to imagine it than it would be to endure it. Better to stew in my loneliness forever than go on living with humiliation on that scale afterwards.

The knuckles of my left hand were still tender. I'd scrubbed them with a nail brush to get the sensation of his kiss off them, because I had too much imagination by half.

Why had I told him about my marriage? Why did I feel so completely relaxed with a total stranger? How could I talk to him so easily?

*Why did I trust him?* The question came back to me again and again, especially when there was a noise in the darkness. Like every old house, the cottage made sounds as it settled down at night. The first night I'd been convinced someone was creeping around, though Bridie had told me it would be the boards on the stairs creaking as the air cooled.

*Because you're bloody desperate,* sneered Saint Frances.

I waited for the rebuttal from The Tart, but there was nothing. Only the sound of the rain dashing itself against the window.

I went back to bed. For the first time in years, I cried myself to sleep.

The rain had blown away by morning, and it was difficult to recapture that sense of despair when the sun was shining and birds were chirping in the Virginia creeper around the window. The Tart insisted on calling it 'creeping virginity', saying there was far too much of that around here already without having it crawling up the walls and trying to get in.

She was getting altogether *too* bold, that woman. I'd have to have a stern word with her one of these days.

I sat up in bed, wrapped my arms around my up-drawn knees and smiled. At least I could have Mark as a friend for as long as he stayed; and today, I was going to try my hand at drawing again.

It had occurred to me that I could do a few quick sketches of him while pretending to be drawing something else. It was better than scaring the bejeezus out of him by asking him to model for me. If I organised things right and was careful not to glance too often at my *actual* subject, I thought I'd likely get a couple of chances without being caught in the act.

Instead of dawdling over a bath, I used the shower. Then I chose a long rose-coloured skirt instead of jeans and pulled my best pretty blouse off its hanger. I pressed the worst of the wet out of my hair with a towel and combed it carefully, sitting in the armchair by the open window. Everywhere, the world looked freshly washed and sparkling. Even the trees by the river looked greener after the downpour.

As soon as I was ready, I tiptoed downstairs into the kitchen. I let Sharp out into the garden and then went to get his breakfast.

Mark was still asleep. After I'd fed Sharp, I made myself a cup of coffee and some porridge, stopping the microwave just before it went 'Ping!' and shattered the quiet.

The sunny patio beckoned irresistibly. Very quietly I opened the back door again and carried my breakfast out to the table there. The wrought-iron chairs were still wet, but I'd brought down my damp towel to be washed and now used it to wipe them down. To go by the cloudless sky, the day should be glorious.

The bees were already busy in the lavender, but I leaned over and broke off a single head whose flowers were nearly spent. I wove the still-perfumed stem carefully through two buttonholes near the neck of my white blouse, where its colour matched the flowers embroidered on the collar. Maybe later I could find a heavy book somewhere so I could press and dry it and take it home as a memento.

Grimacing, I pushed away the words 'take it home'. While I was here, I was going to take *'Carpe Diem'* as my motto. 'Seize the Day.' The Tart would undoubtedly have preferred 'Seize the Guest' but 'Day' would have to do. It would be ridiculous not to make the most of everything, creating happy memories to dwell on when I was back in captivity.

Before I'd finished a very leisurely breakfast, Mark came out to join me. He'd showered and dressed. His ankle was better enough to have allowed him to make some toast, and I'd left a pot of tea to keep warm under the cosy.

After a few minutes of peacefully admiring the view while he ate and drank, he asked if I had any plans for the day.

This was opportune. It allowed me to mention I was thinking of doing some drawing. And, remembering my dark plans of earlier, I added that he could have the job of keeping me company and overseeing the music player.

I was also tempted to add 'I need a model, how'd you feel about posing in the nude?', just to see how he reacted, but scaring him witless wouldn't do much for our fledgling friendship. I went into the kitchen to make a second cup of coffee and refill his teacup.

When I returned, he took the cup with a nod of thanks. "So, you're planning to take up art? Is it something you've done before, or is this a new departure?"

I explained how I'd given it up, and how my attempt the other day had shown me how lamentably out of practice I was. "I was – my husband didn't approve."

He said nothing, though his mouth quirked downward in distaste.

"It was probably as much my fault as his," I said quietly. Now we'd broached the subject, I felt the old familiar nervousness creeping over me, but I tried to keep my tone light. "If I hadn't thrown myself on the floor, he couldn't have trodden on me."

"Please." He looked across at me, grave-faced. "Nobody *deserves* to be bullied. Nobody *asks* to be bullied. If that's what's happened to you, it was *not* your fault *at all*."

I contrived a smile, though I felt nearer to tears; what had possessed me to bring Liam into the conversation and ruin it? "If you're walked over often enough, you start to think of yourself as a doormat. But thank you for saying I didn't deserve it."

One of the empty chairs was sitting at a slight angle, and I could almost feel my husband's presence in it, scowling and vengeful. For a moment my stomach curdled with fear. *I smashed the television.* What the hell had possessed me?

Mark must have seen something in my face. He sat forward, suddenly earnest. "No. Don't. I can feel... I can feel you not listening." He touched my hand lightly with his free one. "I know this is none of my damn business, so feel free to tell me to mind it if you want to. But I hate the thought of you being anybody's doormat. If I had a talented wife, I'd be proud of her, and so should your husband have been."

"Oh, I never said I was talented." I should be snatching my hand away, but I let it lie still, while Saint Frances spat *infidelity* and *hellfire.*

"I'll be the judge of that when I see what you draw," he said teasingly, but his eyes were serious and he was still touching my hand.

With a snort, I told him that going by that drawing I did the other day, the only thing I had in common with Rembrandt was that both of us used paintbrushes.

I hadn't allowed for him wanting to see the finished product though. I'd planned to pretend to be drawing the vase of lavender from the windowsill, but this new development made me think again. If he got to see what I *really* wanted to draw, would he be shocked? Embarrassed? Offended that I'd lied to him, and used him as a model without asking permission?

Would it spoil things between us, end the friendship that had spread two green leaves in the desert of my loneliness?

I tried to put myself in his position. Would *I* want to be used as a model by some stranger calling himself my friend, unknowing, and without ever giving consent, or even having been asked?

*Like hell I would.*

That wasn't the way friends treated each other. And I should have realised that from the start. I could plead the excuse that I'd become so used to getting what I needed by stealth that it had become practically second nature, but that didn't make what I'd planned to do right. Some 'friend' I'd be making myself out to be, if I behaved like that!

I swallowed. "Look. I'm not– I feel bad for asking, but…"

He looked across the table at me. I saw the grin start. "Are you asking what I *think* you're asking?"

If you'd dropped a piece of paper on my face at that moment, I swear it would have caught fire. However, I tried to hold on to at least some of my dignity. "I'm not asking you to do it in the nude!"

His grin turned into an outright laugh. "Well, that's a relief, at least!" But when he was through chuckling, he said he reckoned it was fair payment for his stay.

He was still amused, though, and when we went back into the lounge to set up the 'studio' I was beyond relieved that I'd been honest.

It took a few minutes to decide on a position and a pose he could sustain comfortably. Then, with a mischievous grin, he stripped off his top.

"And what d'you think you're smiling so much about?" I demanded, laying out my pencils on the tray beside me.

"I was waiting for you to say something else inopportune. Like 'Custard Cream', or whatever."

*All-Holy God.* I'd hardly got back to my ordinary colour, and now I blushed like a flamingo.

He had the most wonderful laugh on him. There wasn't an ounce of malice in it. "*I* know why you asked me to model. You really just want to ogle me again."

"You're talking like I'm easily impressed," I sniffed, pretending to hunt for a pencil sharpener while my scarlet face went back to at least something near normal.

He could have pointed out that I'd certainly sounded it last time, but he spared my blushes and stopped teasing. Instead, he ran his hands through his unbrushed hair, getting it into some kind of order, and began going through a series of simpering poses, each one worse than the last, until I was laughing so much I could hardly hold Biddy's leaner-board steady.

Finally, both of us stopped playing the goat. "Will you be warm enough like that?" I asked. "I can turn the central heating on a bit if you want."

He replied in this killing upper-class English voice that he was willing to suffer in the interests of Art.

"It's just that I don't want you going all goose-pimply and starting to complain when I'm busy. That's a man all over, and don't I know it. Three out of the four in our house'd rather spend ten minutes whining to me about the cold than ten seconds getting up and turning the bloody fire on."

"You know how to sweet-talk your sitters, I'll give you that."

I told him sweet-talking sitters wasn't high on my list of priorities.

He'd set up his iPad ready, and as I started drawing, he pressed 'Play'. He'd chosen the Clock Symphony this time, and it was familiar enough to be just a pleasant background while I worked.

And ... relax.

# Chapter 20

A couple of hours passed very pleasantly.

From time to time, Mark moved to sit as I directed. I wasn't unmindful of my ultimate aim, the Lucifer Portrait, but for the time being I just needed to get back into practice.

Eventually, however both of us needed a break. He lay back on the couch and put his foot up on the stool again while I made drinks for us both.

"I hope you'll have *someone* at home who'll appreciate your work," he said as I set down the biscuit-barrel. "I won't be able to see any of your paintings when you get around to starting."

"I don't need appreciating – I've done without it so far. Still, if you... maybe if you left your e-mail address, I could send you a photo of something I do when I've had more practice. When I've got better. If you're interested, that is, not just humouring me." I found myself blushing again. After so long, it was difficult to believe anyone would be *genuinely* interested in what I produced. "If you'd trust me with it, I promise I wouldn't... wouldn't use it any way I shouldn't."

"Fran," he said gently. "You can have my e-mail address with pleasure. And my phone number too, if you'd like it. You can use either of them whenever you want to. Isn't that what friends do?"

He must have seen how sharply I looked at him, because he went on, "What's wrong with that? I don't want us to stop being friends when you go back to Ireland. You managed to keep your friendship with Bridie going after she moved here."

"It's not that – I just–" Suddenly, to my horror, I found tears stinging my eyes. "Look, I hardly bloody know you. I don't want to get my hopes up and find you're just stringing me along for the fun of it–"

"Hey. Stop right there." He grabbed the cushions on the right of him and tossed them to the other end of the sofa, then looked across at me and raised his right arm, beckoning. "Come over here for a minute and let's talk. Just as friends. No funny business, Scout's honour. Come on."

I stared at him, not moving, while The Tart screamed *What are you waiting for?* and Saint Frances sat back with an expression of *I bloody well knew it!*

Out of either bravado or sheer damned obstinacy, he kept his arm up.

Ah, what the hell!

I stood up and walked over. As I sat down beside him, I was stiff with nerves; and though I didn't resist, I moved all of one piece like a doll when he put his arm around my shoulder and pulled me gently down into the crook of his arm. I kept both of my arms closely folded across my middle, paying at least lip service to the fact that I was a married woman and not to him.

For a moment, I kept my head lifted. But it was awkward, and tiring, and I didn't really want to. With a feeling of crossing a bridge that might collapse behind me, I lowered it to rest on his shoulder.

"Let's get a few things clear," he murmured. "I owe you a debt for everything you've done, and I'd like very much to repay it – even a little. I like being with you, I like making you laugh, and I enjoy your company, no matter what you want to do. If you consider me your friend, I'm honoured. So please, talk to me. Honestly."

Putting an arm across him was out of the question, but I weighed up how safe it would be to confide. He waited patiently, the hand of his encircling arm carefully dangling away from me so as not to seem to be constraining me in any way.

"I've had this idea that made me want to start drawing and painting again." I was picking my words very carefully. I didn't look up at him; it was easier not to. "I've always loved fantasy art. I don't know why, it just fascinated me. I wanted to take it up as a hobby – not professionally, I knew I was never going to be good enough for that." I went on to explain about the ruined church in the woods, and how I'd had this idea there, visualised this scene, and I really, *really* wanted to paint it. "I mean, when you look at women in fantasy art they're always beautiful – no matter how evil they are, they're always beautiful as well. So I don't see any reason why the devil can't be beautiful too."

He rubbed his free hand over his mouth. I knew he was trying to control the grin breaking out on it again. "You do know what this means."

"That I need my head checking?" I muttered.

"That you met me and immediately started thinking about a handsome devil." He twisted away, laughing, as I swatted him.

"Oh, *you* should be so bloody lucky!"

"Well, the implication is certainly there."

I swatted him again, and he laughed even more. "So, you're practising for this picture you want to paint," he went on, when he was done chuckling. "I'd imagine you have a specific image in mind, rather than what we've been doing this morning? Fewer clothes?"

"Well, yes. And no," I said hurriedly. "I'm not wanting you to get your clothes off." *Jesus, he already knows you fancy him. You must be sounding like an absolute yoke.* "I mean, not that way. You're honestly not thinking I'm–"

He interrupted my babble, his voice soothing. "No, I'm not thinking you're trying to seduce me, though if you ever change your mind, I'd like to hear about it. It's obvious this project of yours matters to you, so it matters to me. You need a model, and I'm perfectly happy to oblige. Though I've hardly got the sort of physique I'd imagine you're thinking of for the finished product, if all you need is a body to practise with, feel free to use mine."

Though his tone barely changed on the last few words, I was quite sure he meant *in bed or out of it.* Saint Frances, of course, opened her mouth to give out yards on the shamelessness of the man and my sinfulness in encouraging him to think I was up for it, but he didn't tighten his arm around me or give any indication that it was more than an offer.

After a long moment, I nerved myself to look up at him. The smile still lingered, but his expression was mostly serious.

"That's the best offer I've had all my life," I said at last, trying to make a joke of it. "If you're the quality of fella you sound like, that Rebecca was a damned eejit."

He grinned wryly. "Ah, but then she wanted more than a fifty-year-old amateur model."

"May the cat eat her, and the Devil eat the cat!" I muttered, that being one of my granny's quaint old Irishisms, and about the politest that would fit the circumstances.

Then, as both of us needed a bit of a break from what had become a surprisingly intense conversation, I went back to the armchair.

"So, describe this seductive devil for me," he went on, after taking his first mouthful of tea. "I'm an Artiste, remember. I have to get in the right frame of mind."

I'd taken a bite of a biscuit, and nearly choked on it. For pity's sake! Anyone'd think I wanted him to pose for *Playgirl*. "Well. I need to practise a bit first, but if we're going to do the picture, I want you to be... suggestive. Hinting. Not *showing*. It's going to be forever before I can start on actually painting the real thing, so if I could take some photographs I could work from..." He was smiling, and I trailed off uncertainly. "What?"

"It's nothing. Just that the last thing I ever expected to do was pose for naughty photographs at my age."

"Oh, you!" I picked up a cushion and threw it at him. "They're not 'naughty photographs', you eejit. I'm going for 'sophisticated' and 'alluring'. Think of how you normally are, and do the opposite."

He tried to look justifiably offended. "The *opposite* of my normal debonair self?"

"*Absolutely* the opposite. As 'opposite' as you can get it."
"Damn."

I hadn't got another cushion, which was the only reason he didn't get a second one sailing through the air at him.

Still, despite his acceptance, I was very anxious. *Tread softly, for you're walking on my dreams*, or something like that. So far he'd been very understanding, but having exposed my inmost self in this way made me feel very vulnerable.

"I'll do whatever you need," he said at last, his face more serious now. "But I'm just warning you, I tend to laugh when I'm nervous. And I suppose I am a bit nervous about this. It obviously means a lot to you."

But as I explained what I'd thought of – an image of 'Lucifer' on all fours on a bed, lifting the blanket in invitation to show a space beside him – though he listened carefully, I noticed the slight frown.

"Do you not think it's a good idea?" I asked, faltering.

He rubbed the bridge of his nose. "Can I be absolutely honest?"

"That's what friends are for, isn't it? I'm not wanting to put all that effort into making a total eejit of myself."

"I'm perfectly willing to pose for you that way, if that's what you want." He hesitated. "But to tell the truth, Fran, I'm not sure that position's what you need for your Lucifer. It's too feminine.

"Now, switch your artist's imagination on. Pretend I'm young and sexy, with a body to die for. *This* is what *I* see Lucifer doing." He pulled the quilt back onto the sofa, pushed his tracksuit bottoms to the verge of indecency and then rolled onto his side, one hand supporting his head and the other lifting the quilt to show the empty place beside him. For a mad moment, caught up in the pretence, he wore a snarl of invitation.

I sat staring at him as if turned into stone. Even The Tart was momentarily struck dumb; as for Saint Frances, if she was silent, it was only because she was lost for words at the vision of exactly what she'd feared all along.

Suddenly a look of horror came over his face. "God, I'm so sorry." He let the quilt fall, mortified. "I had no business telling you what you ought to draw. I didn't mean…"

The pause felt like half a century. It was probably all of ten seconds.

Then I picked up the sketch pad. "I hope you can sustain that pose, Lucifer."

# Chapter 21

Not that he had to sustain it for long. Unlike medieval painters, I had technology to hand. As I didn't want to risk putting my phone on, he lent me his iPhone and I took several pictures with it.

He took my email address and promised to send them on to me, password-protected of course. Once that was done, and we'd finished our drinks, he could relax and make himself reasonably comfortable while I got in some practice sketching individual parts of his body. It had been so long since I'd done this much drawing, though, that my fingers were starting to ache.

But other thoughts had begun seething.

A cuddle – just a cuddle, because I was getting myself stupidly upset. *Just friends.* His own words. *Scout's honour.*

But surely that meant *he* was thinking... that *I* might be thinking...

Presently I called a break. For one thing, I needed the toilet.

After I'd washed my hands, I leaned on the sink, shaking. Or could it possibly mean *he* was thinking...?

Who the hell was I trying to kid? He'd actually *told* me he was thinking. If I changed my mind about seducing him, he wanted to hear about it.

I felt as though those words would be engraved on my heart for the rest of my life. In Geography lessons at school, I'd read about some desert or other where it almost never rained. That desert was me, and those words had fallen from a blue sky, magically turning the dunes into carpets of multicoloured flowers. At least one man on Planet Earth thought I was desirable.

It wasn't going to happen, of course. But just to have that said to me, to have that gift beyond price dropped into my lap!

If the words alone had that effect on me, what would it be like if I changed my mind? If I said 'Yes', and for one hour of magic forgot *'I. DO. NOT. QUIT.'* and everything that went with it?

My mind replayed that open stare as he lay on the couch. The stare that said, 'This is what you want'.

Because I did want it. Jesus, how badly I wanted it. I'd forgotten just how desperate lust could feel. My groin was a hot pool of wanting, so hot that just keeping myself upright was making my knees ache.

I couldn't tell him to get out, though I knew now that I should. I literally, physically couldn't do it. I had a new friend, and that wasn't what you did to a friend. Almost in a frenzy, I blocked out Saint Frances's bitter, cynical voice saying, *He'd be your friend right till he'd made you another notch on his bedpost, and then he'd walk away laughing.* For all that I wanted desperately to believe him, I still reckoned I was enough of a judge of character to know if I was being duped.

Even if I was wrong, the naïve fool Liam had always said I was, would it be so utterly wrong to snatch this one chance of experiencing sex with a man whose idea of seduction surely wasn't pulling my nightdress up to my waist so he could get at the goods?

But if I *wasn't* wrong, what a chance I'd be passing up! A friend who could laugh with me, and who'd agreed to model for me. And who'd put his arm around me and said that what mattered to me mattered to him. Said it in this incredibly sexy voice, too, though that and all the rest of it was probably just him being all polite and gentlemanly and English, because he wouldn't *really* want someone as fat and ugly as me, would he?

Would he?

'Though if you ever change your mind, I'd like to hear about it.' My soul had shuddered to every word. If Liam had ever spoken to me in a voice like that, I'd have thought I'd died and gone to Heaven.

And this was the man I was supposed to repay by throwing him out on his ear?

And the cuddle. How safe I'd felt in the strong curve of his protecting arm!

There was no cuddling at home. The head of the household had his own special armchair in front of the TV, while I sat in solitary splendour on the sofa – not that I minded that; it meant I was further away from the noise.

On our wedding night – afterwards – I'd wanted to cuddle him, wanted to talk about what had just happened, wanted to make some kind of connection. Even as thick as I'd been back then, I wasn't expecting the earth to move straight away, but

I hoped to find out it had been brilliant for him, and that he thought I was the most amazing woman on God's earth and it had been worth all the wait.

But it hadn't turned out quite like that.

*It's too hot. I'm too tired. We'll talk in the morning if you want.* And he'd rolled over and gone to sleep, leaving me to sneak into the bathroom and clean myself up, hoping that the few hints I'd picked up about the first time being the worst were right. In the West of Ireland, even in those supposedly more enlightened days, you got your information where you could and took your chances on whether it was accurate or not.

Sleep hadn't come quite as easily for me. As tired and sore as I was, various doubts were raising their heads, but far too late. The deal was signed, sealed and delivered, with the evidence on a clean old towel I'd brought along and discreetly laid in position. The days were long gone, thank God, when the proof of a bride's virtue on her wedding night was put on public view the morning after, but even then I must have heard some inner warning that it might be just as well to have evidence available for my husband, just in case.

But breakfast hadn't brought much of an improvement, either. *Of course it was good.* Muttered into the teacup, with an embarrassed glare at me for bringing up the subject somewhere so public, even though we were down so early there was no one else in the room. Looking back now, I could have wept for my innocence and hope. I must have looked like a bloody begging puppy, sitting in front of a fella who disliked dogs.

But worse awaited me the second night. When we finally went to bed, his caresses were as perfunctory as they'd been the night before; he clearly believed that was all that was expected of him. Worse still, he literally hated it when I moaned. 'Making noises was for whores', he said. By that time I didn't feel all that much like moaning anyway, so I simply lay there and endured, praying to a God who disapproved of sex that I hadn't made the worst mistake of my life. Like so many other prayers I was to offer up, it went unanswered.

What the hell had made Liam the way he was, I never found out. True, his family were ultra-religious, but most people in Ireland were at that time, at least as far as external observance went; and I never encountered anyone else with such extreme views. I'd wondered sometimes if he could have experienced some kind of abuse when he was younger, and when the scandals started surfacing, it seemed likelier than ever that he had. But though I noticed he paid close attention every time there was a programme about it on the television and was invariably in the worst of tempers afterwards, he'd sooner plunge both hands into boiling water than discuss the subject. I found that out the hard way on the only occasion I tried. He flew into a screaming rage and told me to shut my filthy mouth about it. It was the one other time I'd honestly thought he was about to hit me.

Mark had taken the cups to the sink and rinsed them when I got back downstairs. "If you've finished with me, perhaps you've something else you'd like to do for a while?" he asked. "That's if you *have* finished, of course."

Then he remarked what a lovely day it was. "Why don't we sit and relax in that sunroom for a while, unless it's too hot – it shouldn't be yet, the sun hasn't gone that far over. We can leave the music on if you like. Get your book and have a read, and then I'll make us lunch."

"*You'll make us lunch?*" I blinked at him. Nobody had *ever* offered to make me a meal. Even my sons had largely been conditioned into believing food was something women produced while their menfolk sat around waiting for it to materialise on the table.

"Certainly. I think you've done enough for me. Now I can start returning the favour." He smiled, turned around and walked towards the back door, adding that he'd see if any of the washing on the line was dry. He was limping far less than he had been.

*Hell, Mark, I know we're just friends and everything, but I wish to God you'd kept that T-shirt on.* His back was a study in subtle musculature, and the shape of his arse...

"Might be a good idea if you got dressed again," I called. My voice was still marvellously casual. "In case the local priest passes and gets the impression I'm enjoying myself."

"Will do." He slanted a grin over his shoulder. Yes, he was walking well enough. He wouldn't need any help to get into the bath if he decided to take one instead of a shower tomorrow. Or out of it either.

*Pity.*

And this time it wasn't The Tart saying it.

# Chapter 22

Surveying the sun-drenched landscape surrounding Middleham Castle, it was hard to imagine anywhere better than the highest point in the castle for eating lunch that had somehow turned into a picnic. Not the most comfortable – for comfort, down on the grass might have been a better idea – but the view was glorious.

The air was clear enough to see detail far away. Unfortunately, this meant low pressure, with bad weather likely to follow. Another of Granny's quaint old Irishisms had been 'If you can see the hills, it's goin' to rain, and if you can't see them, it's rainin'.'

On reflection, it was a wonder sometimes that Grandaddy never glued her false teeth together.

There wasn't much room at the top of the keep, so we'd wedged the picnic basket on the wall and sat tucked out of the way, eating the sandwiches Mark had made and sharing a bottle of lemonade. It was undignified, it was improper, it was juvenile, and it was conduct altogether unbecoming a married woman. But here in the deserted hot well of the top of the tower,

I was finding it difficult to remember Liam McEnally existed, let alone that I was married to him. I felt like a rebellious teenager, and it was *wonderful*.

In a companionable silence, I watched the doings of a couple of horses grazing in the field behind the castle. The ground sloped up to a broken mound that presumably looked out to the moor and the road to the pond. If Mark's ankle had been up to it I'd have suggested walking up there, but although he hadn't complained, the walk around the castle and the climb up here must have tried his endurance, even with the aid of the hiking pole. He'd grunted with relief when he finally sat down, and when I stood up after lunch to admire the view again, he'd stayed seated, basking comfortably in his warm corner. At least he'd had the sense to put sun-cream on before we came out, I thought, and then scowled to find myself slipping into the familiar 'mothering' mode. I bloody well wasn't his mother, and I wasn't planning on adopting him, either.

"So tell me about yourself."

I'd thought he'd fallen asleep. His voice made me jump almost out of my skin.

He *looked* asleep, except that the almost mirror finish on his sunglasses meant it was impossible to tell whether his eyes were open or shut. He was completely relaxed, his hands loosely locked across his stomach and his legs stretched out in front of him.

"Not much to tell," I muttered.

"I know you're married. And unhappy. I'd imagine you have children, but you've never talked about any. I'd like to know more about you. Anything you feel comfortable talking about, of course."

There it was again: caring whether I was comfortable.

I genuinely didn't want to talk about Liam. As for the children, well, it was probably one more reason why I deserved to go to hell, but they were part of the world that I'd tried to leave behind – temporarily – while I tried to find some way to go on functioning. Because changes must be made, even if divorce was out of the question.

"I've three boys." I went on to describe them and their families as generously as I could while not departing from the strict truth.

He remarked it must be strange, not having any of them at home any more. I knew what he meant: the 'Empty Nest Syndrome'. When the last chick flies the nest, the parent birds must refashion their relationship, if by then they even want to, or indeed if it's even possible.

"It wasn't that." I answered the question he carefully hadn't asked. "There were always problems. For a long time, I wouldn't admit it even to myself, and even if I had, there were the children. Even if I'd admitted it to myself and there *weren't* any children, well... I'd promised. And I don't break my promises."

I didn't look down, but my peripheral vision caught the sun's flash on the lenses as he looked up at me, not even trying now to pretend this was a casual conversation. "Never?"

"No," I said in a low voice. "I took a solemn vow before God. 'For better, for worse.' Its being 'worse' is not a get-out clause. I promised."

"Do you love him?" he asked baldly.

"No." I drew a deep breath. "And he doesn't love me either.

"Looking back, I don't think he ever did. I worked for his daddy's firm for a while, and I was flattered he noticed me. But a few dates don't give you any real idea about each other, do they? We got married because… because that was what you did in them days. You didn't find out till after you'd tied the knot that you weren't suited, and by then it was too late."

What a relief it was to admit it! It changed nothing; I'd still be going back. Because *I. DO. NOT. QUIT.* But at least now I'd faced facts, grim as they were, the wishing for the moon would be over.

He looked at me over the top of the glasses. "Then even though it's none of my business *at all*, would you mind explaining why you don't do the obvious thing and leave him now you don't have your children to care for?"

"Because I promised."

In a long silence, he unscrewed the top of the lemonade bottle and took another swig. "Does he know about this?" He was looking at the bottle as he asked, but I assumed he was asking about the state of our marriage rather than the pop.

"I don't know. We don't talk about things like that."

"Ah." Another swig. "Don't you think it might be a good idea to try?"

"God, no!" For all my blether about *How to Save Your Marriage* books, the time was long gone when anything could have salvaged ours. Possibly if he'd gone to therapy years ago with his problems, something might have been done, but if he refused to discuss the subject with me there was no way in hell he'd ever have agreed to discuss it with a stranger. So we'd laboured on, flogging the dying horse, but his raping me had finally killed it. "He's too set in his ways to change. Even if he did, I could never trust him again. I can live with him and do the necessary, but I'm through being a doormat and I'm going to have my painting whether he likes it or not. As long as I have that, I can cope."

"Does he know how you feel?"

"He does now." With a blend of pride and embarrassment, I told him how I'd taken my revenge the morning I left.

"Vandal," he murmured.

"Oh, I don't know. He'll find it easier to replace the telly than his balls. One or the other had to go, and he'd miss his balls less."

"There's that." He narrowed his eyes against the glare of the sun, the sunglasses still halfway down his nose. "So what sort of welcome will you get from this husband who doesn't love you, after you chucked the glassware through his techware?"

I shrugged. "He won't hit me." All the same, the first thing I was going to tell Liam when I got home was that if he put one finger on me again, I'd go straight to the gardaí. I'd pack my bags and go back to Donegal, and that would be it. That should scare him into keeping his fists to himself. As for sex, if he was desperate there was Mary Fitzgarmon up the road; she'd been giving him the glad eye for years, God help the daft cow.

Mark stood up, with an effort, and stared at me, his arms folded across his chest. "Fran, you can tell me to go to hell if you like, but 'going back because he won't hit you' isn't good enough."

"I'm not going back because he won't hit me. I'm—"

He pounced. His arms were around me, and his mouth was on mine. He was kissing me and I was kissing him back, straining to capture the sensation of every inch of him pressing me back against the rough stone wall.

His body was lean and wiry, with almost no spare flesh. His buttocks under the denim of his jeans felt every bit as good as they'd looked, and as he ground against me, one hand thrusting under the waistband of my skirt and the other going around my breast, it was clear he was as aroused as I was.

It needed hardly any invitation to open my mouth before we were snogging like frantic teenagers. It had never been like this with Liam, never anything like this, and my knees buckled at the lemonade-flavoured revelation of his tongue.

*–Hellfire–*

"Now," I gasped when he released my mouth. "Mark, *now–* "

He glanced around hastily, but the castle seemed deserted. He pushed up my blouse to uncover my bra, and bit lightly at my nipples, painfully hard against the lace. I lifted my skirt and pushed down my knickers to let him at me. As he shucked down his jeans, I shut my eyes and felt the hot sun on my face and the hot stone against my back, and raging desire flooded through me again.

He settled carefully into position. I felt the pressure at my entrance, heart-stopping in its promise. "Say 'yes'." His voice was darker than mortal sin.

I clawed the word out. "Yes."

It would hurt. I was still a bit sensitive down there, after Liam's brutality, but that wasn't going to stop me. Even at ordinary times it always hurt, at first, but I got used to it after a minute or two. It...

Oh, God, oh *God!*

*No pain.*

So this was what it was like when you were...

"*Oh, God! Yes–!*" I gasped against his neck. We had to be quick, before I could think better of this, before reality broke in on this divine madness that had seized us.

He didn't need encouraging. I writhed with the urgency of his thrusts, revelling in the raw insane recklessness of it.

Then we heard voices on the stairs.

Saint Michael with his flaming sword was on the way, metaphorically at least. In an instant, 'Fuck' the glorious reality became "Fuck!" the hissed profanity, followed by a withdrawal so abrupt it was almost painful, and the scrambling rearrangement of clothes. It was quicker to kick my knickers off than to pull them up, so I used one foot to push them into the corner behind the abandoned packet of sandwiches. As I did so, I crash-landed on Planet Earth with my legs shaking and the word '*whore*' burned across my brain. This was not what I'd intended to happen, not *at all*. I'd betrayed a vow taken before the altar of God for a quickie up against a wall with a man who might now think all my efforts to keep him at a distance had been some kind of *game*. I'd ruined everything, and for what?

A fecking disaster.

Literally.

It would have been nice for The Tart to have found *something* encouraging to say, but she was probably too flabbergasted to breathe, let alone speak. As for Saint Frances, she'd probably packed her bags and left the castle.

Mark slithered back down to the floor, breathing hard. I didn't dare look at him. I wanted to curl up and die of shame.

My legs refused to hold me up any more. I slid to the floor too and grabbed the bottle of lemonade. My hands were shaking so much I spilled most of it and choked on the rest.

I couldn't even speak. I just sat there, listening to his breathing returning to normal, while on the stair below us, the visitors paused to argue about their hotel's dinner menu.

Finally, he spoke in an urgent undertone. "Fran, I–"

"No!" I jumped in, fending off the agony. "Mark, don't say you're sorry. Please, don't say that. Call me what you like, but for pity's sake, don't tell me you're sorry!"

He turned around and glared at me. "I'll say whatever I feel. And I *am* sorry, Fran – sorry we got interrupted! I hope to Christ *you're* not. I think it's what we both need and I'm damn well not finished with you yet!"

I opened my mouth to say something – anything – but the visitors whose voices we'd heard were nearly at the top. Seconds later, they emerged from the stairwell. A charming, elderly couple, who admired the view, told us they were staying at the hotel in the town and asked if we were staying locally.

Thank the Lord God they'd thought to discuss their dinners a couple of minutes earlier, or they'd have had another sort of view altogether. After that, they'd have had more than steak pie and quiche Lorraine to talk about.

"Quite near." Somehow I kept my voice from trembling, while the professional smile I'd worn at the gallery came in handy. Mark and I had scrambled back to our feet and were standing side by side, but when our arms accidentally touched, he moved away. He took over the conversation smoothly, agreeing that the views from up here were amazing. When they were all looking towards the old fort on the hill, I furtively retrieved my knickers, stuffing them into my jacket pocket.

Walking back down the stairs, we carefully kept our distance. I carried the picnic things, because he'd enough to think about with his hiking pole and his poorly ankle. High on the ruined walls, jackdaws chattered, the only sound to break the silence.

The sun was still shining when we emerged, and that was *entirely* out of order. There should have been a thunderstorm at least, and preferably a tornado, but the damned sun didn't even have the decency to hide behind a cloud.

Silently, Mark led the way around the side of the keep. I'd thought he might want to leave the castle altogether, but he walked into a room I'd looked down at, just before my happiness imploded. There was a wide circular feature in the turf there, probably where some beast had plodded daylong to turn millstones, grinding the corn. I followed him as he stepped onto the grass inside it, where we sat down awkwardly.

"I'm sorry if you – if you're upset," he said stiffly at last, staring between his knees at the turf. "I should never have... Fran, I didn't mean this to happen. Not like this, anyway. If you think it's spoiled things, I understand. I'll go away if that's what you want."

I sat still, my body cold with not touching his. *I'll go away if that's what you want.* Did he mean 'Well I've had it up you and now I know it wasn't even worth the effort, I'm out of here'? Was he disgusted, as I was, at how easy it had finally been? Did he think I was a liar and a hypocrite, as well as a slut?

I wanted to howl, to curse, to cry. Actually, I could have sobbed my heart out, but that would be the worst reaction of all.

If I was to salvage anything from the situation, I had to act like an adult rather than a child. Mark had done nothing I hadn't asked him to do – hadn't been *dying* for him to do, if I was honest – so how could I act as though he was to blame? He might be responsible for kissing me, but I was the one who'd lost my head completely.

"I don't know how to deal with this," I admitted at last. "I'm not upset, not with you, not at all. I'm just really bloody confused."

He turned around at that and looked earnestly at me. He was pale, presumably from our narrow escape, but seemed worried rather than angry or disgusted. "I don't want you to be sorry," he said. "I wanted you like hell and I thought you wanted me too. You seemed to be enjoying it as much as I was. There's nothing wrong with that, though it was a damn stupid place to get carried away, and for that I apologise."

"There's a lot wrong with it when one of us is married!"

"There's a lot wrong with your marriage, by the sound of it. Is it so wrong to snatch a little joy out of life?"

I thought about putting *that* argument to the parish priest back home in Donegal, who'd preached about a woman finding fulfilment in attending to her husband's needs. I doubted he'd approve of extending the idea to embrace the needs of any near-perfect strangers I happened to fancy as well. And as for attending to *my* needs in any of this, well, let's just not go there.

(Not just *unpremeditated* sex, but *unprotected* sex. God above, after the lectures I'd read the kids when they were growing up. I'd have to visit a clinic when I went home, in case I'd caught anything.

... Literally, ANYTHING.)

I definitely couldn't get pregnant. That was the one positive. Soon after I'd had Fergal I'd started early menopause, and the messy, painful business of periods was one thing I was glad to be over and done with.

Mark was saying something, his face suddenly rigid. Something about a clinic. I forced attention.

He'd had himself checked over recently, when he'd begun to be suspicious about Rebecca; thought he should mention it, in case I was concerned. Glory Be, at least I needn't worry about that, then.

"Fran, can you just *say* something?" he demanded. "Tell me I'm a bastard, if that's what you think, but I need to know where we stand! For heaven's sake, let me in!"

"That's where I went wrong a few minutes ago," I answered drily.

"No, that's where you went *right* a few minutes ago!" With sudden energy, he twisted around and knelt in front of me, with only a muttered aside of 'Shit!' – his ankle must have twinged. "Just for once you went with your heart, and you are not going to tell me that was wrong!"

"It wasn't my bloody *heart* giving me the orders," I snarled. "I'm not blaming you, Mark. Not for a minute. Yes, I was wanting you to kiss me, I'll be honest, I was. But I wasn't expecting to melt like bloody snow in summer the minute you touched me. I'm ashamed of myself."

He sat back a bit more on his heels, wincing at another twinge, and studied me. "You're ashamed of being a woman? Being sexual?"

"I'm ashamed of being *weak*. One kiss and that's it. So much for 'forsaking all others'!"

"What about 'to love and to cherish'? Your husband didn't keep his end of the bargain, from what you've said. You've kept yours for all these years – if you'd done this before, you damn well wouldn't have reacted like this afterwards. I'm your first infidelity, and you're blaming yourself for it. I'd imagine you even think you'll go to hell. Well, if that's the best your loving God can do, you can bloody well keep him!"

"Keep God out of it!" I said crossly.

"I would, but it's you who thinks he's got nothing better to do than pry into people's lives, ensuring they're not getting up to a bit of illicit happiness. That's one of the reasons I gave up on him years ago."

Now, normally I'd have agreed with him. It had been a good while since I'd blindly believed in everything the Church preached about sin – such as the prohibition against homosexuality, which was surely a matter of how people were made, not what they deliberately chose to be. But at one swoop I'd broken the promises I'd made before the Altar of God, vows I'd held sacred no matter how unhappy the keeping of them made me, and that had changed everything I'd ever believed about myself. "Adultery is *not* 'a bit of illicit happiness'! It's breaking my fecking wedding vows!"

"Bugger the wedding vows! What we need to sort out is what you want to happen now. Will it make you happier, and help you forgive yourself, if I leave? Because I get the feeling that's what you want. Not what *I* want – what *you* want."

I pressed my hands to my face, flooded by joy and relief that he didn't want to leave. But *forget* I'd committed adultery?

He ought to go. He really, really ought. If I was a good Catholic wife, I'd sling him out on his ear, take myself to the nearest church and go to confession. But then a good Catholic wife wouldn't have thrown a glass vase through her husband's television and marched out on him in the first place, would she? And she definitely wouldn't have moved from kissing to shagging faster than lightning buttered on both sides.

"I think we both need to think about this," I said in a quiet voice.

"I've already thought about it." His expression was infuriatingly calm as he sat back. "How long do you think it'll take you?"

With difficulty, I restrained myself from smacking him around the ear. How the hell long did he *think* it would take for me to come to terms with what I'd done?

I didn't think I ever would, but if I told him that, he would leave. If he did, not only would I have broken my vows, I'd have lost something almost as precious: a friend. The friend who could be my path back to painting. If that wasn't to happen, I had to pick my way with the utmost care through this minefield.

Weakness had got me into this. It wouldn't get me out of it. He had to believe me strong, stronger than I'd ever been. Stronger than I possibly could be.

*The only one who can save me is me.*

I told him he couldn't leave. I was going to draw him, and he'd promised.

Startled by my ruthlessness, he glanced at me. "You still want...?"

"Yes, I do. Unless what's happened has changed other things, you're still my friend and I still want to draw you."

His right hand ran through his hair, disordering its neatness. "But after... I can't..."

"You can run, or you can stay."

I saw the flash of fire at the word 'run', but he didn't bite back. Instead, he got awkwardly to his feet and said he was going somewhere to do some thinking. He wouldn't be long.

I'd played my cards. After watching him limp away, I lay down, deeply aware of the sensation where my flesh still throbbed with the memory of his. Finally and awfully, I understood why a woman could want sex so much; the sensation of him sliding into me had been heart-stopping. I'd not climaxed, and I was pretty sure he hadn't either – there hadn't been time – but what I'd experienced had been a feast for my starving senses. It had been what I'd always imagined, but never actually felt.

*God in Heaven*. If sex was this explosive, no wonder the Holy Catholic kept it under lock and key. The only pity was that they didn't put half as much effort into encouraging married couples to experience it, rather than trying to ignore its existence. If you had that waiting for you at home, there'd be a hell of a lot less temptation to go looking for it elsewhere.

Not that that *justified* going looking for it elsewhere. The self-discipline I'd prided myself on had shattered like glass.

*Nowhere near the worst thing you've to be sorry about*, Saint Frances told me savagely.

Sorry? *Was* I sorry? Was it truly so terrible to have – in Mark's words – snatched a little joy out of life?

**Too** *bloody little altogether,* muttered The Tart. *Pity those auld feckers didn't come up ten minutes later.*

The Saint steamrollered on. 'Interruptus' or not, there had been 'Coitus', and I Had Asked For It. I Had Sinned.

That was undeniable. Adultery was serious, and rightly so. But so were life, joy and love, and it seemed to me that up there on the top of the keep I'd caught a fleeting hold of all three even as I grabbed a man I wasn't married to and parted my thighs for him.

Love for Mark? No, I hardly knew the man. I realised with surprise it was love for myself I'd discovered. And having discovered it, I found myself rebelling against the demand of 'religion' to push that dangerous damn thing back into prison where it belonged.

My mind in turmoil, I lay studying the blotches of lichen on the stone in front of me. Season after season they had grown there, in snow and wind and rain and sunshine, as enduring as the castle itself. I had to be strong too, I had to endure. This discovery was too important to throw away like a handful of grass cuttings on the wind, even if it felt as though madness had taken me over.

*Was it madness, or was it sanity?*

It had been a sin, yes. A serious one. But over the years, I'd come to hope in a rather more sympathetic deity than the heartless idol Mark seemed to think I worshipped. This God, I felt, would understand how three and a half decades' worth of dreary fidelity could end in one blazing moment of madness.

*Was it madness, or was it sanity?*

Still no reply, though the jackdaws high above seemed to be saying 'Mad, mad, mad'. I knew the hope of taking up painting again was in danger of slipping through my fingers, and how was I to bear it if it did? If all this collapsed now, my painting would go with it. Then the sky truly would go dark, as dark as if the sun had gone away forever.

The actual sun slipped fractionally further across the sky. An ant ran across my arm. Maybe even ants had some concept of catastrophe when their nests were attacked; maybe a collective intelligence as sophisticated as theirs extended to some form of anguish. Death, by comparison, was nothing, just an end of feeling and functionality. But loss was universal.

Visitors occasionally stopped and peered at me, probably worried by my stillness, but I smiled reassurance, so they went away again. I heard the distant voices of the elderly couple again. They were heading for the souvenir shop.

I wouldn't move until he came back, and I knew which path I was to take from now on.

Eventually, he returned.

He hunkered down directly in front of me. His ankle must have given him even more grief about this, but if it did, he ignored it.

I just looked up at him with no expression at all. Waiting.

"I'm staying, if you'll let me," he said simply. "But I'm not ashamed of what we did and I'm not staying under false pretences. If you keep me in the house, I'll do everything I can to persuade you to break your promises."

For a long moment, we just looked at each other.

"You mean the important promises," I said at last.

"Of course the important promises. I'm the devil. I don't do the small stuff." He let the tip of his tongue just flicker out of his mouth. "I shall be the Sssserpent in your Eden."

I hooted a bit, for form's sake, and said he was about as terrifying as Kaa in Disney's *Jungle Book*, but the sight of that flickering tongue had sent my mind in all kinds of unseemly directions. Still... "No force?"

"None. Jusssst perssssuasion."

Another long silence. I wondered if we'd both gone completely mad, or if it was just him and I should tell him to go forth and multiply.

Then, slowly, I felt a smile spread across my face. "You have a bargain, Mr Satan."

The answering grin spread across his own. "Then it's 'game on', isn't it?" He gave me his best, lazy lowering of lashes. "Oh, and you got it right earlier on. The name's Lucifer."

# Chapter 23

*H*AVE YOU GONE COMPLETELY, TOTALLY, AB-SOLUTELY BERSERK, Madam?* yelled Saint Frances, as Mark and I finished the stroll around the castle, sharing the last of the lemonade. We'd said no more about the 'Devil's Bargain', but we both knew things between us had changed irrevocably.

There was no reply from The Tart, for once. Perhaps she was too busy dancing joyfully around the battlements.

*I'm not losing my friend,* I said stubbornly.

*Never mind your 'friend', you've lost your bloody marbles! D'you think it's in keeping with 'forsaking all others' to invite some oversexed little bastard into someone else's house when you KNOW he's only staying because he wants to get your knickers off? – **Again?***

*It's about damn time **somebody** wanted to get my knickers off. Besides, I don't think that's what it is.*

*I know damn well what it is. He's got as much shame as a tomcat! And you're not much better. What would Father O'Mahoney have to say about this, eh? You dropped your knickers quicker than Siobhan Adams behind the bike shed, and now you're planning to carry on living with the dirty little shite even after he's told you right upfront he'll try to talk you into letting him at you again! Are you desperate, or just absolutely fecking MAD?*

*I was fecking mad thirty-four years ago. And what the feck Father O'Mahoney knows about being stuck in a hellish marriage would fit on the back of a stamp, even if it was written in big block capitals.*

*That's got nothing to do with it. You made your promises, and God was listening! And as far – wait! You're not going in THERE?*

The tirade tailed off in a shriek as I followed Mark though a single dark doorway in the west wall of the keep into a small, windowless room. It was completely bare, and illuminated only by the daylight from outside. I stood still, wondering, while Mark wandered around behind me.

One fingertip touched my neck, just under my right ear, and stroked very lightly for about two seconds. Then it was withdrawn.

"Not much to look at in here," he said casually, ducking to leave again. "Come on."

Saint Frances was unimpressed. *I know his bloody game. He knows now you're easy, so he's just getting you softened up. Gagging for it. As if you haven't been since you met him!*

The Tart must have finished dancing around the battlements. My fall from grace seemed to have injected her with a zest for life that almost made it worthwhile being an adulteress. *'Any time, any place, anywhere, there's a wonderful knob you can share...'*

*It didn't say **that** in the commercial*, The Saint rebuked her. *She was showing our age by remembering it, too, since it hadn't been on the telly for decades.*

The Tart replied that if a more up-to-date slogan was required, 'I'm Loving It' would do nicely thank her very much, and followed up with a few more that had me blushing like a flamingo. *'When it absolutely, positively has to be there overnight,'* she leered. *That's a good one. Or what about 'And all because the lady loves...' unbridled sex with a handsome young devil.* She added that I'd be singing loud and long one of these fine days (except she said 'LOOUUUD and LOOOONG' highly suggestively), or my name wasn't Frances McEnally. *Come to think of it, you aren't a McEnally at all, you're a McKenna. The McKennas are well known for their powers of vocalisation. It's a well-known fact.*

Trying to ignore both of them, I followed Mark meekly back out into the sunshine. Gosh, his arse looked lovely in jeans.

*'A man who looks at a woman lustfully has already committed adultery with her in his heart,' Jesus said*, The Saint reminded me in arctic tones, declining to continue the theme of corruptible commercials. *And it's the same for a woman, too.*

*Bit late for her to be worrying about admiring his arse now, isn't it?* The Tart pointed out cheerfully. *If she's going to hell anyway, she might as well take the detour through heaven first. At least she'll have some fabulous memories.*

Saint Frances started attacking what she knew was my weakest point. *So what's happened to 'I. DO. NOT. QUIT.' all of a sudden?* she asked sarcastically. *Or was it always 'I Do Not Quit Until I Get An Offer I Don't Want To Refuse'?*

Well, the only other offer I'd ever had had come from one of Liam's drunken cousins trying to grope me in the kitchen at his brother Thomas's engagement party. Even then, though, I hadn't been tempted to go looking for what I'd have defined merely as 'trouble'. God, no. Having found out what sex consisted of, I was in no hurry to go hunting for more of it, especially with someone who'd care even less about my pleasure than Liam did.

But suppose the cousin had been sober and handsome instead of plain and stinking of the whiskey he'd tried to force into my glass, telling me it'd take some of the damned stiffness out of me? Would I have been tempted to go out into some quiet corner of the dark garden and lie down with him, for the momentary delusion of being desired?

No. It wasn't just the offer of sex I found so tempting now, though having tasted it I couldn't help but want more, but the offer of *intimacy* – something I'd never experienced in all the long, empty years of my marriage. Because though the physical act was far from nothing, it was far less potentially destructive than all the emotional stuff it let loose. While I'd expected nothing more from sex than a few minutes' endurance now and then in a wasteland of loneliness, I could carry on with marriage under the heading of 'business as usual'. But now I'd tasted the forbidden fruit, learned I could laugh with a man and talk with him and feel no fear of his temper, that was almost more intoxicating than the feeling of him penetrating me.

*That* was why I'd caved. That was what I'd wanted, to have the complete experience, regardless of the cost, even if it destroyed everything I'd believed about myself. All for a reward that might still be snatched away from me if I'd been mistaken, and prove as little worth the sacrifice as the few minutes' grunting in a darkened garden would have been.

But I thought I could trust Mark. I hoped, I believed, he was not offering me false coin. He was offering me what Liam, in his ignorance and selfishness, had never cared about. Slowly it had dawned on me that my mantra of *'I. DO. NOT. QUIT'* was, in fact, no better than the cry of those sad women I'd read about in magazines who stayed with their abusive partner for years, deluding themselves they were 'doing the right thing'.

The realisation that my marriage was abusive was a massive one in itself. So much so, that I'd have to explore it in detail later and decide what I was going to do about it. My immediate problem, however, was what more – if anything – was going to happen between me and the Devil, strolling with me on the greensward of Middleham Castle as though he hadn't a care in the world apart from a slightly dodgy ankle.

"The statue!" We'd seen it as we came in, but saved a close inspection for last, like the best chocolate in the box.

King Richard's face was careworn beneath its crown. I was surprised he'd been portrayed without arms, but presumably there was some deep meaning behind this.

"I want a photograph of you with him." Mark took a phone from one of the pockets of his jacket and switched it on, thumbing immediately to the camera. "No. Sit at his feet, looking up at him. I think that would be different."

The king had been carved standing on a boar, which the explanatory leaflet said was his personal badge. The boar was lying flat on its side and appeared annoyed by being stood on.

Its temper wouldn't be improved by having me sit on its head, and putting my bare arse on the royal badge felt anything but respectful.

Sitting on rough stone isn't comfortable at the best of times, particularly if you've not got any knickers on. Today was worse, because the pressure reminded me, if I'd needed reminding, of the part of me that was still tingling a bit, even now.

Oh, but it had felt so bloody good!

By way of elaborating on the theme, The Tart remarked that medieval clothing had some outstanding features, especially when you were sitting down and looking up from this angle.

I tried to picture Mark in medieval clothes and pulled myself up with a stern *don't go there.*

*He'd need a bigger codpiece than Liam.* The Tart had gone there, sat down and made herself right at home. Probably helped herself to any cake she found in the cupboard, too.

The photograph taken, I'd have liked to make a second circuit of the castle, but I noticed Mark was standing less easily than he had been, even with the aid of Paul's hiking pole. Although he helped me to my feet without difficulty, there was a faint frown line dug between his brows.

"Ankle playing up?" I asked. "Come on, tell the truth and shame the… yourself."

"Well. If you put it like that." He grinned. "It's not brilliant. I could do with putting it up for a bit."

I quirked an eyebrow, trying to recapture the easy, merely teasing rapport we'd had earlier. "If that's a chat-up line, it's not a very subtle one."

"I *meant* my ankle. At least, for now." Damn, there went the Voice. "But I still intend to make you change your mind. And you can be sure that if I do, it'll be up for much, much longer than it was last time."

"You can try." My attempt at bravado failed miserably.

"Oh, I can do better than 'try'." The thunderclouds had gone shades darker. They were no longer luminous, but pregnant with rain.

"For now, let's leave it at 'try'." I led the way determinedly to the gift shop at the exit. "Any souvenirs you fancy?"

"I fancy giving you a souvenir." The words were breathed in my ear as the door opened. "And I won't even charge."

"As long as it hasn't got 'A Present from Middleham' on it. Come to think of it, I hope it's long enough to write 'A Present from Middleham' on."

"I'll leave it to you to say. But I'm sure you noticed there's *plenty* of room."

"If I write small."

"You clearly need much more time for observation. You could use a large font in capital letters and still get the quotation marks in."

This sort of talk should send me running like a redshank. Though I was now in rather a weak position for claiming to be virtuous, surely a woman with any vestige of respectability at all should be slapping his face and telling him to shut the hell up and get away from her, rather than engaging in risqué repartee and thoroughly enjoying it?

It wasn't surprising I found it hard to concentrate on my inspection of the things on offer in the shop, though I'd have liked to buy something small and unobtrusive for a souvenir – a bookmark, perhaps. Mark remained beside me, seemingly paying close attention to whatever I looked at, but I was too wound up waiting for his next move to concentrate on anything else. Not that he did anything at all. He carefully maintained a very small distance between us. Not even our fingers brushed.

It was absolutely… exasperating. Intriguing. Unendurable!

"You do know you're a swine," I said as we walked out of the castle without having bought anything.

Yes, that was a smirk if ever I'd seen one. If only the detail I required for my painting had been slightly different, it would have been bloody *perfect*.

"'You ain't seen nothing yet', as they say."

"No, and I don't intend to. Wait here and I'll get the car." I'd had to park it a little distance away, and could spare him the walk.

"It's not far. Besides, it's hardly in keeping with my demonic image to stand around waiting for a condemned soul to turn up with the transport. This, if you must know –" he brandished the hiking pole theatrically – "is my trident. Cunningly disguised, so as not to spread alarm and despondency." He fell into step beside me. The obstinate lift of his chin said there was no point in my arguing.

Around us, the pale stone houses baked sleepily in the late afternoon sun. One of the cottages we passed had window boxes bursting with geraniums.

"I'd have thought a car was a bit tame for you, actually," I needled him. "Aren't you more used to fiery chariots or something?"

"Oh, certainly. Scarlet and gold fiery chariots, drawn by jet-black dragons with flaming eyes. But I dare say I can slum it in a car if I have to."

"It's a long walk back to that cottage."

"There again, dragons are *so* 'last year'."

"I thought they might be."

So much for the devil being terrifying, I reflected, hiding a triumphant grin. With a sprained ankle, he's just a tame little pussy-cat.

# Chapter 24

Mark was obviously relieved to sit down again and put his foot back onto the support of the stool. I told him it was all his fault for over-exercising an injured joint.

Turning away, I supposed bitterly that I'd better do some housework. I hadn't run the vacuum around the place since he arrived, and I could dust, too. There was a good new can of polish under the sink.

A gigantic beast of frustrated energy was snarling inside me, so I might as well put it to good use.

I strode into the kitchen area and put the kettle on. This was something safely neutral for me to do, in case I was tempted into doing something that definitely *wasn't* neutral and would have incalculable consequences.

He watched me – I could feel his eyes boring into my back – but didn't say anything. I could *feel* the cage of respectability and fidelity closing back around me, stealthy, inexorable and ready to set like concrete.

Racking my brains for an innocuous remark about the weather, I made the drinks and got out the biscuits. Opening the fridge to get out the milk, the first thing that met my gaze was half a cucumber encased in shrink-wrap, lying forgotten on a shelf. I glowered at it and shut the door with entirely unnecessary force.

Frustration and desperation were building up a head of steam inside me. I was not going to let this happen, I fecking-well was *not!*

Forcing myself to ignore the stare I knew was still fastened on me, I somehow got the drinks carried to the coffee table without throwing them up in the air. I made the return trip for the plate of biscuits, but made the mistake of looking down at them on the way.

Rich Tea. As if it wasn't bad enough that Fate had snatched away my one and only chance of Living Dangerously, I was giving him *Rich fecking Tea!*

I uttered an expletive no good Catholic wife had any business knowing, let alone using. The plate sailed through the air like a Frisbee, showering biscuits in all directions. Fortunately it landed in one of the armchairs.

I hurled myself at Mark, straddling him even as I thanked any available deity that I'd not got around to getting my knickers back on. He just about got his T-shirt off before I landed.

He showed just the right amount of regard for the buttons on my blouse. I only found the fifth one when the vacuum cleaner sucked it up days later. It was just as well it hadn't landed in the lampshade, because I'd never have got it out again, and explaining that away to Bridie would take some doing.

You could tell he knew exactly how to get a bra undone, because mine sprang loose as if the hooks had evaporated.

His hands only left my breasts long enough to push his jeans down again. "Help yourself to that," he growled.

I was past shame. I whimpered as I lifted myself and moaned as I impaled myself.

He paused only long enough to drag my skirt off over my head, and when I showed signs of wanting to cover my very imperfect nakedness, he pulled my wrists away and let his stare track down every inch of me. Then he attacked my breasts again, licking and sucking at them till my nipples stood in hard aching points and the sensation and the excitement had me thrashing like a landed salmon.

I'd never done anything like this, never felt anything like this. I was drunk on passion.

"Ride me. I want to feel you riding me," he breathed, pushing his hips up. "Do whatever feels good."

I hadn't the breath to tell him the whole damn thing felt beyond good already, but he must want me to do something. So I braced my hands on his belly and started experimenting.

*Janey Mack.* There was a little interval of his deep breaths interspersed with my gasps and whimpers as I worked myself on him, my excitement ratcheting up another notch every time I buried him to the hilt inside me. He hadn't even the decency to ignore me like a gentleman but went on playing with my breasts while he provided a running commentary that should have had me covering my ears, if nothing else.

I'd never climaxed with Liam inside me, never come close. But as I found the exact action that would work the miracle, I knew it was going to happen now.

I don't know how Mark knew, but he did. Almost in the instant that I started to come, he grabbed hold of my hips and started slamming home inside me, and the commentary dissolved into bursts of expletives that almost drowned my caterwauling.

If my husband thought moaning was for whores, then the Lord God Almighty knows what he'd have called me if he'd heard me then. I made noises I didn't even know the words for as Mark finally came inside me.

I spiralled back to reality, shuddering with the reaction. Aftershocks from the orgasm coursed through me, and I felt his hands on me again, stroking my breasts and thighs so that flickers of renewed excitement shot through me.

"Frances McKenna, you are a fucking beautiful woman," he said at last. "And now I'm going to start showing you just how fucking wonderful you can be in bed."

# Chapter 25

After breakfast the next morning, I was more than willing to be persuaded of the attractions of a long, hot, sensual bath – shared.

Mark set his iPad on the landing to play on a loop and ushered his by-no-means-unwilling victim into his hot and bubbly lair. There he spent a good half-hour making sure that every nook and cranny I was owner of was completely immaculate. After a brief dip into the bath with me for a sponge-down of his own, he finished off his hard work by laying my very clean and very pink body out on a bath-towel on the floor, where, properly disregarding my feeble protests on the indecency of it, he gave me a gentle introduction into the hitherto forbidden joys of oral sex.

Though I was far from unappreciative of the pleasures of the bedroom (not to mention the bathroom floor) there were other, subtler pleasures we could now enjoy. Instead of staying primly separated as strangers should, we could share the couch while we listened to music. We could touch accidentally during our ordinary daily interactions and, rather than apologising, draw pleasure from the casual contact. And kissing; prolonged deep kissing was another novelty. I felt like a hummingbird, dipping into the pot of nectar every time we passed.

Later that evening, we took Sharp for a walk. In deference to Mark's ankle, there was a short stroll we could do, down the lane and around the square to come back again from another direction.

We held hands. Now and again, we stopped to kiss. I felt as though I was seventeen again.

At one point, a grassy bank offered us an opportunity to sit for a while, enjoying the sinking sun. As there were few cars passing, and the lift of the landscape hid us from any houses nearby, we weren't going to pass up the chance to kiss some more, and while we were about it, he slipped his hand inside my jacket. I was trying to have a conversation, but it was becoming more and more difficult with his hand cupped around my breast and his thumb stroking gently to and fro.

"So you've decided that it's your diabolical duty to separate me from my marriage." I moaned softly, but continued with an effort. "But you-hoooo haven't explained what you're off-offering me in place of it."

"'In place of it'?" He considered. "The same thing I offered to Eve in the Garden of Eden. Your selfhood. Your integrity. The chance to be something other than somebody's pet. The chance to be yourself. The chance to say *this is what I want* or *this is not what I want* without having to take into account someone you yourself say doesn't love you.

"It's not easy, I'll grant you, but nothing worth having ever is."

"But let's be honest, you're not claiming to love me either."

"No, I'm not." God, this had to be the weirdest conversation ever; wasn't an opportunist male supposed to feed into a woman's obsession with being loved rather than telling her the truth? "I don't know you nearly well enough. But we're on holiday, and it would be a pity not to take what's available, even if we'll never see each other again. I can't offer you anything, Fran, except to give you pleasure. And perhaps the hope of a better future for yourself, now you know what the possibilities are."

I couldn't help smiling. "Do I hear the Devil telling the truth?"

"Oh, I won't lie to you. I can promise you that. Devil's honour. 'Great is truth, and it must prevail', after all." He closed his finger and thumb on my nipple, and I jumped. "But I wouldn't have missed this for anything. I can't wait to get my mouth on this again, and you're strung as tight as cheese-wire with wanting me to."

"You're a horny little devil, I'll give you that." I swallowed.

"You're no slouch in the horny stakes yourself, despite your lack of practice." He slid his tongue into my mouth to give me a preview of what else he couldn't wait to do; his fingers strayed to the buttons of my blouse – my second-best, as I still hadn't found the button that had flown off the other one. "You never know, you could take up devilry yourself when you get home. If you can't stomach the thought of giving your husband lessons, you could find yourself a handsome young farmer and give him some."

"Janey Mack, Mark Reeves, aren't you talking out of your arse! A handsome young farmer looking twice at me, even if I felt like going out whoring round the countryside!"

"Why not? You've got a handsome young*ish* construction manager looking at you, and I assure you he's enjoying what he's looking at." He had the blouse open by now and was working on the fastenings of my bra.

"Will you leave that thing where it is, you little wretch? Or are you still trying to get us arrested?"

"Who's going to see?" There was no sound of cars or walkers, just the ecstatic song of a bird high in the tree opposite us and the occasional bleat of a sheep, and the satisfying small *ping, ping* of hooks coming undone. We had the world to ourselves. "Now, doesn't that feel good?"

"It feels grand, but I bet this is a fecking bus route."

"Of course it is. It's an *incu*-bus route – the underworld's version of 'Ring and Ride'." Gloating at his own wit even in a situation as promising as this, he pushed my jacket open, disregarding my invocation of the Holy Family at his lurid behaviour in a public place.

"Well, I've enjoyed the riding so far, but I'm damned if I remember ringing. – Will you get out of that, you daft haddock?"

"You called me up, now you put up with me. How does *this* feel, then? Even better?"

"It feels bloody disgr– Oh, feck it. Holy God, I've never sworn so much in all me life till I met you." My fingers gripped his hair, and I groaned a few more rather inappropriate appeals while I enjoyed myself thoroughly.

Unfortunately, the sound of a car approaching the nearby bend in the road interrupted proceedings. I pushed him away, clutched the sides of my jacket together just in time, and told him he was a fiend out of hell.

"Well, you summoned me up, Mistress," he replied, looking innocent as the car swept past. He probably meant to be smiling at the world in general, but the only word for *that* look was a smirk.

On the way home, there had been mention of events involving the hearthrug and Ravel's *Bolero*, which Mark coincidentally had on his iPad. These were scheduled to feature later on in the evening, and I was rather looking forward to them. Although I'd naturally heard the piece, its alternative uses had never been brought to my attention before.

Back at the cottage, some washing on the line was dry and had to be put away. This provided a perfect opportunity for Saint Frances finally to have a few words with me about my behaviour.

Few of them were polite and none complimentary. It was hard to judge who came in for the most vitriol, Mark for his disgusting and ungentlemanly behaviour, or me for hurling myself gaily into whoredom with him instead of casting him forth into outer darkness, where there was grinding and gnashing of teeth, and preferably far more imaginative punishments than that if everyone got what they'd earned.

*You mean '**weeping** and gnashing of teeth',* chortled The Tart. *You can leave the grinding to us. Flat on his back, down on that hearthrug, and we'll grind till we're saddle-sore!*

Her opponent said that was *totally* disgusting and we were both going to Hell.

The Tart could also whistle, it seemed. Her chosen melody was 'Dancing Cheek to Cheek' – specifically the lines '*Heaven, I'm in Heaven…*' Though doubtless she'd have preferred 'Dancing Groin to Groin' if only someone had written it.

Saint Frances did not applaud her taste in jokes *or* music.

The Tart said who was joking?

The Saint said I damn well ought to be, because I'd cast aside nearly thirty-four years of God-sanctioned marriage for a quick shag with a total stranger who couldn't even be bothered to pretend he was in love with me, and that was *outrageous*. Not to mention Mortally Sinful. Yes. That was 'MORTAL SIN, as in 'YOU GO TO HELL FOR IT'.

The Tart said was that thirty-four years of God-sanctioned boredom in the bedroom, and misery out of it, that we were talking about?

The Saint said that wasn't the point.

The Tart asked what was, then.

*She promised. She swore an oath in front of God.*

*Yeah, and so did he. 'Love and cherish', as I recall.* The Tart rolled her imaginary eyes. *'Wowza', as Fergal would say.*

I found a ladybird on the second towel. Stupid damn thing. If it stayed in here, a house spider would probably eat it, so I went to the window and tried to coax it into flying away. It didn't seem to want to. Perhaps it liked the fluffy feeling of the towel under its feet.

*She's a slut,* hissed Saint Frances. *One fecking kiss and there she was, opening her legs for him. God above, even Mary Fitzgarmon would think she was a scandal. Psha! She's been gagging for it all along. Might as well go on the streets and get money for it if she enjoys it that much.*

*So what's wrong with taking advantage of it while she's got the chance? Like Liam bloody McEnally ever suggested laying her naked on the hearthrug and shagging her to 'Bolero'. Or the Minute Waltz, even, though given his staying power he'd probably have struggled to stay the course. Still, I suppose the theme tune to 'Ultimate Force' might be his idea of musical erotica. – Hey, what about it?* She nudged me in the ribs. *When you go back, see if you can introduce some variety. Just remember not to get between him and the screen, and keep the sound turned up so he can't hear you breathing. It'd be a pity for him to miss any of the gunshots or the macho bullshit.*

"Dinner," I said loudly, and the pair of them shut up, though they probably wandered off into my subconscious, still bickering.

# Chapter 26

Given that Liam's idea of adventurous sex was leaving the bedside lamp on, I'd never got closer than a dictionary definition of the concept of a 'safe word'. Since Mark was playing the Devil, *Exorcise* felt appropriate. He said seriously that he hoped I'd never need to use it, but since I was breaking new ground every time we had sex in a new position, it was a good idea for me to have one.

This brought it home to me forcibly that he'd had far more experience than I had. He'd been married, for one thing; a marriage that, although initially happy, had broken down when his wife failed to get pregnant. She was determined on being a mother, and his failure to oblige even with IVF had shattered their relationship. After that, he'd had a few one-offs before encountering that maggot Rebecca. So my (for want of a better word) 'experience' with Liam was hardly in the same league, and just occasionally I *did* feel slightly intimidated. Though so far I'd never had cause to use it, having the 'safe word' to hand was reassuring, and Mark had told me repeatedly that if I felt any degree of discomfort with what we were doing, I should use it at once.

He ordered me to take my time over showering. That, of course, was because he'd be preparing the scene for the seduction downstairs, and as I closed the bathroom door behind me, I couldn't help but speculate what on earth I was in for if we needed all this thingumajiggery to set the scene.

Not that I was complaining. I felt as though I'd hatched out of a cocoon and spread my butterfly-wings in the sunshine. Life for the next few days – I refused to look any further than that – would consist of a flowerbed of scent and colour, and now I'd cast my marriage vows to the winds, I meant to make the most of every moment.

Aware that for once I had to dawdle rather than the other way round, I took my time. I washed and rinsed my hair three times rather than twice, and was lavish with the conditioner. Then, after I'd towelled off the worst of the wet, I wrapped myself in a towel and hurried into my bedroom to finish the process.

I hadn't had the first idea when I ran away from home that I'd need anything at night other than a clean nightie, worn just in case of an emergency. I'd grabbed the first one from the drawer that came to hand.

It was my habit to put on a nightie after I'd showered. I did it now, without thinking, but as I went to the wardrobe where Bridie kept her hair-dryer, I caught sight of myself in the mirror.

Though not the same one (I'd burn that damned thing when I went home!), it was identical to the one I'd been wearing the night Liam raped me. I'd bought two so I could wash one and wear the other. And the mirror showed me a fat, plain woman wearing a shapeless, frumpy nightdress, a brutal reminder of what Mark was trying to pretend was some kind of bloody sex-goddess.

My newly-acquired self-confidence collapsed like a hot-air balloon with no heat source beneath it.

I forgot about the hair-dryer. I switched the light off, sat down on the bed and slowly rolled over to lie on it. I'm not sure which of us I despised more, him for his lack of discernment or me for letting myself forget what I actually looked like: a defeated old baggage who'd eaten herself out of almost every item of clothes in her wardrobe. Jesus, no wonder Liam hardly touched me these days.

Surprisingly, I didn't cry. I think I was too desolate even for tears.

Undoubtedly he must be wondering by now why I was taking so long. Well, he could wonder. Right now, I couldn't even muster the courage to go down and face him and tell him that both of us had made the most horrible, *horrible* mistake.

I'm not sure how long it was before I heard his footsteps on the stairs. He checked the bathroom (empty) and came to my door. He stopped outside, obviously listening.

"I used to sit on the middle step," I told him, staring at the ceiling. "So I was 'neither up nor down'."

A pause.

"Why did you have to do that?" he asked through the door.

"Because that was who I was."

Another pause.

"That must have been a terrible thing to be."

"It was the *only* thing to be. He fell asleep, you see. Even when I was hoping... he just fell asleep."

"He shouldn't have."

"He didn't care. I was just a – another of the household appliances. And not a very efficient one, either."

"Then he should have cared. *I* care."

"You're different."

"I sincerely hope I'm just a normal human being. I try to be."

A third pause.

Outside, the wind was beating against the walls, though there was no rain. It sounded like something alive, something fierce. It felt as if it might have been called up, might have come in response to the anguish that seemed to have taken on such a life of its own that there were two of us lying here side by side on the bed.

"It was being so lonely, you see," I explained past the sudden lump in my throat. "That was why I ate so much. I had the music, though."

"Music isn't enough. It isn't enough for any human being. You needed more than that."

"'For better, for worse'. 'Till death do us part.'" My voice dropped abruptly to a growl. "The death of what? You tell me that. Respect? Love? Affection? Hope? They all die, but you're still married. And you comfort-eat, and then you're fat, and because of that, you're worthless. 'Go on a diet', they all say, but what would have been the *point?* He never fancied me even when I wasn't fat."

"Then he was a fool." His voice was still level, but it had dropped too.

"No. It was me. I wanted too much."

The slight squeak of the door-handle told me he'd gripped it. "For the love of God, Fran, you wanted to be treated like a *woman*. Like the precious, valuable human being you are. I don't know what he did, I don't know why he did it, but so help me God, if I ever meet him, I'll smash his teeth through the back of his head."

"I'm his *wife*. 'To have and to hold, for better, for worse'." The anguish finally took over, finding a voice that was close to a shriek. "Sanctioned by Holy Church, blessed by the priest. St Paul set the tone for lust: better to marry than to burn. Not sure if he ever said anything about marrying and *then* burning, but hell, I burned. You'd never guess how many nights I burned. Eve, that's me all right. You'd never guess it to look at me, would you? The original spawn of sin. A charnel house of carnal desires. Set on Earth to find my fulfilment in tending to my husband's needs. That's as long as I remembered not to moan, of course. He didn't like me moaning. Ladylike silence, that's the thing. Moaning is for whores. He actually told me that."

"And you're planning to go back to *that*?" he exploded. "To some bastard who's not fit to care for a dog, let alone a bloody wife?" I heard him getting himself back under control. When he spoke again, his voice was tight. "Right. You know what the word is. If you don't use it in the next thirty seconds, I'm coming through this door and to hell with the consequences. You summoned up the devil. Exorcise him or live with it."

*Exorcise, Exorcise.* I should say it. I'd broken my marriage vows, I'd been a fool, I deserved the pain.

"Exorcise." My mouth shaped the word, but no sound came out; only a long wail of desperate need.

The door slammed back. Mark marched over to the bed and threw himself down beside me. "Up."

I 'upped'.

"Down."

I 'downed'. Lying down, with his arms wrapped tightly around me.

"Now cry."

So I did. Sobbing in the arms of the devil, who didn't fetch handkerchiefs or say 'there, there' or 'it'll be all right', or show any sign of realising that his chest was soon soaking wet. Sobbing till the storm spent itself, until at last I fell asleep there, draped across him like a rug that snored occasionally.

Outside, the gale was slowly blowing itself out too.

At some point in the night, he must have managed to manoeuvre the bedspread to keep us both warm, and eventually, he fell asleep too.

And from start to finish, he hadn't so much as kissed me.

# Chapter 27

*God, that feels disgusting.*

My face appeared to be stuck to something with some kind of resin.

Reluctantly, I opened my eyes. Then blinked in horror at the expanse of bare skin that greeted my appalled gaze.

A chest. A male chest. *Mark's* chest.

My arm was thrown across his ribs, his arm around my shoulders. My face was practically welded to his right breast by…

Oh, hell. Oh, bloody, sodding hell. All that work he'd put into the foreplay – I'd seen the flickering glow of the candles waiting downstairs – and what had he got for his trouble? An unstrung woman snivelling all over his torso and falling unconscious there in a pool of her own slime.

The headache – not to mention the ghastly taste in my mouth – told me *exactly* what had been responsible for my downfall. There'd been a bottle of wine in the fridge and I'd sneaked a glass before I went into the shower, hoping to ease my inhibitions. Predictably, since I rarely drank, it had had its effect.

I took a solemn vow in that moment never, ever, *ever* to touch alcohol again. I'd become a Quaker. I'd join an Institution. I'd leave all my money to Alcoholics Anonymous. I was done with the Demon Drink.

You couldn't make it up. I'd spent the night in the arms of the most gorgeous bloke I'd ever clapped eyes on, and all I had to show for it was the dreadful suspicion I'd revealed far, far too many extremely intimate things for my own peace of mind and topped it all off by passing out on top of him. I didn't even have the consolation that I'd at least given him a blow-job to make up for missing out on 'Bolero'.

Yes, and leaving all the candles to burn themselves out downstairs! All-Holy God, the house could have burned down because I couldn't handle my drink.

Stuck to him so emphatically, there was no way on the green Earth I was going to be able to detach myself and sneak away to die of shame somewhere without waking him.

Which way of escape was best? It was like removing a sticking plaster. The slow rip, or the quick yank that gives you all the pain at once.

I decided on the quick yank. It would let me get away from him faster, for one thing.

It wasn't as painful as I'd expected. More 'disgusting', really. I stared down in mortification at the hair on his chest, which was now matted with the fruits of my lack of emotional control the previous night. From the corner of my eye, I saw that his eyes had flicked open. I couldn't summon the courage to meet them. He must think I was an absolute slob.

There was a silence that seemed long, though it was probably only a couple of seconds. Then his free hand clasped my shoulder, and I was gently and firmly propelled backwards to lie flat on the bed.

I got ready to open my legs. It would be something for him after the no-show of the previous evening, and then afterwards he'd probably pack his stuff and leave, shrugging off the disappointment I'd been. A chap can put up with 'fat' if he's not too picky, but 'crazy' is something else altogether.

*Remember, moaning is for whores.*

He got out of bed and walked out of the door. I watched dumbly, too exhausted even to try to understand.

The sound of his footsteps going downstairs, and his voice talking to Sharp. The back door opening, to let the dog out into the garden for his morning constitutional. Then the faint noise of cupboards opening and closing; and a moment later, his footsteps coming upstairs again. The bathroom door opening. The hot tap on the sink had a distinctive squeak when you first turned it, but it didn't run for long.

Then the bedroom door opened again, and he came back in, carrying the very same things I'd brought him to clean himself up with when he'd first arrived. His face was serious and composed. He soaped the wet flannel and washed my face and neck with it very gently and carefully, seeming not to notice I was blushing like a flamingo again. Afterwards, he rinsed the facecloth in the bowl and cleaned the worst of the soap off before patting my skin dry with the towel.

His gaze dropped to his chest.

"Let me," I said in a small voice.

He handed over the soap and flannel without a word, and I returned the service he'd just done for me. I realised after a moment that there was a soothing element to the activity, that we were re-establishing contact with each other in a kind, constructive, non-threatening sort of way. It was about all I felt able to cope with right now.

He thanked me quietly when I was done and said he was going to make breakfast. "Would you like toast today, or do you want porridge again?"

"You shouldn't be–"

"Coffee, you have in the morning. Milky, and you take sweeteners. Toast would be something different, if you like it."

"Two," I replied, defeated. "Just butter."

"Just butter it is. You'll have to wait while I feed Sharp, though. Can I bring you up your book?"

"No, I'm fine." I'd have to visit the toilet, anyway. "But when you're coming back up, could you bring me a couple of Paracetamol?"

"Ah. The 'morning after the night before', I take it." He smiled teasingly. I realised, mortified, that he must have realised what I'd done. "I'm sure you didn't drink enough to give you a *very* bad hangover."

"Just a headache."

"I'd imagine. I'll be as quick as I can."

"Mark, I–"

"Shush. Not now. It's all right."

In despair, I watched him walk to the door. How could he possibly say it was all right? How could he possibly speak to me in the gentle tone you'd use to an animal in pain after I'd made such an absolute exhibition of myself the night before? If he'd had the brains he was born with, he'd have waited till I'd fallen into that drunken stupor, gone downstairs to get a decent night's sleep and rung a taxi first thing. He should have been long gone already. And who would be to blame?

The usual suspect, that's who.

*Yeah, you cocked **that** up altogether,* The Tart agreed ruefully. *It was the only cock-up of the evening, too.*

*Only because she added the sin of drunkenness to the sin of lust,* said The Saint, with vengeful satisfaction.

"Oh, shut up." I'd accidentally spoken aloud. Nervously I glanced at the doorway, but Mark's footsteps were audible downstairs.

*The truth hurts.*

The Tart lost her temper. *D'you know what you are? You're a ventriloquist's fecking dummy for Liam McEnally, so you are. He's spent thirty-four years coaching you and you've got it word perfect. Well, it's about time you gave it a rest. His day's over and so's yours. So fecking button it!*

In the stunned silence that followed, I got out of bed and went to the bathroom. Dismally, I inspected the damage. Although clean, my face still showed some of the evidence from the previous night; it was hardly surprising that my eyes were red from all the crying.

I wouldn't have time for a bath or even a shower before breakfast. Perhaps if I had a good long soak afterwards, it would do something to restore me.

It was probably inevitable that The Tart got her oar in on that idea. The silence from the other party suggested someone around here was sulking. Even the reminder of how much fun could be had from a game of Hunt the Soap failed to elicit so much as a censorious grunt.

As for the bathmat – I couldn't even look at it.

Back in my bedroom, I caught sight of my reflection in the triple mirror on the dressing table. Yes, I'd had to seize *that* nightie when I was filling my suitcase, hadn't I? White cotton, buttoned right up to the neck. (That said, these days pretty well everything I owned buttoned up to the neck, to save myself from any possible accusations from Liam that I was flaunting myself.) And even without its horrible associations, what in the Name of God had possessed me to put it on after my shower last night, when I'd been expecting a night of unbridled passion on the hearthrug? What had I been *thinking* of?

Talk about a bloody passion killer!

Despondently, I got back into bed. It was a certainty Mark wouldn't be joining me in it with mischief in mind this morning.

Could matters be improved? Oh, yes. Open all the chaste white buttons on the nightie. All three of them. At least an inch apart, too. If that didn't drive him into a frenzy, nothing would.

I could always take it off altogether, but perhaps he'd changed his mind, anyway. After last night, who could blame him? Shagging a lump was one thing. Shagging an *unhinged* lump was something else altogether.

I was a married woman, and however much I'd been enjoying this lunatic, dangerous fantasy world, that was all it was. A fantasy. And fantasies have to come to an end.

A bloody shame. Still, nobody dies of disappointment. I could testify to that. He'd live.

I wasn't sure I would, but getting involved in this at all deserved its punishment. I'd earned it. I'd accept it. However many billions of Our Fathers and Hail Marys it involved, and the rest of my life enduring Liam's occasional outbursts of lust while I lay there underneath him, gritting my teeth and thinking of a very different body and a very different man...

It still felt completely unreal to have breakfast made for me. It wasn't *done.* I fidgeted, wanting to get up and offer to butter the toast or something. It wasn't hard to forecast his reaction if I did, however. I'd be sent smartly to the about-turn, and potentially with a smack on the bum to speed me along.

"Breakfast coming up for the sexy señora," sang a voice on the other side of the door. It seemed he believed he was good at accents. Sadly, this was untrue.

That was all we bloody needed, Manuel from 'Fawlty Towers'. I pulled the bedspread hopelessly over my head. *He's mad. I'm doomed.*

"No good hiding. I know you're in there." There was the sound of a tray being set down, and a set of fingers pretending to be a spider insinuated themselves under the bedspread, searching for a foot. "You are my prisoner. Zhere is no escape."

"No, no, I'm ticklish!" With a shriek of panic, I erupted back into daylight. "No, really. I hate having anyone touch my feet."

"Aha. Zhe prisoner has revealed her weakness." He leered fiendishly at me. "Zhe prisoner has committed a serious tactical error!"

"You know, you're bloody mad." I picked up a pillow and hit him with it.

He fended it off with one elbow, narrowly saving the contents of the tray from being hit. "Mind out, you daft woman. You nearly spilled the coffee!"

"It would have been your fault."

"*Mine?* Who assaulted me with it in the first place?"

"Yes, but you asked for it!"

"Zhe prisoner vill desist from arguing und assume zhe position." His accent had gone from Spanish to Russian. Or perhaps it was supposed to be German. It was hard to tell, really.

"I assume you mean the position for eating breakfast."

"I do for now. Later, zhe orders will be different."

"You've been reading too many of them rude books." I started tidying the bedspread, this being a grand excuse for not looking at him till I'd got the blush back under control.

"Zis will all be demonstrated to zhe prisoner in due course."

*Bring it ON!* howled The Tart.

Saint Frances found occasion to mention hell again. Both The Tart and I ignored this, so she went off and sat in a corner, muttering darkly about the Seventh Commandment and mortal sin.

When the tray was finally settled across my lap, there were two things on it I hadn't expected. The first was a coronet of honeysuckle in an egg cup. The second was my mobile phone.

Mark sat on the bed and looked at me seriously, his silly accent gone. "I know you've got your reasons for leaving this off, but I'm not convinced they're the right ones, so let's just talk about them."

I took a bite of toast and muttered that I wanted to be left alone.

"Well, that's fair enough, and probably safest, but I do get the feeling you need to be in control of it. Leave it off because that's what you want to do rather than because you feel helpless when it's on.

"It's a *machine*. A small device that was probably made in China. And you're letting it boss you around." He poked the mobile and then flicked it with one finger so that it spun on the melamine. "Look. It doesn't bite. It just does what you tell it. Not the other way around."

I stared at it, nibbling the toast. "And your point is?"

"Take control of that. It's a start, but it's a good start. First off – disable your location finder, just in case. Then check your texts and messages. Any you don't want to read or listen to, delete. If it rings while you've got it switched on, decline the call. You don't have to read, you don't have to listen, and you *don't* have to accept a call you don't want." He smiled.

"On the other hand, you may be missing something you'd like to get. You may have a message from your friend – what's her name? Bridie? I'll bet she's wondering how you're getting on." He gave my hand a quick squeeze, then stood up and went downstairs. Presumably to make his breakfast and eat it in peace, at a safe distance from emotionally disturbed women who weren't interested in listening to *Bolero*.

I ate the toast and drank the coffee, still staring at the phone. Then, quickly, before I could change my mind, I switched it on.

Texts, texts, three voicemails, missed calls, texts, more missed calls, several voicemails, more texts, even more texts, more missed calls, all from my family. Jesus, hadn't I told them I was safe enough?

Nothing from Bridie.

I deleted everything, then showered and went downstairs.

"All done?" Mark glanced at his watch. "Right, I want us to go shopping."

"Shopping?" I looked up from fussing Sharp, who was showing how pleased he was to see me by insisting I tickle his tummy.

"Yes. I have this uncontrollable compulsion to go shopping. Preferably somewhere largish. I think Richmond's the nearest decent-sized town – how far is it from here?"

*He* was asking *me*, and I was from Ireland? I gave him the sarcastic eyebrow, and he gave it to me back and said he wasn't a walking atlas of the United Kingdom just because he came from London.

Since neither of us knew, he got Google Maps up on his iPad and consulted it. "You don't mind driving? I'll pay for the petrol."

We squabbled over who was going to pay for the petrol. I won in the end, but he only let me on condition he paid for the parking and bought me a coffee somewhere.

The weather had turned showery. Still, the countryside was beautiful. About a third of the way along the road from Leyburn to Richmond we saw a red flag on a pole by the side of the road. I asked what it was for. He said it was a live firing range warning on the MoD range there, and you don't fool me into thinking you don't know that, Beautiful Russian Spy.

A spirited exchange followed, mostly to conceal my delighted embarrassment at being described as a Beautiful Russian Spy. I don't know where he'd got the description from – most likely from watching too many James Bond films – but for some reason it tickled me no end.

We were still squabbling cheerfully when we reached Richmond. To his annoyance, we found that parking was free, although time-limited by a parking card that could be borrowed from various shops around the square. He announced his intention of compensating for this outrage by finding my secret stash of vodka and drinking it out of my belly button when we found a parking space.

"Not in Richmond market square, for God's sake," I objected. I wasn't even going to dignify the idea that I had a secret stash of vodka by referring to it. "And what the hell size bellybutton d'you think I've got?"

"Certainly not in Richmond market square. I would be foiled by the capitalist pig parking attendants. As for your belly button, I am assured that one sips vodka sparingly from such an exquisite vessel. Surely they must have taught you that in the Kremlin?"

"Never mind the parking attendants, you'd be foiled by the capitalist tourists with their mobile phone cameras filming us. And if you've got any fancy ideas about cocktail sticks, paper umbrellas and ESPECIALLY ice cubes, you can forget them." The thought of what sort of attention we'd gather if we put the seats flat and started doing a James Bond seduction scene in the middle of Richmond market square in broad daylight was mind-boggling – not to mention the amount of vodka that would dribble down into the car seats. I'd drive back to Dublin smelling like a distillery.

When I pointed this out, he said he'd had no idea Beautiful Russian Spies were so utterly lacking in the spirit of adventure.

I replied that I had a lot of the spirit of adventure, and even more of the spirit of wanting to avoid being prosecuted for public indecency when I got around to having one. Having previous form at the top of Middleham's keep, I thought I'd better make that clear.

The bickering continued while we strolled. We passed a clothes shop, and I had a look inside at what was on offer. Mark stayed beside me, only sighing theatrically once or twice. I poked him in the ribs and he squawked dramatically. The expression on the face of a nearby saleslady suggested she didn't know what tourists were coming to these days.

"I thought you wanted to go shopping?" I demanded when we were out on the pavement again.

"I do. I want to go shopping in interesting shops."

"Well, after you, I'm sure. I haven't been here before. *I* don't know what interesting shops they have."

"I got the bus here from Darlington. I had a look around. I don't suppose you'd class the Military Museum as interesting, by any chance?"

"You got that right. If you want to go there, I'll catch a coffee somewhere and wait for you."

"Only kidding. I've already been there. The shop I want is along here." There was a narrow lane leading off the square, and he turned into it, with a purposeful look on his face that made my heart sink for some reason.

There were quite a few charity shops that might have some CDs I could buy to take home with me. First, however, I supposed we'd better pay a visit to whichever shop had caught Mark's interest. He probably wanted to buy another pair of jeans to replace the torn ones. He wore nice clothes – he wouldn't want to buy from just any old shop. And he might want my opinion about something, even though I was nobody's idea of a fashion expert and a shop assistant would be a better bet for advice.

As soon as I realised what sort of shop it was in front of us, however, I tried to do an immediate about-turn. Unfortunately, he was ready for that. He was right behind me, had one arm around my waist before you could say 'naughty lingerie', and pressed a ten-pound note into my jacket pocket with his free hand.

"Here. There's a café back in the square. Go catch that cup of coffee we mentioned, unless you want to come in and try things on for me. I won't be long."

"I– you–" My tongue seemed to be tied in knots. And my face, yet again, had gone up in flames. "No."

"You're making the assumption you can stop me."

"And you're assuming you can make me wear... it. Whatever. At least, I hope it's for me." I tried to make a joke of it, though I'd never felt less like laughing.

"It definitely is for you. But *make* you wear it? No. Need you to? No. Want you to? Yes. So you can feel as sexy as you'll look."

"Oh, bloody hell," I said weakly, while The Tart went *Woo Hoo!* and followed up with assorted other noises of the strongest approval.

It now dawned on me he hadn't walked us past that clothes shop for nothing. And once in, he hadn't gone away to inspect the menswear section, as Liam would have done. He'd been right beside me. Watching what size clothes I looked at.

Swine.

"You could, of course, tell me I'll be wasting my time buying it," he murmured in my ear. "But unless you say so before I get through the doorway in there, I'll take it I won't."

I opened my mouth to assure him he would be wasting not only his time, but also his money. Because I was a married woman and what we'd done up till now had been the most terrible mistake, and... and... and...

Nothing came out.

"Better make it quick." He took his arms from around my waist. "Unless I hear from you before that door shuts behind me, I'll meet you at the café. Get yourself a piece of cake, and don't rush eating it. Just don't order the parkin unless you're starving to death."

There were only a couple of paces to the door. He walked without hurrying and without glancing back.

*If you say a single fecking word, I'm never speaking to you again,* The Tart said fiercely.

The coffee was a little strong for my taste. Mindful of his warning, I didn't have the parkin, though there were homemade mince pies I couldn't resist sampling.

Afterwards, though.

'Afterwards' was presumably going to feature the Bolero, deferred from last night.

Afterwards was going to be…

*'Glorious?'* suggested The Tart.

*'Monstrous!'* muttered Saint Frances.

I ignored them both. The word was 'Terrifying'.

# Chapter 28

Mark had suggested taking Sharp for an evening walk as far as the hermitage. Not because he himself needed the exercise, as he was planning to have plenty later, but because he had no intention of leaving me anything to worry about instead of enjoying 'Bolero'.

I worried about his ankle instead. He said it was much better, but he put some extra bandages from the First Aid box on top of the support bandage he was still wearing, and said he needed to work through the discomfort.

The steps down to the bridge were uneven. They wouldn't be easy for him to navigate, even if he had brought the hiking pole.

"Are you sure you can manage?" I asked doubtfully, as the two of us came to a halt at the top of them.

"I'm positive I can." His voice from behind me had taken on that dark, silky quality that made my heart judder.

"I *meant* the *steps*."

"So did I. The slowest steps imaginable. Right until neither of us can wait."

"For Heaven's sake!" For some reason, I was finding it hard to concentrate on my footing. I clutched nervously at the trunk of a nearby tree. "Do you *want* me to break my neck?"

"Well, I was planning on a fate that would be a lot more lingering." He'd taken mercy on me, however, and his tone was back to teasing, though the words were not. "Come on, give me your hand. I don't want you ending up in hospital."

"If I do, it'll be your fault." Relinquishing the tree, I reached back towards him. He caught my hand, but instead of grasping it to steady me, he lifted it to his mouth and licked delicately between each splayed finger.

The sensation caught me by surprise. I gasped involuntarily.

*"Step one,"* he whispered.

The muscles in my arm tensed, but my hand remained still. Palm upward in his grasp, and spread like a prayer.

He leaned forward. Not like last time. Not demanding.

Asking.

His mouth was gentle. I could feel his breath fanning softly across my cheek as he kissed me. After a moment, his eyes closed. The lashes were surprisingly long and dark for a man's, lying motionless.

*Step two.*

He released me after only a couple of seconds. "I believe you were saying something about showing me a bridge," he murmured, though his mouth remained mere inches away from mine.

"Yes. It's – not far now. Just down here. There's a church a bit further on, if your ankle's up to it."

His eyebrows rose. "I can't think of many less appropriate places for you to be leading me to. I'm afraid I'm quite past redemption if that's your plan." His lips brushed against mine again. "In fact, quite the opposite. *I'm* busy leading *you* to perdition."

A shaky laugh. "You're doing a good job, but I shouldn't tell you that, should I?"

"No." The next kiss was slightly longer. "You're tempting the Devil. And considering this is a public place, this is a hell of a time for you to give me a hard-on."

It was getting to the point where I wondered if my face would ever go back to its normal colour. I might as well dye it fluorescent pink and have done with it. "At least I'll have something to grab if I feel myself slipping," I managed.

"Please. Slip away. You're getting my hopes up."

Without my ever quite intending it, my hands found themselves on his body. Taking in the feeling of warm fabric, with the hard muscle behind it. Just his sides, but that in itself was a gesture I'd never meant to make; it was already too easy for my fingers to start getting a grip on the shirt, ready to pull it up so they could slide onto his bare skin. One more step on the slippery slope back into hell disguised as heaven.

*Step three.*

He drew back and gave me a lazy smile. "It'll do for a start."

"The church." Damnation, why wouldn't my voice stay steady? I turned around and started down the steps. "I only want to see you spontaneously combust as soon as you set foot on consecrated ground."

"If I did, you'd miss an *awful* lot of pleasure."

"There is that," I admitted. "So perhaps it's just as well it's only a ruin."

"I can't tell you how relieved I am. Perhaps that's a sign of things to come. With the emphasis on 'come'."

I wasn't going to fall for that one. The bridge. Must get on to that damned bridge.

And a far safer topic of conversation, too.

If I could find one.

A few minutes later, we were standing in the middle of the footbridge. After a last glance around to make sure there were no sheep anywhere within sight, I released Sharp. He gave a little joyful 'woof!' and galloped off towards the far bank.

The bridge was made of wood. Being very slim, it was also very springy. It reacted to every footfall in a most unnerving way. Like probably everyone setting foot on it for the first time, Mark responded to this by bouncing to see how much reaction he could get.

"If it snaps in half and plunges both of us to our deaths, I'll know who's responsible." I clung nervously to the rail. I'd found the bounciness of the bridge disconcerting the first time, with only me on it, and I wasn't good with heights. Even standing on a chair worried me.

Mark peered over the side. "'Plunges us to our deaths'? If you fell off here, you might break your ankles landing awkwardly, but that's about it. The only way you could drown in that depth of water would be to lie down flat on your face and put a very heavy rock on the back of your head."

"You have no poetry in your soul," I said crossly.

"But then I have no soul. That's why I want yours so badly. As well as your body, of course."

I glanced at him. He was watching me steadily.

After holding his gaze for a moment, I turned back and leaned on the rail. Below, the river went burbling onwards. I wondered where the leaves were by now. Caught up in some eddy, perhaps, or still floating helplessly towards the ocean. Most probably, they'd sunk to the bottom somewhere the flow lessened, to join the litter of the years.

"You said this wouldn't work if we didn't both tell the truth. The whole truth, and nothing but the truth."

"I did. A strange thing for the Devil to say, but it must have been one of my off days."

"So I want to ask you something and I want you to tell me the truth. The *entire* truth."

He was leaning on the rail beside me by now. Without looking at him, I caught the shrewd, sidelong glance. "I detect my victim indulging in thinking when she should be indulging in enjoying."

"Maybe." I was staring down the river, winding away to the sea. "I think you could fool me easily if you wanted to. You probably know that. But I want to know something ... before we go any further with this. And I'd prefer you to tell me the truth. Even if it isn't very nice. I can handle that. But I can't handle being told a lie and believing it and then finding out afterwards it wasn't true."

"Go ahead." Now he, too, was staring down the river.

A pause, while I marshalled my thoughts. My companion waited too, patient and silent. "You told me why you came here," I said at last. "Because of Rebecca."

"Yes." There was no inflection in his voice at all.

"That must have hurt," I went on. "An awful lot. I can understand why you felt you had to get away. You're probably still hurting, because nobody gets over something like that in a rush."

"I still think about her sometimes," he admitted.

The admission, however painful it was to me, at least showed he was being honest. If he'd have said otherwise, the conversation would have been over, because I wouldn't have believed a word of it.

"If she was that beautiful, I'm sure you do." Catching his surprised glance, I clarified. "Of course she was beautiful. You don't get much success sleeping your way up the ladder if you're ugly."

He winced. His ex-girlfriend had been having an affair with his department manager, which was the reason for him suddenly becoming superfluous to her requirements. "There is that."

"Well, so. You're still getting over being dumped by a beautiful young woman you were in love with. And now, a week later, you're in bed with a fat, middle-aged and not particularly attractive woman with marriage problems. Now call me cynical if you like, but that sounds to me like a serious case of rebound, pity or ego boosting. Probably two out of the three of them, at least." I swallowed.

"I don't think you'll deny the 'rebound' part of it; I don't think you could. If you want to sleep with me for pity, it's not the best reason I could think of – actually, it hurts – but I can understand it. If it's just you seeing the opportunity and taking it for an ego boost, that's not a good reason from your point of view. If I'm the best you can do to rebuild your confidence, you're not aiming nearly high enough."

There was another long silence. At the far end of the bridge, Sharp came into view briefly just to check I was still there. Reassured on that score, he disappeared again, presumably in search of rabbits.

"I think you're asking the impossible," Mark said at last. "I'm not trying to get out of giving you an honest answer, but giving you a percentage score of my motives isn't possible right now. I'm not sure it ever is for anyone, realistically."

"I'm not asking for percentages. I want to know what you're *really* thinking when you take me to bed. I want to know if you're saying all those things because you know I want to hear them, or because they're just part of the patter, or because in your heart of hearts you're still talking to *her*."

The sun peeked through at that moment. He put up a hand to shade his eyes as he stared at me – evidently he'd forgotten to bring his sunglasses, but then it hadn't looked much like he'd need them when we set out.

"Apart from the fact that if I *was* just stringing you along I'd hardly be likely to admit it because then you'd quite justifiably sling me out on my ear, you think I'm the sort of cruel bastard who'd think *any* of those things?"

"Maybe you wouldn't tell me, but they're all absolutely possible. I don't want lies, Mark. I can enjoy being in a play if that's what this is – and I know it's just fun for you, because you sure as hell aren't in love with me – but when you say the things you do, I can't help myself, I start believing them. So if you care about me at all, please, if they *are* lies, don't tell me any more. I can't bear it if you're lying to me."

He looked down at the river again. His long exhalation had something close to anger in it. "Fran, I don't know what sort of twisted swine you're married to, and quite frankly I don't give a toss about him. The only thing I care about is how much damage he's done to *you*, how impossible you find it to trust me or believe in yourself.

"Let's get this clear. I'm not over Rebecca, or more accurately, I'm not over what she did to me. Still in love with her? No. After what she did to me, no. Actually, I don't think I ever even knew her, so I was never really in love with her anyway. In love with who I thought she was? Maybe a little. Human nature; it'll take a while, but it'll wear off. Talking to her when I'm in bed with you? No. One hundred per cent, no. I'll give you a cast-iron guarantee on that one.

"Fucking you for pity? No. Maybe there's some 'sympathy', it's a bit more human. I'll hold my hand up to that one. I *do* think you deserve better. I *do* think you deserve to find out that a man can do more for you in bed than your husband has ever done, by the sound of it. And I like to think I'm achieving that, at least.

"Taking the opportunity? How many men wouldn't? I'm not a saint! Of course I want sex, of course I want pleasure. I see an attractive, sexy woman and of course I want to get her into bed with me. But you insult me almost as much as you insult yourself when you imply I'm sleeping with you because I'm desperate."

Aghast, I broke in. "I didn't mean you–"

"I know you didn't, Fran." His voice gentled on my name, like a caress. "You have so little self-belief you don't even understand how to accept someone cares about you. You want me to admit you're just a score, because that's something that fits in your universe. Well, to hell with your universe. I don't know if I could love you. It's too early to know something like that. I'm too messed up at the moment to make that kind of statement, and you're too messed up to believe it if I did. But I know that I care, that we get on together, that you make me laugh, and that I find you physically attractive. I love making love to you. I want both of us to get something out of the mess we're in, if nothing more."

He raised his hand and began ticking off the points on his fingers. "Fat? So you're carrying a bit. It doesn't worry me, I love seeing you naked. Fuck, *I'm* not Brad Pitt!

"Middle-aged? It happens. You're not decrepit, for God's sake, any more than I am. There's only a few years' difference between us, and *I'm* not finished enjoying myself! None of us can stop the music, Fran, we just need to dance while it's playing.

"Married? To hell with your marriage. It sounds to me like it's hell anyway.

"Woman? That's the important bit. That's the *really* important bit, and it's time you accepted it and stopped being ashamed of it!

"Marriage problems? There's help out there if you want it, if you really *are* determined to go back in spite of whatever I do or say. Whatever you can get, counselling, the lot, take it and see if it helps, though personally I think you'd be wasting your time. In the meantime I think I've made a start with helping, and I've a lot more I can do if you'll let me. At least I can show you what you *should* be getting. I can give you confidence in yourself. I can show you you're a fantastic lover who deserves to have a man make her happy!" He turned and glared at me. "And so help me, if you dare come back at me with some 'So you only want to sleep with me as sexual therapy' crap, I'll throw you off this bridge!"

My laugh was shaky, though not as shaky as I felt after so much emotion had poured across and through me. "I thought you said I'd break my ankles if I fell from here."

"So I'll promise not to suggest any positions where we put pressure on your ankles while they're in plaster. Honestly. You're such a negativist."

He closed the small space between us. The temperature had come down to something closer to the seasonal average, and we were both wearing jackets and jumpers. "You only wore that because it's got no buttons," he whispered.

"Less to undo when you take it off."

My arms slipped around him, under his jacket, which was conveniently undone. I rested my head on his shoulder for a few minutes, and felt his arms come around my shoulders, holding me close.

There was still a dog that needed exercise, however, so presently we disengaged and walked the rest of the way across the bridge. When we got to the other side, Mark firmly and gently took hold of my hand, so that we walked linked through the woodland; just like a 'proper' couple, I thought. And when a pair of runners passed us, probably doing some cross-country training, he didn't let go as if he didn't want anyone to notice.

I was so preoccupied I nearly walked past the church. Only the distinctive shape of the hermitage caught my eye.

"So this is it?" Mark looked around with interest. "Not much left, is there?"

"Not a lot. It's sad, really. The church got turned into an alehouse."

"Oh, I don't know if it's all that sad. Have you read that poem by William Blake? 'Dear Mother, dear Mother, the Church is cold, But the Ale-house is healthy and pleasant and warm'?"

"You should be confessing and doing penance for all your sins." I poked him in the ribs. "Not proving how wicked you are."

"Spare me. If there is a God, and my dark misdeeds are any concern of his, he and I can sort it out between us. And besides, I haven't got up to any particularly dark misdeeds since yesterday. Though I'd like to remedy that." His arms slipped under my jacket this time. "Soon."

I swallowed. I was in no position to lecture about sins. It was I, not Mark, who was guilty of one of the worst imaginable. But hard as I'd tried to convince myself to stop, to harden my heart and tell him to leave, I couldn't make myself do it. I knew our time together was running out fast. Sin or not, I could only seize these enchanted 'todays' until there were no more, and all that remained was a succession of desolate tomorrows.

I was a married woman, guilty of infidelity. I was standing right beside a church, with the vows I'd made in another one lying around me like shards of shattered glass. Sooner or later, I'd have to pay the price. That being so, didn't it make sense to make the most of the joy now?

For a man, he was on the short side; a lot shorter than Liam. I didn't have to look up far to meet his eyes, which were fixed seriously on my face. "I'm scared," I whispered.

"Scared of what?" He kissed me gently.

"I don't know. Everything. Infidelity. This is a big thing for me." I sighed against his ear. "It's a bit late now to worry, I know, but this isn't a game, not for me. It's not something I can just shrug and walk away from. This changes everything about me, everything about my life. I have to go back after this and find some way to deal with living. So I'm scared, right?"

"Well, I'd never have guessed *that* if you hadn't told me. Fran, come *on,* this is me you're talking to! I can't make you trust me. I can only ask you to. But I can promise you I'm not doing this for a game either. It may not last, but that doesn't mean it's not worthwhile while we have it."

The shattered glass rang out on a sweet, wild note; I was going to hold on to joy, and damn the consequences. With a feral moan, I pushed my hands under his jumper, wanting to feel bare skin.

His mouth was no longer gentle. Nor were his hands, which pushed me backwards, overbalancing me. I don't know whether it was by accident or mischief that I ended up pressed against the back of the ruined hermitage, but I pushed him off, scolding him that even for Satan, there should be limits. He laughed, nodded, and took the ball out of his pocket; Sharp was close by, plainly hoping he'd throw it.

"This was where I had the idea for that picture." I watched the dog race after the ball, heading back the way we'd come.

"You mentioned it. There you are. Divine inspiration."

"'Divine' is hardly the word," I said crushingly. "I was thinking what it must have been like living in that hermitage. Being completely on your own, practically all the time. Nothing to do except pray, and worry about sin and the Devil. In those days, they really believed in the Devil, didn't they? They honestly thought he went around incarnating. Tempting holy people, just out of spite. Creeping into people's beds and having his wicked way with them."

"You should know. You called me up," he breathed, his teeth closing lightly on the angle of my neck. He was now standing behind me, his arms around my ribs. Things hadn't improved in the seemliness department of his second-best pair of jeans either, to go by the evidence; if those runners came back, he'd better stay behind me, or turn his back, or do *something* to maintain public decency. "You wanted an insatiable sex slave, Mistress. Now face the consequences."

Now was the time when a snappy comeback would come in handy. For the life of me, I couldn't come up with one. Getting a satiable sex slave would have been the bonus of a lifetime; drag in 'insatiable'... though for a slave, wasn't he very bossy when he felt like it! "Oh," I said weakly. I wasn't sure if that was 'Oh good' or 'Oh God'.

"What you mean is, *Show me*," he purred into my ear. "Your desire is my wish, Mistress."

*God in Heaven.* Didn't he have the sexiest voice in the world when he talked like that?

For a devil, presumably one from the hottest regions of hell if his behaviour so far was any indicator, he was a cool customer. I envied his apparent carelessness as we walked back down the path, our progress interrupted now and then by Sharp's returns and the necessity to throw the ball for him. Every few minutes, however, Mark whispered suggestions in my ear that severely worsened the wobbliness factor. When we came across a leaning dead tree, caught and held by others part-way through its fall, he pressed me back against it with his body until I could feel every detail of the rough bark through my clothes, not to mention the details of what was pressing hungrily against my groin. Seizing my wrists, he pinned them above my head and kissed me until I was whimpering and breathless.

It was a mercy the runners didn't come back. Given that carrying a weapon in public was illegal, even if it was tucked in your trousers, he might have got arrested.

And his was loaded, too. He'd made a point of mentioning that.

Several times, in fact.

I came to a decision. Right now it was 'Oh good'. But I had a feeling that pretty soon it was going to turn into 'Oh God'. And probably, at a guess, on a rising volume. So maybe they were both right.

Neither of my voices commented as Mark and I crossed the bridge and walked back across the field and up the lane. Maybe they'd headed for the mental equivalent of the nearest pub for a drink, comparing their black eyes and arguing over whether to watch a nature documentary or one of the soaps. Saint Frances had probably decided I was a lost cause, though she still looked in now and then to make sure I wasn't enjoying myself too much altogether.

It was just as well they weren't here, actually. This was going to be scary enough without an audience.

Now, I truly *was* on my own.

# Chapter 29

"Fran, listen to me for just a moment." Mark put his hand on my arm as I was about to go upstairs for my turn in the shower.

I hesitated. Surely, after the lovely day we'd had, there wasn't going to be a problem?

He said quickly that there was nothing to worry about. He just wanted to talk about something.

"You've been talking about it all afternoon, *acushla*. For the love of God, don't tell me you've a headache now."

My feeble attempt at a joke at least earned me a smile, but his expression was serious. He pulled me back from the stairway and put his arms around my waist. "Fran. I haven't forgotten about last night, and I'm not minimising how upset you became. I think perhaps I hadn't realised quite how much damage you've suffered through your marriage.

"You clearly have a *lot* of hurt you need to work through at some point. I'm asking you, if you won't leave your husband, at least get some kind of help for yourself. If he won't go to counselling, go on your own."

He lowered his forehead to press against mine and went on, his voice quiet. "In the meantime, it's occurred to me it may seem insensate for me to just try to repeat what we tried to do last night without asking if you're really all right with it. If you're not ... look, I'd so much rather you said so. We can do other things, just be together in other ways. I want to make you happy, not twist the knife."

Aw, wasn't he the lovely man? Not just interested in giving me a good time in bed, but actually looking out for me in other ways as well. And saying that if I'd gone off the idea of *Bolero*, it wouldn't be the end of the world.

I cupped my hands around his head. "Look, you've spent all bloody afternoon getting my hopes up. Don't think you're backing out of it now, because I'm telling you, there'll be a riot if you even try."

He looked at me for a moment longer, as though making sure I meant what I said; then he smiled, let go of me and said in that case, he'd give me something to remember.

This time, I didn't make the mistake of putting on that damned nightdress I'd brought from home. It was already in the bin, anyway, so I couldn't have, but next time I went to a town of any size I'd look around for something to replace it.

At some point, he'd left a large shopping bag on my bed. I'd seen him carrying it in Richmond, of course, when he came to the café to pick me up again, but neither of us had said anything about it. Still, I had to admit I was eaten with curiosity to know what was in it. There was an awful lot of bulk in it for the sort of thing I suspected he'd bought in that naughty lingerie shop.

It turned out there were a couple of bags in it. The wretch had been spending his money like it was water when I wasn't there to kick his arse and tell him not to.

The bulk was from a folded 'throw', probably from India or somewhere like that, woven of shimmering red and gold silk. In the light from the bedside lamp, it sparkled as if it was on fire.

Singularly apt, for a seduction by the Devil...

There was a smaller carrier bag, from a pharmacist's. Perfume, and not a small bottle at that. 'Beautiful'.

*All-Holy God*. I put it down and wiped the tears away.

Then, my hands shaking, I opened the bag from the naughty nightie shop.

The mirror now showed me a very different woman. Ivory silk with dark red lace flowed over my curves, and a matching dark red velvet negligee hung from my shoulders. My best pendant – a tanzanite and diamond pear-drop Ciarán had bought me for my fiftieth birthday – hung between my breasts, and now I knew why I'd saved it so faithfully for a special occasion.

Occasions didn't get more special than this.

I didn't have much by way of make-up. An overheard comment from Liam years ago about the pointlessness of putting lipstick on a pig had put an end to my buying cosmetics. But I had a few bits saved up for 'just in case', and such as they were, they were better than nothing. My newly dark eyes looked exotic, to go with the outfit I was wearing.

Who wouldn't feel sexy wearing such clothes, even if they were over fifty and overweight?

Bolero beckoned.

High heeled shoes weren't for the likes of me, but I'd shamelessly borrowed a pair from Bridie's room (I knew she'd egg me on if she knew, bless her) and luckily they only pinched a little bit. I wouldn't have wanted to go hiking in them, but just for getting downstairs and as far as the hearthrug, I could put up with them. The years since I'd worn any such thing made me feel slightly wobbly, even though they weren't even that high, just a couple of inches, but I managed to achieve a *fairly* elegant walk. And having them on, to set off the rest of the outfit, just made me feel drop-dead gorgeous as I paused at the turn of the stairs for Mark to notice me and admire.

Which, of course, he did. If his eyes weren't actually out on stalks, they certainly looked as if they would have been if they hadn't been attached to the back of their sockets. I felt like a million euros as he stood up, whistled, and came forward to meet me.

He must have been spending on his own account, too, the monkey. He had a loose white shirt on him that looked like silk, and good black trousers that said *style*. Wasn't I going to have the time of my damned life, between him, the hearthrug and the music?

*Love me, Lucifer. Love me.*
*With pleasure, Beautiful.*

I carefully negotiated the next few steps, trying to combine concentrating on not falling over on my high heels and keeping up the film-star look. As soon as I was within touching distance, he reached out and took my hand.

And that was the precise moment when we heard a car turn into the drive, and pull up on the gravel.

For one terrifying moment, I thought that somehow – by some unimaginable fluke – it was Liam.

There was a window on the landing. I flew back up to it and looked down, shaking with fear.

My knees almost buckled with relief as I saw that the vehicle below was a Land Rover. Bridie had told me Peter drove one. Some divine agency – definitely not Satan, in the circumstances – must have put it into his head to come and check up on me.

Confirming it, Sharp erupted from his basket and hurtled towards the door. He was whining with eagerness, and his tail was wagging madly.

Mark had followed me upstairs. His eyes met mine. He must have reasoned from Sharp's reaction it was probably Peter arriving, or even Bridie and Paul coming home for some disastrous reason, so I saw his initial look of tension melting into a huge grin of relief.

Well, it wasn't the disaster it could have been, and thank the Lord God for that, but it was bad enough. What the blue bloody blazes was Peter going to think, coming here to find me dressed like a dog's dinner when I was all on my own? Gesturing Mark to hide in my room, I fled into the bathroom. *No way* could I answer the door wearing what I was right now.

Without a doubt, my host had a key. It was his house, after all. But I blessed his sense of propriety in the current circumstances – if his parents had been here he'd likely have walked straight in, but as there was (supposedly) only me in residence, he rang the bell and waited.

I dumped the negligee and the beautiful ivory silk nightdress in the laundry-basket and hauled a towel out of the cupboard and dropped it in on top of them. With frantic haste, using pads I'd found in the medicine cabinet, I scrubbed my make-up off, and wrapped a towel and Bridie's dressing-gown around myself. There was no sign of Mark's presence, thank God.

When I got downstairs again, Sharp had stopped barking. He was still by the front door, though, and he looked up at me eagerly.

Peter must have decided I was asleep or having a shower or something, for he was just walking back to his car. He looked around as Sharp galloped out to him.

"I'm so sorry. I was just getting in the bath," I panted.

His apologetic smile made me feel like an absolute heel. "Mrs McEnally, I'm so sorry to have disturbed you! I should have called first, but I was passing, and I just thought I'd check everything was all right with you." He patted Sharp absently.

I said everything was grand, told him to call me Frances, and asked if he'd come in for a cup of tea. He declined gracefully but suggested he'd be glad to meet me some other time when it was convenient; perhaps I'd like to visit the stables one of the days?

"That would be grand. Thank you."

Was it something English about constantly apologising? By the time he finally took himself off home, he'd said sorry at least three more times for ringing the bell of a house he owned, that I was staying in rent-free at his parents' invitation.

I got Sharp back into the house, shut the door and burst into tears.

# Chapter 30

Though the mood that evening was ruined irretrievably, the setback didn't prevent us trying to wring out every drop of joy from every available moment. However, our time together was limited.

Mark made beans on toast for breakfast the next day and brought it up to me. It went cold. We experimented with reheating it afterwards in the microwave. It wasn't a success, but we ate it anyway.

The sausages and bacon came in handy for lunch, though for some reason we didn't pay them our full attention. The bacon got scorched under the grill, and the sausages nearly burst into flames. The kitchen table was found to harbour a squeak, and Sharp had to be locked in the back garden for a while after he put Mark off his stride by staring curiously at us, though I'd never have known if he hadn't said.

I finally got to experience a shared bath, but my lover (God Above, *me* having a lover!) didn't care for the idea of being left smelling of roses afterwards. We drove into town and bought some exotic bath oil instead.

Neither of us noticed that the water slopped over the edge of the bath quite a lot. He said it wouldn't do his ankle any harm, though that was a bit of an exaggeration. And – much to my astonishment – he helped me to wipe the floor dry afterwards.

We made love in the back of the Fiesta in a farm gateway after dark like a pair of teenagers, giggling and desperate and horny. As 'comfortable' went, it wasn't, and we probably wouldn't have persevered with the attempt but for me saying it wasn't possible. This again didn't do his ankle any good, and I insisted on strapping it up again and putting a packet of peas out of the freezer on it. His having to sit with his feet on the footstool again the next day didn't prove an insuperable handicap; after all, I wasn't sitting across his ankle.

And, at long last, a few days later he finally showed me what the big deal was about 'Bolero'. The cottage was a cup of dark magic lit only by the scented candles burning on the hearth, with the wind gusting outside and the rain spattering against the windows. And after foreplay that made me feel it was impossible to contain all the longing he'd aroused in me, I spent the fifteen minutes of the piece itself enduring the most exquisite torment I could imagine with my Lucifer matching the speed and force of his thrusts precisely to every phrase, until the climax that broke over us was hardly separable from the climax of the music itself.

Afterwards, sobbing in his arms, I thought I'd never listen to it again without my pulse speeding up – if I could ever bring myself to listen to it at all.

In between times, over the next few days, we kissed and talked and listened to music; we went for walks (short, because of his ankle) and drives (long, because the scenery was stunning), and I practised my sketching. The red and gold throw proved perfect as a prop for his 'diabolical' posing, and he posed for me so realistically with it that it wasn't long before I succumbed to his devilish blandishments and joined him underneath it. After that, I wasn't in any condition at all to care about artwork, so that too had to be left for another day.

But how many days were left to us? Slowly but inexorably, they were slipping away. Real life still existed outside this enchanted idyll, and we were doomed to have to take it up again, though I pushed the thought aside with growing desperation whenever it occurred to me.

Our final evening.

I stood by the window of the bedroom, looking out across the dale. This was the last time I'd see it through the eyes of a lover. Tomorrow, I'd drive Mark to Richmond and leave him there. I'd offered to park up and wait to see him off on the bus, but to tell the truth, I was relieved when he'd refused. There was enough agony in store without the long-drawn-out suffering of watching each other's faces through a bus window, waiting on tenterhooks for the change in the engine note that will bring an end. I'd pull up in the square, drop him and his rucksack, and go.

And that would be that.

I tried to ignore the sensation inside me of a sadness so deep it made me feel hollow. I realised I was mourning my loss even before it happened, and felt ashamed of my selfishness.

At least I'd a home to go back to when Bridie and Paul returned. It wasn't a very happy home, true, but it was mine, and with a bit of luck and determination I could improve things for myself there. Mark, however, was going back to London to live in a damned hotel room and work for a chap who'd nicked his girlfriend. Presumably he'd get his own place sooner or later, but even though he'd been reluctant to talk too much about it, I could imagine how badly he'd been wounded by the betrayal – and that on top of his failed marriage. It must have eaten his masculine pride from the inside out to be unable to get his wife pregnant, even by IVF, and finding out (as he had) that shortly after divorcing him she was shacked up with another chap and three months up the duff must have just about put the tin lid on it. He was constantly worrying about my hurts, but bejeezus, he must have more than enough of his own.

I glanced back at the bed. Mark was still asleep, curled up in the fur throw. He'd moved over to my side of the bed when I got up, mumbling drowsily about keeping it warm. I usually got up very early to go to the toilet and got back in, grateful in the last couple of days for his warmth to snuggle up to. September was approaching fast; mist hung over the river down in the dale, and the leaves on the trees looked weary. Soon a warmer quilt would be a necessity, and the summer clothes would be either got rid of or put away for another year.

After tonight, however, there would be no more warmth to snuggle up to. He'd be on the bus back to Darlington, and then the train back to London and the dreary drudgery of living. I'd be left here, and though the cottage and the Dales were still as beautiful as ever, after experiencing what I had here, the gilt would be gone off the gingerbread with a vengeance.

"Fran?"

I jumped almost guiltily. Mark had woken up and was frowning at me in concern. "Is anything wrong?"

"Just looking at the mist," I said evasively, though the half-truth was painful; we'd promised each other from the start to tell the truth. "It looks like something out of one of those old Hammer film sets, down over the river."

He pulled the red-gold throw around his shoulders (we still threw it on top of the quilt), slipped out of bed and padded across to join me, shivering a little in the cool of the early morning. "It does. I'll tell you what, when we take Sharp out for his walk perhaps we could see if we can pick some blackberries."

"I can make us a crumble." Of course, that was exactly what he was hoping I'd say. Men and their bloody stomachs.

"Excellent. As long as I get to name the stakes for who picks the most blackberries."

"Oh, you." Swatting him was becoming a habit, I thought with a pang. "Are you always so bloody competitive?"

"I am when there's such a wonderful prize on offer."

Hell, even now he could make me blush. "That's assuming you win."

"If I win, you get on top. If you win, I get on top. Sounds like I win either way."

"You have such a one-track mind."

"Certainly. And your train's calling at exactly the same stations, lady, so you are not in a position to talk."

Even with the throw around both of us though (and I was wearing a new nightie I'd bought in Leyburn), it really wasn't warm enough to linger, even to enjoy the view. Especially when there was plenty of warmth left in the bed, and plenty for us to do in it.

Afterwards, I rested my head on his chest while my heart slowed from its frantic pounding. Heavy-hearted, I recognised a new intensity in the way I was holding on to him, as though trying to imprint every atom of his existence on my skin.

I think he recognised it too. He kissed the top of my head. What point was there in talking?

We took Sharp for a walk.

The air was clear and bright and fresh. The sunshine had in it the first foretaste of autumn, and Mother Nature the Artist, now selecting colours from that season's palette, had already touched some of the trees here with gold.

In patches, the hedgerows were a tangle of brambles, hung with spider-webs still jewelled with dew. The rain that had fallen lately had swollen the blackberries, which hung in rich purple clusters among the already fading foliage; we decided it made more sense to gather them on the way home.

At last, acknowledging we could put it off no longer, before we set out we'd exchanged e-mail addresses so he could send all the photographs from his iPhone to my laptop, where he'd shown me how to create a hidden folder. In it we'd stored them as protected files with innocuous titles. I also added a few photos I'd taken of him in less exotic locations, similarly renamed, and created a document there with his e-mail address on it. One day, when I'd finished The Portrait, I'd send him a photograph of it by way of a reply.

My worst fear was Liam taking it into his head to check my contacts, call lists or e-mails, or to even to spy on my phone calls, so we carefully went through my phone to make sure the photographs were gone past retrieval by anything short of a professional. Liam wasn't a technical wizard like Fergal, for instance, so even if he managed to get into my laptop I doubted whether he'd even realise there were such things as hidden folders – I hadn't known about them, and I was far more computer-literate than he was. There were no phone calls or texts to worry about, though Mark insisted I should add his phone number to his e-mail address on the document 'just in case'. In the circumstances, it would be natural for my husband to be suspicious, to try to find out where I'd been and what I'd done. He'd have more than enough to hold against me without finding messages from a lover.

Neither Mark nor I said much as we strolled. To try to distract myself from thinking about what I'd have to face tomorrow, I wondered what I could do if this second attempt at making my marriage work failed. Once I was at the far end of a divorce, I could go wherever I wanted. Maybe a trip abroad would be the thing. New places, new people; maybe I could even go to America, to see the autumn foliage in Vermont – this was on my 'bucket list', along with the Northern Lights, Santorini, the Himalayas, and the pyramids of Egypt. If I got half of the proceeds out of the sale of the house (property prices in Dublin had risen to insane levels since we'd moved there), it would be enough to let me travel for quite a while. Then, wherever I settled afterwards, it wouldn't be in Dublin. Somewhere close enough for me to travel regularly to see the grandkids, though.

Maybe the time would come when I'd think about meeting up with someone on my travels, but I couldn't foresee it. After this, I was done with love. I couldn't be having with feeling like this again, only to get my heart broken a second time.

It seemed Mark had been thinking along the same lines. "Are you sure you'll be all right if it *doesn't* work out with Liam? Where will you go?"

"I don't know. It's a pretty bloody scary idea." I managed a wan smile. "It'd feel strange, taking my pictures down off the walls, and everything. It's been my home for so long, and it's got my imprint on it. That said, lifers probably personalise their prison cells, but it doesn't make their imprisonment any less real."

Ideally, I told him, I'd like to go home to Donegal, but that'd mean hardly ever seeing the grandkids. "So I'll take my time and look around. Find myself a little place somewhere on the East Coast, down Wexford way."

"But you'll manage?" he asked, his tone surprisingly urgent.

"Yes, I'll get by." I couldn't help sighing, but tried to sound cheerful as I went on, "I've more of an opinion of myself now than I had before, thanks to you, and I think I've toughened up. There *is* life outside of marriage. So if we divorce, I reckon I'll manage."

He said nothing. I hoped to God he'd manage too.

I told myself that from his point of view, it very likely *was* just a rebound thing, and whatever feelings he had were nothing more than a healthy dose of lust mixed in with the ego-repairing flattery of a woman plainly finding him so attractive. Yes, I thought he'd miss me for a while, but it wasn't as if we hadn't been honest from the start.

I'd read enough horror stories about the miserable outcomes of people mistaking holiday romances for 'the real thing'. He'd offered me a whistle-stop tour of paradise, not a retirement cottage in the Garden of Eden.

He was Lucifer, and tomorrow he must return to Hell.

Alone.

"Hey." We'd let our hands part. He caught hold again. "Let's stop talking about it now. I've got much more interesting things to talk about."

"Such as?" I kept my mouth prim, but I knew what the subject was going to be.

He leaned over and kissed me. He'd popped a blackberry into his mouth. His lips tasted of it. "How much I want you."

He continued that theme for some time, clearly loving the fact that he could still make me blush. After a while I even got brave enough to respond in kind, though at one point the conversation had to be suspended briefly when we passed a couple of walkers going in the other direction.

Now, however, I had to be on guard over every sentence, making sure that one terrible truth did not slip out along with all the others.

*'I love you.'*

We had lunch in the café in Leyburn, where we'd eaten a couple of days after we met. It wasn't the same table, but then the food didn't taste the same either.

It wasn't the chef's fault that the previously delicious soup tasted like ashes this time around.

I swallowed it down anyway, because you don't waste food. Opposite me, Mark ate his cheese salad baguette in silence, occasionally glancing at me with a smile that didn't reach his eyes. Today, there was no sunshine across the storm clouds; none.

It was hardly surprising, I reflected. He was going back to London, and to a life without the woman he'd been in love with – even if her best qualities had only existed in his imagination. He even had to work with the man who'd stolen her and dealt such a cruel blow to his pride. The love affair might have been an illusion, but the ending of it would still be hell to live with.

Who could be expected to look forward to that kind of future?

I hoped desperately that the time we'd had might have gone some way towards restoring his faith in himself. That little wagon Rebecca, throwing him over and hurting him so badly for some upper-management wannabe with a personal assistant! *If ever I meet her, I'll shake her till her bloody teeth rattle,* I thought furiously.

"Hey." He reached across and took hold of the hand that wasn't holding my spoon. "Beautiful looks cross. The soup's not that bad, is it?"

"I've had worse," I said, attempting to make a joke of it. "And you shouldn't call me 'Beautiful' in public. People will think you need an eye test."

"You're assuming I give a toss what they think. I couldn't care less if everyone in the place hears that I think you're beautiful. Come to think of it, I might go out and shout it in the middle of the square, just to maximise the effect."

I tried to smile. "I should send that baguette back. The cheese is giving you hallucinations."

"I've seen you naked. I know just how beautiful you are." He didn't even bother to lower his voice.

Several conversations at nearby tables stopped abruptly.

I looked at him, embarrassed and a little puzzled. This sort of talk was wonderful when we were alone, but surely he knew how uncomfortable it was for me, having it made public property? I asked him if something was wrong.

"Nothing I can cure." He set down the last piece of the baguette and drained his teacup. "Have you finished?"

"Almost." I bolted the last spoonful. He'd already got to his feet and was heading for the till.

He paid for both meals. Ordinarily I'd have put up at least a token protest, but today was different and I was getting nervous.

We set out at a fast pace back towards the car. His legs were longer than mine, and I had to trot to keep up. We dropped into the seats, but he didn't even pass me the car keys. We sat for a couple of minutes in a cocoon of silence that suddenly seemed almost hostile.

Mark said nothing. He sat staring at the dashboard, his expression closed.

"Have I upset you?" I asked at last in a small voice.

Saint Frances stirred. *He's had enough of you, you slut*, she whispered. *It was only a matter of time.*

"Oh, Fran. No, of course you haven't. I don't think you could." He sighed, and his head dropped forward. "I'm sorry. It's just this damned situation."

"I'm sure you'll find somewhere soon," was all I could think of to say. "And you never know, you might be able to find another job."

"Damn the house-hunting, and damn the job!" he exploded. "Fran, it's *you* I'm worried about. I keep thinking about you going back to that ogre you're married to and getting stuck in the tar-pit again. I can see him playing on your conscience about keeping your word and doing your duty and all the rest of the crap that's kept you tied to him for thirty-odd years. And what if he hits you because of the television? Will you make excuses for that, too? Forgive him seventy times seven? Are you actually going to have a life worth *living?*"

I swallowed. I'd been trying not to think along those lines myself – about exactly how Liam would react when I walked in and told him I was staying on the condition he'd put up with my painting. Assuming that once I was back in the real world, I still had the courage to say it, and didn't collapse back into the pathetic, spineless heap I'd been for far too long.

I didn't *think* he'd hit me. I suspected his first slap had shocked him almost as much as it had me. Maybe he would have done if I'd been there when he first walked in and found the television in smithereens, but he'd had time since then.

The trouble was – time to do what?

To realise I wasn't that much of a loss?

To dwell on how irresponsible I'd been, bolting out of my own home like an escaping prisoner without giving a damn how it would upset everyone else in the family?

Or to realise how truly desperate I must have been to act in the way I had; how hard I'd worked around the house, and how lonely he was without me? How important it was that things *should* change when I came home, so that with a bit of effort both of us could be happier?

*To realise how tough it is to cook his own damn meals, you mean,* snarled The Tart. *And as for 'lonely', he'd have been as lonely as hell – till he could buy himself a new telly. He'd have missed that a darn sight more than he'll have missed you!*

Mark, meanwhile, was watching me closely. "I don't hear any denials here," he said, his voice harsher than I'd ever heard it.

I raised my eyes to his. His face was twisted with pain that I recognised with a shock was on my account.

"I have to go back," I said simply. "Even if it doesn't work out, I think I ought to."

# Chapter 31

Mark glared at me. "Would you mind explaining *why*, exactly? Because I'm still not getting it!"

"I'm not deluding myself, Mark. Honest to God, I'm not. It isn't like I could rewind time and make everything like it was before. He won't forgive and forget. I don't think he'll even try to understand why I did what I did – he's got all the empathy of a house-brick. But I have a responsibility to myself to finish this properly – one way or the other.

"It may work out. It may not. But at least I'll be able to say I tried everything. And whether you understand it or not, that matters to me. My *word* matters to me." My hands were twisting together in my lap, and with a conscious effort I stopped them.

"Yes, I broke it when I went with you. But that's between you, me and God, and it's a different thing, in my eyes, from blowing the whole damn thing up without even giving it one last chance. There's more than me will be affected if I give up. There's a family involved, and for their sake, I want to at least try the last shot in the locker.

"If it doesn't work out, I'll leave. I will, honest I will. But first, I'll give it one more try."

He slewed sideways on the seat, grasping my shoulders. "Then promise me, *promise me*, you won't go back and let him bully you."

"Swear to the Devil?" I knew my smile was twisted. "I swore to God once, and look how that turned out."

"Oh, this is *much* more serious. Because I'm the one who's proved he can take you to heaven."

I burst out laughing at that, even if it was laughter that trembled on the edge of tears. "Oh, Mark Reeves, you can tell you don't believe in God. That's got to be blasphemy."

One eyebrow quirked upwards. "Can the truth be blasphemous?"

"Don't ask me. I'm just a common-or-garden sinner, trying to pick my way through the minefield of morality without blowing myself up in the process."

"Right. Let's put it this way. If you were God, and one of your kids came to you when they were dying and said, 'Mom, I've led a hell of a life, but I couldn't do anything about it because I'd made you a promise fifty years ago', how pleased would you be?"

I said nothing. I hadn't thought of it in that way before.

His eyes searched my face. "Oh, Fran. What a terrible, terrible God they taught you to believe in."

"He can't be all that bad." I lifted a shaky hand to touch his mouth. "He let you get away with murder in that hermitage."

"There is that." He caught hold of my hand and kissed it. "Let's go home. I want to share a bath with you and then kiss every inch of your body before I make love to you."

"Even for a devil, you're awfully good at temptation."

"It's my speciality."

*Love me, Lucifer. Love me.*

*With pleasure, Beautiful.*

# Chapter 32

It was morning, and the fantasy was over.

I threw an arm across my eyes, shutting out the mocking sunlight. How *dare* the sun be shining when he was leaving? How *dare* the birds be singing in the trees across the lane?

His dark head was resting between my breasts. His right arm was thrown around me possessively.

I should tell him. Now, while I had the chance, tell him everything.

Only one thing could possibly be worse than spending the rest of my life wishing I had.

Spending it wishing I hadn't.

He had enough problems. He didn't need the guilt of finding out how desperately I'd come to depend on him, to value his company, to enjoy our easy banter; how desperately, in fact, I was in love with him. He'd been honest with me, and I had to repay that honesty with deceit – had to pin on my best and brightest smile, and wave him goodbye as though the time we'd spent together had never meant any more to me than the pleasant interlude it'd undoubtedly been for him.

Falling in love had never been part of the deal. You could summon up demons, but they belonged in the underworld and they had to return there.

I could survive. I *would* survive. Even if my lunatic idea of trying to improve my marriage didn't work out, I still had the boys and their families. I'd surely be able to find myself another little job somewhere that would get me out of the house and give me some independence. I'd have my painting too – I *would* have my painting, whatever Liam thought about it, and if the worst came to the worst and we couldn't even share the same house as civil strangers, well then, we'd have to divorce and sell up. My name was on the deeds too, I owned a half-share in it. Couldn't I buy myself a little flat somewhere with my half of whatever we got from the sale? If I had to work full-time to support myself, I could look around and see if there was somewhere I could set up my own little business. There were other towns, there were other places where my qualifications and experience would be valuable. I could look forward to peaceful evenings listening to music for pleasure as opposed to a means of drowning out the television, and one thing I definitely *wouldn't* have to fork out for would be a bloody TV licence. Financially, I might struggle for a while, and maybe I might be a bit lonely now and then, but I'd have so much by way of compensation.

Painting, at last – after all these years!

I had dozens of sketches, as well as a number of photographs, in preparation for my planned 'masterpiece', whenever I should feel up to having a try at it. One photograph in particular had wrapped itself around my heart: Mark had appropriated one of the dining chairs and sat himself in it like a throne, with the golden throw flung across him and a look of wicked humour in his face. All he needed was some kind of demonic familiar at his feet, and he'd be the King of the Underworld for sure. Maybe, if ever I got around to making it one of a series of portraits, I'd even throw in the box of 'coffee spoons' for good luck.

And apart from the painting, the idea of having no one but myself to please was still both thrilling and scary. I could see fresh places, meet new people. *Make* something of my life. Learn a new skill perhaps, go to evening classes. Something that was fun, challenging, that would belong to the new Frances McKenna whom Mark Reeves had dragged from the chrysalis in which I might otherwise have stayed forever. I felt like a butterfly, opening my wings on a new world.

But a world without him in it.

*Can't be cured, must be endured,* I told myself fiercely. *You can get through this. You knew it was going to hurt, and you went ahead and did it anyway. So now keep your head up and pay. You can't say it hasn't been worth it.*

Oh, it had been worth it. However much it cost. All I had to do was get through today, and everything else would be easy by comparison. No amount of grieving could ever be worse than the pain that was waiting for me today.

I felt the flicker of his eyelashes against my skin, telling me he'd woken. The previous night he'd set the alarm on his phone for the first time, since the luxurious days of going by our own internal clocks were over, but both of us had beaten the alarm. Without a word, he slipped from the bed, heading for the shower. As he left the room, he paused for a few seconds, looking through the window at the dale bathed in the early morning sunlight and the utter quiet. Maybe he, too, was wondering how everything could look just as it had the day before, while for me, absolutely nothing was the same. Or would be, ever again.

With a movement that had already become a habit and would tomorrow be an agony I dared not imagine, I rolled over into his half of the bed. Still warm with his warmth, the pillow bearing the impression of his head. Tomorrow, it would not be there.

*Oh, love it is a killing thing; did you ever feel the pain?*

Some Irish poet or other had written that long ago, part of an old song if I remembered right. *Oh, love it is a killing thing.* With so many years in which to perfect the design of the human body, why couldn't evolution have spared a thought for this fatal flaw, this gaping gap in the defences through which pain could slip in to tear you apart, sometimes beyond healing?

But that would mean never having known what I'd known since Mark and I became lovers, so Oh, thank you Evolution, because I *can* cope.

*And I will.*

He was quick about showering. When he came back in, he paused again by the window. The light through it cast into strong relief the high cheekbones of his face, the sculpted musculature of his body. *Oh, love it is a killing thing,* but lust can be pretty damn fatal too, and that was one of the images that would come to mind in the long nights ahead. Certainly not one of the most heart-stopping, but the painter in me wished so much to have the time to have him stand there so I could capture that light flowing across the curves and hollows. True, I could borrow his iPad again and take a photograph, but I'd never be able to bear looking at it.

I slid out of the bed in my turn. Thanks to our beating the alarm clock, we had time to spare.

I was quick about showering too, and didn't bother to wash my hair, which would have taken more of those precious minutes now ticking down ever more swiftly to disaster.

He was waiting for me when I got back.

Words were unnecessary.

From start to finish, we held each other's gaze.

*Love me, Lucifer.*

*With pleasure, Beautiful.*

At the end, we held hands. Once again, he was careful. Even as his face contorted, his fingers tightened only slightly, because mine were so much smaller and more slender, and could be hurt so easily.

There was also time for a walk with Sharp after breakfast – if a shorter one than usual.

More blackberries had ripened in the hedgerow, but we didn't pick any. My first ever attempt at a crumble using them hadn't been the success I'd hoped it might be, though I made them at home with apple often enough, and plums when they were in season. That said, it was his fault it had got too brown on the top. If he hadn't been such a damn brilliant kisser, I'd have been paying more attention to the timer.

No more blackberry crumble, ever again. I'd not have the heart for it. Perhaps I'd try peaches one of the days. Or pineapple, I liked pineapple. Mark said pineapple was lovely in a crumble, though we'd never got around to trying it.

*Oh, love it is a killing thing.* I'd known that before I started, at least as a concept, but you've got to be in it before you know how painful a way it is to die.

He packed his rucksack in silence. He didn't have much with him, since this had been planned as a walking holiday.

I put a packet of Nice biscuits in on top, in case he wanted something to nibble on the way home. Maybe he'd get something to eat on the train, though I'd heard the food was very expensive. Why hadn't I thought to buy something to make him up some sandwiches?

Perhaps he could get a takeaway or something when he got home.

Damn, it was hard work keeping up this front. Now and again I found my eyes brimming, but I either blinked them clear or contrived to have a discreet dab with a sleeve. Thank God I'd no mascara on, or I'd have looked like the Bride of Dracula.

He gave Sharp a last rub behind the ears. "Behave yourself, Dog." It seemed to me that the dog's expression was a little worried, the wagging tail less certain than usual. I'd always had too much imagination for my own good – but then, I knew Sharp was sensitive to emotional atmosphere.

Mark told me where to turn when we were driving, even though I knew the way to Richmond by now. When he spoke, his voice was toneless. It was hardly surprising he was sorry to be going back to London. Who wouldn't be, in such circumstances?

Now would be a really, really useful time to believe in an intervening God, who could, if enough prayers were sent to the right address, lean down and put things right for someone who deserved so much better from life than he'd received. I'd given up long ago believing that intercessory prayer was any use, but I found myself praying anyway, a mindless frantic gabble to a deity who'd turned a deaf ear for years to my prayers to him to make my husband love me.

But though the worst sin in what we'd done was undoubtedly mine (after all, I was the one of us who was married), what was the going rate for coveting your neighbour's wife? Perhaps I'd have done better to keep quiet and hope the Almighty's attention would be elsewhere as the Darlington train sped south to London. I didn't want the train to leave the rails and take its passengers out wholesale because one of them had fornicated with a woman he wasn't married to.

He'd insisted on putting his phone number on the document in my protected folder, but the trouble was, I couldn't guarantee that sooner or later I wouldn't give into the temptation to ring him and end up just looking pitiful and making a total bloody idiot of myself. And if we did keep in touch (just as *friends*, but could such a thing even be possible, could it even be bearable?), when he found somebody else he probably wouldn't let me know in case it upset me, but then if he did, and I lost control and told him, it could end up doing a lot of damage. I wouldn't want to do that. So I let him put it on because it made him feel better for me having it, but silently promised myself that the first time I opened the folder, I'd delete it.

So, no phone number. Best on all counts.

He hadn't asked for mine. The omission was so pointed it had to mean something, but I didn't want to think about it. Either he didn't care or he...

Nothing was going on in the military area to have them flying the red flags today. This was a Bloody Good Thing, because if he'd called me a Beautiful Russian Spy today, I'd have broken down.

Richmond was crowded. Ah well, it wasn't like I was planning to park, thank God. I'd had to drive round for ages last time trying to find a space, and today looked worse.

Just in the nick of time, some eejit pulled out from a space right in front of me, leaving me a perfect place to stop for the couple of minutes it would take. Obediently, I signalled and manoeuvred. Textbook parking. Auto-pilot. Wonderful how it works.

Mark sat in the front passenger seat as though he'd turned to stone. His rucksack was in the back, to save me the bother of popping the boot.

Kiss me. For the love of God, kiss me. Like you're never going to let me go... *Don't kiss me, don't, I can't bear it because I'll have to feel you stop.*

"Fran..."

"I was thinking I might do some shopping while I'm here, but we handed that permit thing back last time, didn't we?

And I don't want one of them capitalist pig parking attendants slapping a ticket on me. So I'll just get off straight away." My voice was as gay as a plastic daisy, and about as genuine. "I'll send you the picture whenever I get it done. I hope the train's not delayed or anything. And thank you, it's been wonderful." I wasn't looking at him. I couldn't. I was staring through the windscreen at the back of a bus, where there was a really, *really* inane advertisement. Fixating on that advertisement was the only thing preventing me from throwing my pride to the four winds and telling him everything, begging him not to leave me. Now on the brink of the ultimate loss, I knew I'd have given up my marriage, I'd have given up my home, I'd have given up everything, if only I could have kept him.

"I'll look forward to seeing it." His voice in response was so wooden it would have made a plank seem animated by comparison. "Thank you. For everything."

He *couldn't* be getting out of the car. He *couldn't* be leaving me without even a kiss, but then it was for the best, because if he'd kissed me, I'd never have been able to let him go.

I listened to him opening the rear door and getting his rucksack out. The front door was still open. I sat staring at the inane advertisement, while every fibre of my mind and body was screaming at me to *do* something.

The rucksack was placed on the pavement.

I didn't know if the bus stop opposite was his, or it would be somewhere else in the square. He had about twenty minutes to wait. Maybe he might buy himself a cup of tea. It was rather soon after breakfast for a piece of parkin if it was as filling as he'd said.

He hesitated, bending to look in at me again. "Fran…"

My head turned of its own accord, even though I told it not to. The sadness and worry in his face tore me.

"We'll be all right. Both of us." The words emerged stilted but steady. "I've got to go, Mark." *Love me, Lucifer. Love me.*

He nodded slowly. *With pleasure, Beautiful.* "Goodbye, Fran."

I didn't answer. I couldn't. I just nodded, jerkily.

The sound of the door closing was that of the guillotine crashing down.

Luckily, I hadn't switched the ignition off.

Check the driver's side mirror and look over the shoulder, textbook correct.

Check again for oncoming traffic, reverse enough to get clearance and then pull out, calm and competent. Observe correct speed limits and safe stopping distances. Remain alert for other vehicles and pedestrians. Find a small country lane with a space to park up in. Watch the dashboard clock ticking down to the bus's departure time.

It can't be that time already; it *can't* be.

Fall apart.

If there truly was a merciful God, agony like this would put an end to me *right now*, but even as I screamed like something impaled, I knew there was no mercy. Besides, there were still the boys and the grandchildren, and they still needed me. If things had been different, I'd have had no hesitation, but the same bonds of love and duty still held me like chains to my existence.

*Oh, love it is a killing thing; did you ever feel the pain?*

# Chapter 33

Middleham.

I was my own worst bloody enemy, I thought drearily, applying the handbrake. Of all the places I could come to, why this one?

*Go easy on yourself,* ***alannah****,* said The Tart gently.

*The Wages of Sin,* muttered Saint Frances. *She brought the whole thing on herself. If she'd listened to me, none of this would ever have happened.*

Oh, no. Not if I went on weeping forever to pay for it, I'd never have wanted that. Never to have been loved as Mark had loved me; never to have felt beautiful, desirable, wanted!

I pushed the heels of my hand across my eyes, shoving away the tears. *Can't be cured, must be endured.*

Walking around the castle fell squarely under the heading of 'self-flagellation', but I bought a ticket anyway. I could remember scraps of our conversation and repeated my parts of it when appropriate; I even laughed at his replies. A family I passed probably thought I'd escaped from an Institution, but

Mark was explaining about the Wars of the Roses, so I had to pay attention to him. I still wasn't sure I understood the whole thing, but I had more of an idea now than I'd ever had before, so that was a plus.

We'd been talking about music that day and got on to the subject of Gilbert and Sullivan; I knew some of their songs from old 78 rpm records of Granny's. Mark had apparently played the part of the Pirate King in a school production of *The Pirates of Penzance*. I'd had to badger him mercilessly before he consented to sing a single verse (he'd said it was the only bit he could remember, but he was lying). I'd come in with 'Hurrah, hurrah for our pirate king!' right on cue.

He'd said I was off-key.

I sang it again now, my voice reedy and tearful in the empty, echoing space between the walls. A group of tourists who'd been about to come into the keep turned abruptly, shepherding the children hastily away from the mad Irishwoman singing all by herself in a ruined hall.

I'd have loved to see a teenage Mark wearing a curly wig and a pirate hat, and brandishing a cutlass. I bet he'd gone for broke playing the part. Maybe when I'd got better at my sketching, I could draw–

At the thought of drawing him when I'd never see him again, I turned aside and pressed my forehead hard against the rough, cool stone of the wall beside me while the tears ran.

But I couldn't stay here forever. After drying my face with my handkerchief as best I could, I wandered outside, a lonely ghost reliving the glories of the past.

A spatter of rain sounded on the grass as I sat – or rather collapsed – on the circle of turf in the remnants of the kitchen again. He squatted opposite me, looking down at me gravely.

So the castle *was* haunted, after all...

*Love me, Lucifer.*

*With pleasure, Beautiful.*

Why had I fought the inevitable, wasting so many hours of the time we'd been granted?

I could forgive myself for that, though. We'd talked once, about relationships – genuine relationships – having the same kind of sequence as a piece of music. When a symphony or something is played, each section of the orchestra has to come in at just the right time. Not a second too early, not a second too late. Otherwise, the entire piece will be ruined, and the audience leave at the end murmuring *What a pity.*

The little room in the wall of the keep was still dark and empty. I ducked into it and stood alone, waiting for his breath on the back of my neck. *Love me, Lucifer.*

*With pleasure, Beautiful.*

The statue was still in its place, of course. The King stared pensively at nothing, borne down by the weight of the scaled creature on his shoulders. I couldn't remember what the leaflet had said this represented, but if it was grief, I could sympathise. Bloody hell, I could sympathise.

We'd gone to the gift shop on the way out. I hadn't bought anything – Mark's nearness had been too much of a distraction. Now I looked around listlessly.

Some of the tourists who'd given me odd looks earlier were in there. Two boys were arguing about whether to have toy swords and shields or bows and arrows.

Their mother was looking at the merchandise. "It just seems a shame," she said, obviously continuing a subject that had already been under discussion. "You'd think they'd have some things for Ricardians, especially with all the interest there's been since he was found. Even a picture of a boar or something."

The boys decided on toy swords. Mother chose a book. Father had the privilege of paying for everything, still eyeing me in case my madness resurfaced.

Intending to go home, I left the castle. The sound of church bells made me pause.

Mark and I had never visited the church at Middleham – under the circumstances, it seemed inappropriate. I'd even deferred attending Mass since I'd got here, uncomfortable about taking the Sacrament until I could make a full confession. On a more personal basis, however, I felt God could make up His own mind about what I'd done. All the prayers I'd aimed in His direction for the past thirty-odd years seemed to have got lost in the post, so what right He thought He had to cut up rusty now I'd no idea.

Still, a visit would delay my return to the cottage and its half-empty bed.

"Yeah, well, don't start, God," I muttered as I pushed open the church door. "If You're wanting to hurl a thunderbolt at me, just get it over and done with, willya? I can't be having with the wait. And for Christ's sake, don't nag."

I stood still in the dimness so He wouldn't have any problem aiming, but it seemed He was withholding punishment. Maybe the Lake of Fire would eventually be enough, though it felt as if I was already in it. But as Lucifer's harlot, I supposed I ought to be thankful He'd not made me burst into flames as soon as I stepped into the porch. At a guess this contained some kind of holy water receptacle, even though it was a Protestant church.

Talk about living dangerously.

The structure of the building (dedicated to St. Mary and St. Alkelda) must have been familiar to King Richard. Obviously a lot of it would have changed in more than five hundred years. There wouldn't have been pews in his time, and the walls would have been bright with paintings, bringing the bible stories alive for a congregation who largely couldn't read or write. The basic building was still the same, though, hushed and cool.

Mark's voice in my ears: *'Dear Mother, dear Mother, the church is cold...'* This one wasn't cold, just dim and remote. Someday, my memories of the past ten days would be similarly dim and remote. Though that was a terrible prospect, maybe it would be for the best, because then they wouldn't hurt so much.

I genuflected to the altar out of habit, though as the church wasn't Catholic I didn't need to. It seemed polite anyway, acknowledging that whoever lived here was Looking. Glaring, more like, but at least He wouldn't be able to complain I'd disrespected him.

How things change, over a couple of generations. In my parents' time, you'd have been scared to set foot in any church but a Catholic one, and no woman would be seen there without a decent head-covering.

I slipped into one of the pews.

I didn't kneel. He might take that for repentance, and I didn't repent a damned thing.

For a few minutes, I sat in silence. All kinds of feelings were churning inside me.

"I know, I'm going to hell," I said aloud at last, despairingly defiant. "You don't have to tell me. But I tried. I stuck it for thirty-four years. You know what it was like. I told You often enough, before I gave up trying. And…"

In spite of the attempt at defiance, a lump found its way into my throat. I had to swallow a few times before I could continue. "I'm sorry I broke my vows. If You're disappointed about that. But I'm not apologising for anything else." I swiped tears away with my hand; my handkerchief wasn't good for much by now. "I suppose in one way I'm headed for hell before I die as well as after, because I'm going back to Liam and I'm scared sick at the thought of it. But if I *do* go to hell afterwards, Mark was worth it. And I'll bloody well remember him when I'm there, too!"

For a moment or two I stifled the boiling resentment that was anything but appropriate for where I was, but I was booked for the Lake of Fire anyway, so what was the point of not saying my piece? "If You're supposed to be the God of love, at least You could fecking sympathise a *bit!*"

*Whores are supposed to repent before they get sympathy*, Saint Frances pointed out primly.

No response from The Tart. Presumably she'd been afraid to come in, in case *she* spontaneously combusted passing the holy water font.

I rested my aching forehead on the back of the pew in front. There were tapestry kneelers on the floor – a pleasant touch, even if the details weren't clear because my eyes were swimming. I blinked. One a few feet away had an odd design on it: a white pig on a green background. Why put a pig on a kneeler? They could have used one of the Evangelists' animals, a lion or an eagle or something.

A few more blinks brought the design more clearly into view. Not a pig, but a white boar. King Richard's badge.

The lady's complaint in the castle gift shop: 'Even a picture of a boar or something.' There'd been a lot of interest in Richard after the discovery of his body under the car park in Leicester. Even I'd heard about that.

How difficult would a boar be to paint?

Inspired, I went back to the cottage. Paul had given me the password for the Wi-Fi, just in case, so I got out my laptop, signed on and searched for images.

It took me nearly two days of steady practice before I was happy with my first design.

My degree course had included painting in both acrylics and watercolours. Unwilling to spend too heavily on something that might not sell, I drove to the nearest shop that sold art materials and bought better watercolours, some decent pens and a few sheets of good quality paper. Another shop provided me with a couple of modestly priced picture frames. Then I drove back to the cottage again.

I sat down at the table, organised my things properly, and – my heart beating rather quickly – picked up one of my paintbrushes.

Two days later, I drove back to Middleham.

Going into the shop there was an ordeal to me.

The manageress was out at lunch but was expected back in half an hour. I sat in the car, my stomach churning with nerves and nausea as I watched the clock tick down.

When she returned, however, she seemed impressed by my White Boar painting – to my relief, though I tried to hide it. My experience in the gallery had given me some background about picture sales, so we made the appropriate agreement. She made a note of my details and said she'd be in touch.

I walked back to the castle and told Imaginary Mark about what I'd done. He said *Attagirl, Beautiful*, which made me cry again, but it was a good sort of cry.

The jackdaws were still at the top of the keep. They sounded impressed by my achievements too. A lone magpie declined to comment, but a couple of crows said 'Cor!' in an incredulous sort of way, probably wondering why I was back again so soon and *still* talking to myself.

*Too much sex,* sniffed the Saint. *She's lost nothing, to my mind. He probably shags anything desperate in a skirt.* ***And*** *I wouldn't be surprised if he's given her something.*

*Yeah. He gave her something, all right. Self-respect. Self-confidence. And pleasure, too – more in ten days than Liam bloody McEnally did in thirty-four years.* The Tart sprang to my defence. I was pathetically glad of her.

*Humph. She'd better report this little romp to the doctor when she gets home. It'd pay her to get checked out for souvenirs, even if she can't get pregnant. You never know, with a dirty little bastard like him.*

I came to an abrupt halt in the middle of the keep. "How bloody *dare* you talk about him like that!" I hissed. "I've had enough from you. *More* than enough! Piss off back to Liam and leave me alone, I don't need you any more. Actually, I don't think I ever did, I just didn't realise it till now. I've grown up. I'm taking charge of my own life. I've had a bellyful of your bitching and your criticism and your judging everything I do. If I ever decide I want a God again, I'll go for Mark's, not yours, but right now I want to find *me*. This is *me* talking, and *you* listening, and *I* say your day's over. So *feck off and don't come back!*"

*Yeah, and good riddance!* yelled The Tart, reprising the dance around the battlements.

My voice had risen wildly over the last few sentences, echoing off the damp grey stone. Luckily, on a day like this there was no one there to hear me. The only other sound was the patter of the falling rain.

My painting was in the shop window already when I walked past it on the way back to the car. The price tag was astonishing, but in small lettering a label said 'Hand Painted Original', which probably accounted for it. The boar had come out really well, considering, and the touches of gold paint on his tusks and hooves had worked. I'd touched the York roses with gold, too, one in each corner of the ivy border. I'd tried doing a rosemary border at first – *there's rosemary, that's for remembrance* – but it hadn't worked very well. The ivy looked good, though, and from the novel I was reading back at the cottage, its symbolism of 'fidelity and wedded love' was appropriate for King Richard.

Partly elated, partly worried at seeing my work open to public view, I got into the car and drove back to the cottage. An empty cottage, and a lonely one too for the next few weeks, but it would give me the space to start my slow climb to becoming an artist.

I couldn't have Mark with me there. That door had closed. I could only hope he'd be proud of me, and that wherever he was, he would be happy.

# Chapter 34

The weeks that had stretched before me like an endless idyll slid into the past more swiftly than I would have believed possible.

But they were quiet weeks, and in some ways exactly what I needed.

Of course, I missed Mark every waking moment. The nights were hell. Once or twice I even resorted to buying a bottle of wine and drinking a few glasses in search of anaesthesia. But though on the worst of the nights I drank and cried till I passed out, waking hours later with a sick stomach and a blazing headache, there hadn't been a single moment when my heart had stopped aching. So I poured the rest of the wine down the sink and made a conscious effort to pull myself together.

Progress with my artwork was intermittent. On some days, nothing I could do would make my pencils and paintbrushes serve me; on others I could feel the tingle that said what I was doing would turn out well. But the good days gradually got better and more frequent. My confidence grew, and there were fewer times when I looked at what I'd created and felt it had been wasted effort.

Much to my amazement, my first painting was snapped up within the first couple of days, and the manageress ordered two more, again on a Ricardian theme. These sold too, again fairly quickly, and she ordered another three. I put one online and that was bought, so I started thinking of expanding in that direction. Practice meant I needed less time to produce each work, while the payments bolstered both my cash ledger and my confidence. I kept all my paperwork carefully, knowing Ciarán would be able to advise me on any tax issues when I went home.

I didn't paint every day. I met up with Peter and he gave me the tour of the stables he'd suggested. With the now functioning sat-nav to bolster my confidence and tourist leaflets to give me ideas for places to visit, I explored the Dales and beyond. On one memorable occasion, I drove to the Lake District. On another, I went pony-trekking – given my weight and inexperience, astride a beast the size of a small Shire – a luxury I wouldn't even have considered without the income from my paintings. The sky above was cloudless, and skylarks sang in it, too high in the blue for me to spot them. My friendly horse plodded placidly, the rolling, heather-clad dales spread out around me as far as the eye could see, and the world was wonderful to experience. It might not have Mark in my corner of it, but it was still beautiful and deserved my appreciation, and I was as happy that day as I thought I still could be.

Though the weather after that was changeable, there weren't many days when I couldn't manage a few miles' walk with Sharp in the evening. Combined with the fact that when I was painting I was so absorbed and happy I didn't even think about eating, the exercise began paying off. The waistband of my skirts began feeling significantly looser.

But all good things come to an end. It hardly seemed possible that a month and a half had gone by when Paul and Bridie returned, sun-bronzed and happy, and saying how well Sharp looked. Paul's contentment was low-key, as always, but Bridie was as full of stories as her tablet was of photographs. It took a whole evening to hear and see everything she had to tell and show me, sitting out at the patio table while a low sun softened and deepened the colours around us, slowly filling up the valley with shadow.

Later, however, when we had to come indoors because of the midges and Paul went upstairs to have a shower, Bridie set aside the tablet and went to the fridge to bring out the bottle of fruit-flavoured water I'd got into the habit of keeping there.

"We've talked our hind legs off about our doings," she said, filling a glass and handing it to me – she had a can of cold lager for herself. "Now, young Fran, tell me what *you've* been up to. I hope it's not much more than 'resting', but whatever it is, it's done you good. There's half of your waistline that's taken itself off, and took ten years of your age with it."

I had all the cover story prepared. I had lots of drawings to show, a few paintings, and the story of my success at the shop. I had photos of Windermere and my friendly horse. I had the visit to the stables at Middleham and the walk around the castle. I could talk my own hind legs off if necessary.

I opened my mouth to start the light, entertaining, beautifully edited recital of what an uneventful six weeks I'd had.

"Oh Jesus, Brid," fell out instead.

At first she went berserk at me for giving up so easily. Once she'd calmed down, however, she had to admit that in the circumstances, there hadn't been much either of us could have done differently. A holiday romance was one thing (she punched the air when I admitted to it, and I could foresee an entire raft of embarrassing questions later on), but committing your whole life on the strength of it was something else.

"He gave you his phone number and all! Bejeezus, what more could the man do to tell you he wants to see you again?" she ranted, when I said I was going back to Ireland to patch things up with Liam. "For feck's sake, woman!"

"He c-could have said 'I want to see you again'!" I retorted, mopping my eyes.

"Did *you* say it? Ah, no, of course not. You, being a first-rate eejit, never even got around to just idly mentioning you'd fallen head over ears in love with him!"

"Of course I fecking didn't, Brid! He n-never mentioned loving me, he never said any-anything like that. As a matter of fact, he was honest and said w-we should just take what's on offer while we can and enjoy it. Does that sound like h-he was in love with me?"

She glowered. "It sounds to me like the pair o' you were too fecking proud and scared and all-round brainless to tell each other the truth!"

"We di-idn't talk about it," I said defiantly, emerging from my now sopping handkerchief. "He said it was too soon to talk about being in l-love!"

"Well, at least one of you had enough sense to scratch with." Her mood softened, and she came over and sat beside me on the sofa to pull me in for a hug. "Bejeezus, *alannah,* you ran away from trouble at home and more came up from London and found you."

The journey from Australia had been a long and tiring one, and my kind host and hostess weren't young. I could tell Bridie was drooping by this time, so I told her to have a shower and get to bed. We'd talk more about things tomorrow.

"I'll not be sorry to put my head down in my own bed," she admitted, yawning. "They've a lovely house over there, but God above it's getting hot already – pity knows how they cope with it in the summer. It was that lovely to walk out of the plane at Heathrow and breathe cool air again."

"You won't be saying that when there's four feet of snow down. Peter told me about that winter when everyone was snowed in."

"So we were, but we had plenty of warning and got food in, and thanks be to God we've good neighbours, and Jonjo got through to us with a tractor and made sure we weren't short of anything. Bless him and Maria, they're the best people

I know, short of yourself. –Paul!" she shouted. Her husband had come downstairs again earlier on, but, sensing a confidential conversation going on, had gone into the sunroom to read for a while. "Come out of that and let's be off to bed, if you're not asleep already.

"Are you heading for bed, Fran?"

"I think I'll stay up a while longer, if you don't mind." The book I'd been reading when they arrived was still lying on the coffee table; it was about Richard III, and now I'd visited Middleham, it all felt so much more real. I was rather sorry I was nearly at the end of it.

She wagged her finger at me. "Now, don't be thinking that just because we're home, you've got to start doing things to please us. Carry on doing *what* you want to *when* you want to.

"And don't think you're going to slide out of having a good long talk about your future, me girl. You've finally had the guts to leave, and found out there's more to life than being married and miserable. If it's up to me, you're not going to throw away the next thirty years the way you did the last."

"I'll tidy round and make sure everything's locked up," I said as she walked into the kitchen.

Her look said she knew an evasion when she heard one and wasn't buying this specimen. "Well, now, wouldn't I be expecting to get up in the morning and find the place looking like a trash-heap and the back door left open for the world to walk in and out, just like you leave it every night."

"Bridie Byrne, you've a bloody sarcastic tongue on you when you get going."

"And you must think I was born yesterday, Frances McEnally." She ran a glass of water to take upstairs with her and paused with one foot on the stairs as Paul emerged yawning from the sunroom. "Just you remember, *alannah*: You get one chance at this life, and if you find something that makes you happy, bloody well go for it."

I hadn't gone searching for love, but I'd found it regardless – or rather, it had found me. Then I'd lost it again, and now had somehow to live the rest of my life without it.

I had his phone number.

I was going back to being a married woman, and the days of love had to be put behind me. There, one day – and dear God, make it soon – they would be no more than a pleasant memory rather than the tearing agony they were now whenever I thought about him.

In time, if I lived long enough, a day would come when he no longer even crossed my mind. In the meantime, I. DO. NOT. QUIT would have to sustain me again, just as it had for the past thirty-four years.

I opened my laptop, found the hidden folder and opened the Word document. Keyed the number into my phone and pressed the 'Call' button, and listened to it ring out, just once.

*Love me, Lucifer. Love me.*
*With pleasure, Beautiful.*

Then, before he could answer, I cancelled the call. I deleted the number from the document, saved it, and got rid of the call record too. I couldn't retrieve either now if I tried. Short-term memory being what it was, the numbers I'd pressed were already gone.

That was it, then.

Over.

*Love me, Lucifer. Love me.*

# Chapter 35

It was dreadfully hard saying goodbye to Bridie, Paul and Sharp, and leaving the cottage where I'd experienced so much. By the time I finally managed to tear myself away, both Brid and I were in tears. As I glanced miserably at the cottage disappearing in my rear-view mirror, the sunshine and the little puffy fair-weather clouds seemed to tell me I should stay for a while longer.

If only I could. If only things between me and Mark had worked out. If only... well, 'if only'.

But they hadn't. I had to make the best of things as they were rather than mope around crying for the moon.

The overwhelming feeling was one of going back into captivity. There was none of the sense of freedom, adventure and downright irresponsibility that had propelled me on the outward trip. The feeling of rebellion, however, was still present. It might *feel* as though I was trudging home with my tail between my legs, but feck it all, I wasn't going to be put into a prison. I was merely going to begin negotiations. If the negotiations weren't successful, or if whatever agreement Liam and I came to didn't last, I'd be off again – and this time, I'd not be going back. Ever.

Despite my having that thought to cling to, the motorway stretch was long and tedious, and the journey through a wet North Wales seemed everlasting. And I was sure that when I reached Dublin, there'd be no enthusiastic welcome. No one would kill the fatted calf for *this* prodigal, except perhaps the grandkids when they were allowed to see me. Every mile covered was taking me closer to a blazing row.

Now, though, I had options. If he so much as raised his hand to me, I'd be away off into a B&B before you could say 'divorce'; if he'd tried to block my savings account he hadn't succeeded, so I'd enough money left for that, as long as I wasn't too choosy. The day after that, I'd be back on the ferry. In the long talk the three of us had had the day before, Bridie and Paul had practically made me promise to come back, even saying they'd buy me the ferry ticket if I couldn't afford it myself. I needed somewhere to stay, they had a room, and as for my earning my keep, well, we'd deal with that when – if – it happened.

I couldn't imagine what I'd ever done to deserve such kindness, but there must be a special place in Heaven reserved for the likes of Bridie and Paul Byrne.

"Oh, *God!*" At long, long last, calling hollowly on the God who'd most likely washed His hands of me altogether by now, I turned the car into our road. It was almost surprising that nothing had changed during the weeks that I'd been away; its dreary familiarity dragged at my spirit. A scowl of apprehension on my face, I drove down to our house. It was a fairly modern semi-detached, spacious but – in spite of the touches with which I'd tried to give it individuality – rather soulless. Or so it seemed to me now, looking at it with the jaded eyes of a recaptured inmate being marched back to it in manacles.

Liam's car was in the drive. He hadn't bothered putting it into the garage, which was unusual for him at the weekend. Still, there was enough space for me to edge the Fiesta into, so I did, trying desperately to stifle the sudden feeling of suffocation that surged over me.

As the engine note died, I wound the window down despite the slight drizzle that was falling from the gloomy early-evening early-autumn sky – a sky so different from the one over Yorkshire that very morning! – and, breathing in the familiar damp air of home, allowed myself ten minutes to gather my forces.

I wasn't going to apologise. I'd been the injured party from the start. I wasn't even going to pretend. I'd had plenty of time to plot my campaign, and to work out my response to what I reckoned would be the inevitable 'So you've come back, have you?'

It would be 'Not for long, if we can't work things out.' I'd leave my suitcase in the boot, and just take in my shopping notebook, in which I'd made a note of my demands. I'd put up with his gloating for a bit. Then when we'd got that out of the way and *if* he was willing to listen, seriously listen, I'd read him out my list of things that had to change. If we were still talking after that, I'd invite him firstly to comment on them and secondly to come up with a list of his own, because in fairness he might have some grievances *I* hadn't known about that had contributed to making our relationship go sour. Afterwards–.

'Afterwards' was rather hazy, mainly because I didn't believe matters would get that far. I was moderately sure that the course of the evening would go 'encounter, confrontation, presentation of list, explosion, dismissal of list, sulk to end all sulks, wife (soon to be ex-) gets back in car, wife (soon to be ex-) spends night in hotel'.

Oh well. Better get it over with. The sooner I started looking around for accommodation, the more choice I'd have.

I wound the window back up, got out and locked the car. After stretching my back and rolling my shoulders – I wasn't as young as I'd used to be, and long journeys like these took it out of me – I walked to the house, noting that the lawn needed mowing and the fuchsia hedge was running riot, which it would if given half the chance.

The front room was dark, but I hadn't expected it to be anything else. At least it was clean enough, though as I peeped in through the front window I thought sourly that this needed a good washing. The lounge was at the rear of the house, and as the television lived in there, so would Liam. Most likely he'd be stuffing himself with chips and beer and watching some war film or other, if there was no football game on of course. If there was, I might as well take myself away to the pub till it finished. He'd not want his fecking football interrupted just because I'd taken it into my head to come back at last. Jesus, Mary and Joseph, it was terrible the way I'd started cursing.

It was dreadful, how limited his amusements were. Apart from going to work and to the football, he hardly put his foot out of doors if he could help it. If anybody took his television away he'd go insane within twenty-hour hours, out of a combination of panic and boredom. If only he'd had other hobbies, hobbies that I could have shared (or at the very least, hobbies that I found less annoying), it might all have been very different.

*Can't be cured, must be endured.* I opened the front door and entered the house.

The pile of mail on the corner table in the entrance hall was smaller than I'd expected it to be. I'd attend to that later, if there was a later in which it would still be one of my duties.

The living-room door was shut, but the sounds coming through it told me an inane game show was in progress. Presumably Liam had heard the opening and closing of the front door, but he probably thought it was one of the boys coming in. Or perhaps he'd dozed off. At least there wasn't a match on, so I'd no need to head for the pub and sit there sipping a drink I didn't want while I waited for it to be time for the reckoning.

The old Frances whispered I should take myself into the kitchen and wake him up with a propitiatory cup of tea. The new version said brutally that if he wanted a cup of tea, he could bloody well make one for himself; he must surely have learned how by this time. And besides which, if he was as mad at me as I thought he might be, I could end up getting it in the face. He'd have enough ammunition to use against me without handing him more, scalding hot in a cup.

Now for it.

# Chapter 36

Liam stared at me, groggy with sleep but too taken aback by suddenly waking and finding me here to get up from his armchair.

Unsurprisingly, the new telly in the corner was even bigger than the old one. I eyed it with amused contempt, remembering almost with surprise how cowed I'd felt by its predecessor. It had no power over me at all now – none. It was just a bigger fecking target.

Equally predictably, amazement metamorphosed into rage in his face. I watched it slither into caution. I was no longer the spineless rag he'd wiped his feet on for so long. I was aware of my wrongs and prepared to act on them. He mustn't scare me again, at least not straight away, not till I was safely buckled back into harness.

But there was relief too. I'd come back. That meant submission, a return to the proper state of things where I was his wife and responsible for keeping the house as it was meant to be. At a guess he'd hired someone to come in and clean once or twice a week, because the place actually didn't look too bad, but now he had his unpaid servant back, all that was at an end.

"You finally decided to come home, eh?" He tried to make a joke of it, but the resentment jarred horribly.

"Yes, I'm back." I couldn't make my mouth use the word 'home'.

As soon as it evidently dawned on him that he was in control of the situation again, and that it was important to start off the way he meant to go on, he stood up to make the most of his superior height. "So you couldn't stay away from your family any longer, eh?"

I realised as he got to his feet that he'd been planning for the day I was forced to crawl back to him. That he meant to get the maximum enjoyment out of it, his fury feeding on his sense of injury.

At a guess, he'd fallen asleep because he'd been drinking. A number of beer cans stood on the mantelpiece – the very same mantelpiece that he'd insisted I keep spotless, citing it as the first thing a visitor to the house would look at. I looked at it now, and my lip curled. He'd got that right, at least.

Presumably he'd showered after work that morning, but hadn't bothered to dress afterwards, just thrown on a dressing gown. The remains of a curry sat in the overflowing wastepaper basket, presumably from last night. And at some point during the intervening weeks he'd got himself a tattoo on his chest – the badge of the football team he supported. At a guess, it was the fruit of some drunken binge with his mates after a match.

I watched him lurch forward, his mouth hardening, and wondered how I could ever have cried because he didn't love me. My flesh crawled at the thought of having to perform my 'wifely duties' again.

"My return's conditional, before you go any further," I said coldly, holding up my hand to stop him in case he'd any intention of grabbing hold of me. "I walked out of here once and I can do it again, and the next time I'll not be coming back."

"The next time you'll not be *allowed* back – I'll change the locks on you!" he yelled. "What d'you think the front door is, a fecking turnstile? If you want us to be husband and wife, you'll *be* a wife, not a fecking season ticket holder!"

Even a mountain with snow on its peak can hide the chamber and shaft of an active volcano. Far below, I felt the magma shift. I waited till it stilled again.

"I've been your wife for the past thirty-four bloody years," I growled at last. "In other words, I've put up with being second best to your bloody television and with being your domestic servant, because that's all that 'being your wife' meant to me.

"Well and good. That's what's on offer, that's what I'll take. But if you want me back, I've some demands of my own, and it's take 'em or leave 'em. So that's up to you, Liam McEnally, and if you've the brain you were born with, you'll think and think hard before you answer, because I'm not joking. If you want us to have another try at this marriage of ours, that's my price."

He eyed me. Then he subsided resentfully back into his chair, waiting, and I sat in the armchair opposite him.

"One." I ticked the points off on my fingers. "You've hit me for the last time. So help me God, you lay a finger on me in anger again and I'll go to the gardaí and have you arrested, and don't you think for one minute I won't! And if that happens, the marriage is over. Finished. I'm out of here for good and all.

"Two. Well, I'm guessing you already know what 'two' is."

He flushed, looking angry and embarrassed. "I'd had a drop, right? If you hadn't...."

"Three." I overrode him. I didn't want to hear his attempt to justify raping me. "I'll keep the house clean, I'll do the housework and the cooking and everything else I always did. But you'll keep your mouth shut about what you want doing, and how and when you want it done, 'cause I don't need any lessons from you, Liam, and still less do I need you giving me orders. If what I do's not good enough for you, you either do it yourself or you hire a skivvy, because I already told you, my days as one are done.

"And four." I leaned forward. "I'm redecorating Brendan's room and I'm going to have it for my studio. I'm going to paint in it, any hour and any day I want to. I'll find myself another job and I'll buy my own stuff, but I'll go to hell and be damned before I sit through your bloody war films any more.

"As for your football, the minute it goes on I'll be out of this room and upstairs till I feel like coming down again. Don't even think about yelling up for me to be bringing you a beer, because if you want one you know where the fridge is. You probably didn't before I left, but it looks like you've found out."

He'd been leaning back, waiting for the demand he could quarrel with as a potential breach of the 'marriage contract'. When none came, he looked at first surprised, then relieved, then suspicious. "That's your lot?"

"Those are the deal-breakers," I said evenly, deciding to keep my notebook with its list in reserve. "There'll be a few more along the way, but they'll be little things, grit in the bread now and then. These four are the big ones. If you don't agree to them, or you don't keep them, I'll be away out of here, Liam. And I won't be coming back."

At least he'd taken my advice to think before he answered. He stood up again, and I tensed, but he was only going to the fridge for another beer. He sat down again and drank half of it, looking at me with a puzzled frown. "So everything else will be just... normal," he muttered. "You're not saying we, we won't be man and wife any more, not ever."

"No, I'm not saying that."

*'Love me, Lucifer.'*

*'With pleasure, Beautiful.'*

He drank a bit more. "Couldn't you use Fergal's room?"

"I could have picked Ciarán's." As the eldest, Ciarán had had the second-biggest bedroom in the house. It had the same view over the garden as ours did, and better light, whereas both Fergal's and Brendan's looked over the street and tended to be noisier. When our eldest had married and moved out, the two youngest had quarrelled so bitterly over who should step up into the bigger room that we'd solved the problem by redecorating it and keeping it for a guest bedroom.

He couldn't dispute that. Fergal had hopped out of the box-room faster than a flea as soon as Brendan moved out of his, and at a guess, the junk from the loft was still in there; the loft insulation that had prompted the clearance would have been done by now. Unless Liam had recruited the boys' help to put all the rubbish back up where it had come from, it could stay there indefinitely. They'd have to lay flooring if they wanted to move it back, which would halve the insulation's effectiveness, but there was no use me pointing that out. *I* wasn't going to lift a hand to move the bloody stuff, and I didn't see him moving it on his own.

"I'll not have you making a pigsty of it," he growled. "It's a decent little room, that. Me and the lads were thinking of doing it up and putting a pool table in it."

I let my gaze travel to the mantelpiece and the beer cans decorating it. For a man with such strong opinions on pigsties, he seemed comfy enough living in one. "Then you've a choice, haven't you? A pool table or a wife."

It wasn't all that much of a surprise when he told me not to be a fecking eejit.

After all, a pool table wouldn't cook his meals for him.

The news of my return flew round the family like wildfire. Liam could hardly wait to announce that the runaway mare had at last trotted meekly back to her stable, where the doors would be kept a hell of a lot more tightly locked in the future. It'd be a miracle if I got to keep my car once the insurance ran out.

Naturally, there would have to be a family get-together that very evening. He described it as a celebration, but I could think of nothing less worthy of celebrating. Still, I wasn't to be asked to do anything – we'd buy in pizza or fish and chips for everybody when they were all assembled, he said, and then we could all have a good bit of the *craic* and they could fill me in on everything that had been happening while I was away. The grandkids, in particular, would want to give their Granny a hug. Hadn't they missed me every day I was away?

"I missed them too," I said mechanically, staring into the bottom of a cup whose inside was stained with tannin from not being washed properly since the day I'd left.

Of *course* I'd missed them. I'd adored them since the day they were born, flesh of my flesh. But neither Deirdre nor Mairead brought them to the house that often, and I couldn't blame them. It was hardly a happy environment, where any sounds of childish enjoyment even in the garden had to be hushed for fear of disturbing Grandaddy watching the telly.

I'd done my best to be a better mother-in-law than my own had ever been, but my cautious overtures of friendship had fallen on rather stony soil. Deirdre, I thought, was the more sympathetic of the two, on the whole, but I was quite sure Mairead regarded me as a relic from the Stone Age, and blamed me for not having done more to bring my sons up as modern young men who do their share of the housework.

Ciarán was the first to arrive, with his family in tow. Deirdre hung back slightly, with six-year-old Connor and nine-year-old Aiden, who looked round-eyed at me as though expecting me to disappear up the chimney at any minute.

At least one person wasn't handling me with kid gloves. I felt the tears pricking at my eyes yet again as my tall, handsome eldest son threw his arms around me. "*Welcome home, Mammy!*"

"*Fáilte abhaile, Mamó!*" echoed the children, one eye on their mother. Deirdre was a Gaelic teacher, and they'd been brought up bilingual so that sometimes I struggled to keep up – for all that I'd been born and educated in the northwest of Ireland, where Gaelic had clung on tenaciously, at that time there hadn't been nearly the emphasis on keeping it alive and in daily use among the children that there was now. Apparently deciding I wasn't after all going to vanish like one of the Sidhe at the touch of a mortal, they ran forward and hugged me too, clinging on as hard as though I'd been snatched away into the Hollow Hills and only rescued at the touch of cold iron. Once they were through scolding me for going away and staying so long, they started telling me all about Orlando and Disneyland and the Space Centre at Cape Canaveral. What with them both talking at once and switching between Gaelic and English as the mood took them, I could hardly follow a word either of them was saying, but I fetched out the toys I'd bought them in Yorkshire, along with a box of fudge and some biscuits for their mammy and daddy. Pretty soon you'd never have guessed I'd ever been anything but safe, dull old Granny with her headphones on in the kitchen.

Brendan and Fergal had probably arranged to meet up beforehand and plan their reactions. Their greetings to me were much more restrained. I supposed they'd take their own sweet time about forgiving me. Fergal's girlfriend Ann-Marie was absent, pleading a migraine (this might or might not be true because she did suffer from them), and Mairead didn't turn up either. Presumably she was either reinstalled at home, looking after Aoife, or still at her mother's house. If the latter, it was a poor lookout for the marriage; the youngsters these days didn't have the commitment to it that we used to. Whether that was a good thing or a bad, I suppose depended on your outlook. On the one hand, most relationships go through bad patches that can be worked through if you're prepared to try hard enough, but on the other hand you don't commit yourself to drinking from a terminally fouled well for the rest of your born days, like previous unfortunate generations did.

My own fouled well was trying hard to make the occasion jovial. His forced cheer was making my teeth ache. He'd even gone to the outdoor down the road and bought a bottle of wine. I hoped Deirdre might enjoy that, because I wouldn't bloody touch it and all the lads were drinking beer.

Halfway through the evening it occurred to me why, despite everyone talking, the room seemed so quiet. The TV was actually switched off. God Above, now that was a first in this house; how come the lot of them were still breathing? But there again, probably Liam was scared that if I saw moving pictures on the screen I'd throw something else through it.

*Long may it continue*, I thought cynically, though without much hope.

It soon became obvious that the reason for my flight was to be a taboo subject. Everyone was treating it as though I'd simply been on an extended holiday and they were throwing me a welcome home party. They made polite remarks about how well I was looking, and left it at that.

The only moment of honesty came when I went into the kitchen to make myself a cup of coffee. Ciarán had been out in the garden with the boys, playing football, and seeing me alone, he came in at once, shutting the door to the lounge before he turned back to me.

"Mammy, you worried the wits out of us," he said, keeping his voice quiet. "I know something must have happened to make you go off like that. Daddy did admit he'd given you a bit of a backhand, for which God may forgive him but I won't, but I know what he looks like when he's not letting on about something.

"Now to my mind, the backhand alone would be reason enough for you upping and leaving, but you've stood him for years. You might have gone off for one week to teach him not to raise his hand to you again, but *six?* That's a long time for you, you're too bloody good at forgiving and forgetting. I'll bet his hand was hardly off you before you were blaming yourself for asking for it."

I leaned on the kitchen work-surface, watching my reflection in the glass inset in the cupboard opposite me. I could see my shoulders raised on either side of my neck, the old hunched, defensive posture. I despised myself for it. "I'm not the total wimp you think I am, Ciarán," I said at last, despite the evidence of that image. "I never did think I 'asked for it', not for one minute. And I've made it clear to him that if he does it again, that'll be the end. I've been an eejit up to now, but that's over."

"Well, at least that's worth hearing." He got himself another beer out of the fridge. "But I know you too, Mammy, and you're even worse at hiding things than Da. Yes, you texted me to say where you were and what you were doing, and I appreciated that. It stopped us worrying. But now how about you telling me what *really* happened to drive you away for all this time?"

He was right. I always was useless at hiding things, and Ciarán had always been sensitive to my moods. But I was prepared for this; absolutely the last thing I was going to tell him was that his father had raped me. The relationship between them was fragile and fractious at best, and that would be the end of it. Someday it might break of its own accord, but it wouldn't be me who swung the axe.

"You're right, there was more." I turned from my reflection, pushing down my shoulders and straightening my spine. "We had a royal falling-out over Brendan and Mairead splitting up, and you know yourself how arguments go. When you've been married as long as Liam and I have, you know just where to hit, and that night things went much too far. Some things were said that took a while to get over, and I needed to get away and think things through in peace, let myself settle down again.

"The truth is, Bridie's always been on at me to go over there and stay with her and Paul for a few days, but she was going to Australia for six weeks. Her house would be empty and she'd have to put her dog in kennels. So I asked her if I could house-sit and dog-sit till she came back. What the hell, it was a six-week holiday without having to wait on your daddy hand and foot, and in a lovely cottage in Yorkshire. Why *wouldn't* I stay the whole six weeks when the place was mine for the asking?" I forced a smile. "Not to mention giving Liam enough of a scare to make him think twice before he lifts his hand to me again."

There was enough truth in it to give it the ring of honesty, but my son's troubled frown didn't quite dissipate. Luckily, Connor ran in at that moment shouting that Aiden had kicked the football into the next-door neighbour's garden and was after climbing over the fence to fetch it.

I seized the chance, and gasped, "God, that fence is falling down and Ailinn Dunphy'll raise Cain if Aiden breaks those bloody dahlias of hers!"

Ciarán, of course, had no way of knowing that poor Ailinn next door didn't know a dahlia from a dandelion. Since her husband had had to go into a nursing home, the garden had gone to rack and ruin. She'd been telling me last time we spoke that she'd have to bring in a gardener to set it to rights before he came home, or just the sight of it would give him a heart attack that'd carry him off altogether.

Though it was accurate enough that the fence was in a bit of a bad way, just one more of the projects that Liam and the boys were going to get around to 'one of these days'.

He set down his beer-can and ran out into the garden, shouting for his eldest to get down out of that and go round to Mrs Dunphy, apologise and ask politely if he could get his ball back.

Almost at the same moment, Deirdre came in from the lounge. She and I had hardly exchanged two words during the evening, but she looked at me hard. I felt a guilty blush washing up my face, as though I'd the letter A tattooed in scarlet on my forehead. A for Adulteress.

"You've lost some weight, haven't you, Mammy?" she said politely. "Being on your own must have done you good."

Maybe it was just my imagination, but I suspected there was a lot of silent accusation going on behind that statement. My going AWOL might have done me a lot of good, but it wouldn't have done my grandsons any good at all. Children hear things, particularly when they're not supposed to; and although I didn't see them every week, by the time six weeks had passed, there could have been no hiding the fact that Granny had upped and left Grandaddy.

"It did me a lot of good, Deirdre," I replied with dignity. "And thank you for the compliment. I might see what I can do to keep on with losing weight, and then I'll have to go out and buy myself a new wardrobe. I'm sure I can depend on you for advice about what'll suit me."

"I'd be delighted." Her lips hardly moved. She always dressed beautifully, and I didn't need telling that the sort of shops she bought from wouldn't stock plus sizes, even if she'd be seen dead in there with the likes of me.

I wasn't going to hang around waiting for Ciarán to come back in and start the inquisition again. I picked up my cup of coffee (it was a bit cold by now, but still drinkable) and went back into the lounge. There I sat down beside my husband and forced myself to smile around at my beloved family.

*I. DO. NOT. QUIT.*

It was late before they all left.

Liam and I got into bed. He switched the light off and we lay side by side, still as statues, staring up at the ceiling with the past between us like a wall.

Then he turned over, and I felt his hand on my waist.

I hadn't thought it was possible to get any stiffer, but I managed it.

"Fran, it's been six bloody weeks."

Six weeks wasn't a record by any means. Over three months, we went once. But I refrained from mentioning that fact.

"You said we…"

"I know what I said." I lifted my hips and pulled up my nightdress, the one with three buttons at the neck, just over an inch apart. Fortunately, I'd visited a chemist on the way in through Dublin, and the assistant had been very helpful. The discreet tube was now hidden at the back of the medicine cabinet, for use when I feared I might get lucky.

So at least it wouldn't hurt.

I don't know if he'd been watching mucky films while I'd been away, or what. At any rate, he did make an effort. He wouldn't go so far as to put his mouth anywhere 'dirty', but he tried. And without making the mistake of going so far as to moan, I made the right kind of gasps, so he knew he was doing it right and he'd think I was so excited I couldn't wait another minute.

As he levered himself on top of me, I threw out a hand on the pillow. No hand clasped it in answer.

*'Love me, Lucifer. Love me.'*

*'With pleasure, Beautiful.'*

He was so excited by our newfound pleasure that he couldn't last long. With unutterable relief, I felt him start to come, and let out a few even more ecstatic gasps in response.

When he was done, he rolled off me. But surprisingly enough, instead of just turning away and going to sleep, he turned back towards me. "I'm sorry for the last time," he muttered. "I told you, I'd the drink on me. I've been to Confession and all."

It was years since he'd set foot in a confessional. I had to admit grudgingly that he must have been feeling bloody bad for him to do that. And his apology *sounded* sincere, though I wondered...

I waited till he was sound asleep, and then I crept to the stairs. The step halfway up and halfway down welcomed me as though I'd never been away, and I cried there silently, because of all the ridiculous things, I felt now as though I'd committed adultery with my own husband.

*'Forgive me, Lucifer. Forgive me!'*

# Chapter 37

Time passed, as time does, and I got on with the business of living, as I was duty-bound to do.

To give him his due, Liam seemed to have learned his lesson from his six weeks of wifelessness. He offered to do the washing-up most nights (and made a reasonable job of it) and even helped me to redecorate Brendan's room. When it was finally finished, we could look around with an equal sense of pride and a feeling of a job well done.

He even tried to moderate the telly-watching. I couldn't expect him not to watch the football when it was on, but that just gave me more time for painting. When there was a war film or a gory documentary on, he kept the sound down. I always took care to thank him. After all, he was trying, though his occasional forced attempts at humour still made my teeth ache and now and again, deep in my brain, a small voice said all this was far too good to be true. I'd run off, I'd made him look a fool in front of the family, and he was just going to forget about it all like this?

It took about a month for me to find another job. I ended up doing admin in the Criminal Courts of Justice in Parkgate Street. Though it wasn't exactly exciting, it let me start saving again and paid for my art materials. So I had my painting at long last, with my husband's acceptance if not enthusiasm. As I told myself constantly, things could have been worse. Things *had* been worse – far worse. The problem was, the improvement had come six weeks too late.

And Mark... I still thought of him. Constantly, with a low, helpless, dragging ache that sapped my spirits. I remembered things he'd said, the way he'd laughed, the way he'd held me and comforted me. The way he cut the toast in diagonal halves rather than rectangular, the way he'd used to whistle *Chariots of Fire* while he helped me with the housework.

The way he – *All-Holy God.* Some nights my body shuddered with longing for his. Every now and then Liam tried to improve things in the bedroom, but there were nights when it was as much as I could do to let him touch me without screaming. Still, a bargain was a bargain, and *can't be cured, must be endured*. He couldn't be expected to guess that the wife supposedly enjoying his attentions was far away in everything but body.

Christmas came, and the boys came around with their gifts on Christmas morning. Deirdre was busy at home, preparing the dinner (we were all invited over there, so I'd nothing to do but make a few batches of mince pies), but Ciarán brought Connor and Aiden. Brendan brought Aoife – Mairead had started divorce proceedings, God bless her common sense, but so far the two of them were being amicable and sensible enough about their daughter's welfare, so I was glad of that. Fergal brought Ann-Marie, who asked to visit my studio and politely admired my paintings. Though I guessed she wasn't really that interested in art, I appreciated the gesture.

Christmas went, a blur of visits and entertaining. Some of the rest of the family came to visit, and as they'd travelled all the way from the Northwest we had to put them up; one night the house was so full that Liam's cousin Dominic had to sleep on a put-you-up bed in my studio. I hardly dared shut my eyes all night for fear he'd go sleepwalking and fall over my canvases – or worse still, knock my paints onto the good new flooring, which so far had escaped accidents even during Connor's visit.

And then it was New Year. It'd been the tradition for years that we had the children to stay overnight so their parents could go out together and see the New Year in somewhere in the town.

We had the telly and a DVD set up in what had used to be Ciarán's room, but that was for later. The children still found the idea of Granny being an artist hard to grasp, so I'd bought some coloured paper and pens and some glitter in various colours. We sat at the table in a corner of the lounge, and I taught them how to draw cars and rockets and unicorns (Aoife had a 'thing' about unicorns) and paint them.

After a while, Liam took his headphones off and switched off the television – the war film hadn't even finished! – and awkwardly asked if he could join in. Which of course he could, and soon he and Aiden were arguing about which was better, Star Wars or Star Trek. *That* started because rockets weren't good enough for our eldest grandson, and he couldn't believe his ears that I'd managed to get a degree in art when I couldn't even draw the *Enterprise*.

The evening passed more quickly and pleasantly than I'd have believed possible. It would have been heartless to send the children off to bed before the chimes, so when the art stuff and all the mess had been tidied away and there was only an hour to go, I sat down on the sofa with them and read them stories about Thomas the Tank Engine.

The years rolled back, so it could have been my own boys sitting beside me. These were the same books I'd read from then (by the bitterest of ironies, put away in the loft 'just in case'), and you could tell by the covers which had been the favourites. 'Duck and the Diesel Engine' had half its pages loose.

I expected Liam to go back to the television till midnight got close, but he just sat in his armchair, watching us. I guessed the stories were taking him back a few years too, because there was an expression almost of regret on his face that I hadn't seen before.

The chimes came. If it hadn't been a raw, blustery night with rain blowing on the wind we'd have wrapped the kids up warm and taken them to the end of the street, where they could see the fireworks in the City Centre. But as it was, we were all too warm and comfortable. We could catch glimpses of the rockets from one of the windows while sipping mugs of hot chocolate. The kids were already dropping with tiredness, and their grandaddy had to carry little Aoife as we trooped upstairs afterwards. The boys were to have the double bed in Ciarán's old room, and she was to sleep on a borrowed mattress on the floor.

I should have followed Liam downstairs again, but on the landing at the turn of the stairs, I paused. There was a brass vase on the sill of the window there now, filled with stems of artificial lavender. A net curtain partly concealed the night beyond, but on impulse I pushed it aside.

This side of the house faced due East. If you looked through it at a certain angle, you could just see the lights on the towers at Poolbeg.

The rain had got heavier. Drops of it spattered on the glass and ran down, hurrying to join all the others in a mad race to the sea. I remembered with absolute clarity the rain on the window in the cottage, with me standing there and wishing – as I thought then – for the moon.

*Beware what you wish for, for you may get it...*

I pressed a hand to the glass. Somewhere out there, beyond the heaving blackness of the Irish Sea, were England and the man I still longed for, my *anam chara*, my soul-friend. "Happy New Year, love," I breathed. "And I hope you're having a good one, wherever you are. I hope you're with someone you–"

The word wouldn't come out of my mouth.

I squeezed my eyes shut on tears, while the sudden lump in my throat made it hard to swallow. *'Love me, Lucifer. Love me.'* Jesus, would I ever be through crying?

"I thought you'd fallen down the hole." Liam was standing at the foot of the stairs, watching me. "Come down and finish this coffee before it's stone cold."

"I'll be there in a tick." I hurried to the bathroom, where I washed my face and dried it, and put on a dab of perfume. Just in case, I applied a bit of lubricant as well. It was unlikely my husband would have ideas about impromptu sex in the living room – especially not when the grandchildren were upstairs – but it lasted a while, and might be needed later.

It took a minute or two for me to gather myself together. I looked at myself in the mirror and reminded myself things *had* improved, and I had to be thankful for it. I had to live with a few things that weren't quite so good, but I could put up with those; there were other lives than mine that had to be taken into consideration. Little Aoife, for one. With her Mammy and Daddy splitting up, the last thing she needed was more upheaval in the family.

Bolstered by this sensible talking-to, I was just about to go downstairs when the phone in my pocket rang.

The number wasn't one I recognised, and I'd just heard Liam downstairs answering the phone to Brendan. Sighing, I pressed the 'Answer' key. It was probably a wrong number, since I couldn't imagine anyone working in a call centre at half twelve in the morning on New Year's Day. "Hello, this is the Funny Farm in Eejits' Alley," I said. That'd end the call fast enough.

Silence.

I glanced at the screen uncertainly. The line was still connected.

"If you're one of them naughty callers, you're wasting your time," I said. I'd never had one before, but there was a first time for everything, and I'd always felt I'd like to disillusion one of the sad little shites. "I've an arse like the back end of a car ferry and a face like a squashed grape, and I'm wearing a pair of old Dunnes Stores knickers the size of a pillowcase. If they're your idea of a turn-on, you're in. Otherwise, this is the end of the conversation." My thumb moved to end the call before the abuse started. As soon as we were disconnected, I'd block the number, so there wouldn't be any repeats.

"Fran."

*All-Holy God.*

My knees buckled, and I sat down on the edge of the bath. "Mark?" I whispered, stupidly.

"I'm sorry. I shouldn' 've called. I just – need to know you're all right."

*I am now I'm hearing your voice.* "It's – it's not been too bad." I tried not to let my voice tremble, but I was clutching the phone with both hands because they were shaking so hard I thought I might drop it if I only used one. "I'm just – I'm just getting on with things. And I'm doing my painting. I thought you'd be happy about that. But how are *you?*"

"Lonely." The word hit my heart like a brick. "I miss you, Beautiful. I'm drunk and I'm on my own and I miss you."

"I miss you too, Lucifer." I swallowed. *I miss you every minute of every hour of every day.*

"I just wan'ed to hear your voice." Now that I knew, I could hear the slight slurring. "But you're still married, aren't you? And you're still not going to leave the bastard."

"He's tried, since I got back. He has, really. And things – things are better than they were." I could say that much with truth, though I still wondered occasionally.

"Good. Good. I'm glad of that – 'least I ought to be, oughtn't I? But you know what? I'm not. 'Cause if they weren't I could say *I love you* and I wouldn' be talking to a married woman. So I can't. Bastard."

"I can't leave him, Mark," I whispered, my mouth as dry as the Sahara Desert. *'I love you...'* "Thank you for ringing me. I... I hope things get better for you."

"I shouldn' have rung you," he said desolately. "All this time, I haven't rung... I didn' even know if it was your number. I'm sorry."

"Fran, Brendan sends his love, now Ciarán wants a word!" Liam's voice floated up the stairs from the lounge. The boys were seeing in the New Year together, and presumably the phone had been passed over from one to the other. I'd not the faintest idea whether to bless or curse the timing.

"God bless you, sweetheart. *Is tú mo rún, mo chara.*" Then I hit 'End' and switched the phone off. He spoke no Gaelic; he wouldn't have understood the quickly whispered words, undoubtedly wouldn't remember them.

He'd never know that I'd told him I loved him.

Ciarán was tipsy too, and inclined to be sentimental. It took about half an hour before I could get him off the phone, and every moment of that half-hour I listened with half an ear and answered mechanically.

Liam listened in, sipping his coffee – it was surprising he'd not had a beer, but perhaps he wanted to stay up and wait for me to be available. Beer would send him to sleep.

"Holy Mary, I thought I'd never get rid of him," I said, when I could finally hang up.

Liam put down his now empty mug, which he'd been idly playing with for the past few minutes, and looked at me. "Fran, we need to talk."

"At this hour o' the morning?" I looked at my watch, a sudden unexplained sense of panic welling up in me. "It's gone one o'clock!"

"This can't wait."

The words startled me out of whatever else I might have said. I just sat there, staring at him.

For a minute or two he stared at the fire, his face set. Then he turned towards me and said the last words I'd ever expected to hear on his lips. "Fran, it's not working out."

"...Not...?"

"No." Once again I saw the expression of earlier on, and now I understood it. It was the look a man wears when his cat has given birth to an unwanted litter of kittens, and he's going to take them out and drown them.

"It all went wrong when you took it into your head to do a runner." He held up a magisterial hand in case I interrupted. "I grant you, you had cause, I did something I shouldn't, and I've apologised for it. But we could have sorted that out without you running off and staying away for months.

"Well. You did, and then you had your say. You said you weren't satisfied with things, and they had to change. *I* couldn't see much wrong with the way we were, but I've gone along with what you said and I've been trying to make a few changes.

"So ever since you came back, I've been trying. I have."

"I know you have," I muttered, still not sure where all this was ultimately going. "I've appreciated it."

He sighed. "But the fact is, Fran, I'm sick and tired of tiptoeing around the place trying to keep you happy every hour of the day.

"We had a good enough life. I'll not say we hadn't. We had some good kids, and I'll always be glad about that. But when you ran away and then you came back, I finally started *looking* at you. And I don't know why the feck I was so bloody scared when you left – the place didn't fall down while you were away.

"I've been telling meself it'll take time for you to settle down. I knew it might be a while before you realised how daft you'd been, but I thought if I made an effort here and there, you'd maybe realise it a bit quicker." He rubbed his hand across his eyes. "The day you came home, Christ, I thought you'd finally come to your senses. I was glad enough to see you, but I'd had a few, and I wasn't expecting you, and… you didn't even look happy to be home. It put my back up from the start. You never even admitted you'd done anything wrong running off!"

I was so dumbfounded that when he paused, I couldn't even think of anything to say.

Liam smiled with sudden bitterness. "It's the New Year, Fran, and I don't know about you, but I think we've gone as far as we can with this marriage the way it is. I've had it to here with living with a moulting hen. It's not worth it to get a bit of housework done – *when* you can spare the time from that fecking painting of yours! – and see your face like you're going to the gallows every time I touch you. If you can't get yourself together, there's no point in us going on."

I was staring at him like he'd grown an extra head. I spent half my life cleaning the house, but I was too stunned even to resent the phrase 'a bit of housework'. "You mean… *divorce?*"

"That's exactly what I mean. The truth is, I'm sick and tired of trying to live up to your demands, and it's not like you've improved since you got back. Besides, everybody says I could do better."

Up to this point, I'd been sitting there, completely paralysed by this development. But now I shut my dropping jaw with a click and let myself feel the rage start.

"Daddy's not happy with the way Flanagan's running the business back home," he continued. It was obvious from the way he spoke that he had the speech all prepared. "I can't see Thomas ever getting his health back enough to take charge – the last time I spoke to Mary, she said it'll be God's own miracle if he lives another year.

"Daddy doesn't need the worry of the business as well as all that. So I'm thinking of going back and taking over. Fergal can finish his training and come work for me when he's done. With luck he'll be in the way of being ready to step up to management when it's time for me to step down. I've a decent few years left in me yet.

"The bottom line's this, Fran. I can't be running a business *and* doing bloody housework. I'll likely need you to lend a hand with the business, too. If you're not prepared to buckle down and do more, there's no point in us going on. We can sell the house and split the money. I'll go back home and you can do whatever the feck you like.

"We'll get a decent bit for this house. I'll give you a reasonable amount from it if you can't be sensible. I'll not want anything big, and the prices over in the west are nothing to what they are here.

"I'll see you're not short. That's only fair, and nobody can say I'm not a fair man. And I'll not make difficulties with any of the legal stuff. They say you can do the business for five hundred euro if both parties are reasonable, and I'm damned if I want fecking lawyers making a fortune out of me.

"I daresay you'll be able to afford something," he added, just a little more gruffly. Presumably he was assuming the substandard wife he was proposing to dump like a worn tyre must be feeling a little upset by this time.

In fact, if I'd had a shotgun, I'd have given him both barrels where he sat. But before I could disillusion him, he continued. "If you look out of town and don't go for anything too big, you could get a one-room flat *somewhere*. And you'll be able to do all the painting you want to, without having to think about me at all." He sounded bitter, as though aggrieved at the thought that I mightn't.

I had to draw several shaking breaths before I could speak evenly. "So, you've made your mind up, eh? In short, my choices are 'shape up or ship out'!" I think he was expecting me to cry, but just as on the last time, any tears would just have boiled off the rising magma. "You'll have talked it over with your mates over a few beers, of course, and got *their* valuable opinions. Or is it just 'Liam McEnally the arrogant bastard says this is how it's to be, so just live with it'?" A thought occurred to me then, and I sat forward, a momentary hope fighting the rage inside me. "Have you got another woman?"

"No, I'm just fecking fed up with the one I've got!" he answered flatly. "Every day since you came home it's been like looking through the bars at a fecking geriatric parrot, drooping and moping. I've had enough of it. Any decent woman would thank God her husband was prepared to have her back if she'd run off and left him the way you did me, but *you–!* Christ Almighty, the face you've had on you, you'd think you'd got out o' Kilmainham Gaol and been recaptured, and it was bad enough before.

"You've done your best around the house. I'll not deny that, you have. And with you being a woman, I don't expect you to think straight right away, so you can take your time before you decide. But Daddy's business is going to rack and ruin. I can't stand by and watch that happen – the whole family fortunes are sunk in that, and it's a decent business when the right man's in charge. If I have to go back there and set it to rights, I'll have enough on my plate without having to come home to more trouble, so I'll be damned if I'm dragging you with me all the way back to Donegal to droop and mope and bother me.

"Life won't be easy for you all on your own, but if that's really and truly what you want, you can have it."

I stood up. Part of me – I'll admit it – wanted to rant and scream like a fishwife, to vent my rage and pain at full blast. But I took several more long, quivering breaths, steadying myself, and when I finally spoke, it was in a low, controlled voice. "Right, then. Divorce it is. And you won't 'give me something' from the sale of the house – I'll take half, as it's in both our names."

I'll believe to my dying day that he expected me to cave. That I was so besotted with being his wife that the mere threat of being abandoned to my own devices, of being thrown on the world without his support, would reduce me to a tearful wreck who'd promise anything if only he'd forgive me and take me back.

The blank astonishment on his face made me wish harder than ever that I'd a shotgun to hand.

The selfish, arrogant, thankless *bastard!*

"So that's all you can find to say?" he ground out eventually, when he'd found his voice. "You're not even going to *try* being reasonable?"

"*'REASONABLE'?*" The one word escaped as a scream; I couldn't help it. But then I got myself back under control. The children were upstairs, and didn't need to hear this.

"You were the one who started this conversation, Liam. You're the one who's got it all planned out. You're fed up with me being miserable? You're fed up with me not being quite the full-time domestic skivvy you were used to? You're fed up with me having talents you've never had and finally having the guts to use 'em? You're that fed up with it all *you want a divorce?*"

I let go then, my words escaping in a scalding hiss of fury.

"So help me God, Liam, I've never in me life heard more welcome words than them last four. If you'd twice the imagination you've never had any of, you'd never get near *dreaming* how happy I'll be to walk away from you, if it means I've to starve in the gutter.

"'You could do better'? I wish you luck. I totally fecking do. I can't wait for you to find out there won't be women queuing up to service a selfish bastard who couldn't make a fecking sex-doll happy.

"You say I've been moping since I came back? Well, you're right. You're absolutely right, and I'll tell you why.

"I was in England, at Bridie and Paul's cottage. They were going to Australia and they let me house-sit. And while I was there, I had an affair with someone. And let me tell you, once I'd had a man who actually knew what to do with a woman's body, having to come back to *your* best efforts was enough to make me weep!"

Liam had been a big man when I'd married him and had put on weight since. But when he chose to, he could move extremely fast.

I hadn't a prayer of getting away, even if I'd had anywhere to run.

As the world went black, there were words written across it in letters of blazing red.

***DOMESTIC VIOLENCE.***
***ONCE IT'S STARTED, IT'S NOT FINISHED.***

# Chapter 38

I found out much later that Liam phoned for an ambulance in a panic when I didn't regain consciousness, and told them I'd had a fall. But the staff at the hospital had plenty of experience in the sort of injuries a woman gets when she falls on her husband's fist a couple of times, and it wasn't long before the Domestic Violence people turned up.

Fortunately, nothing was broken, though one wrist was so badly sprained the doctors initially thought it was fractured. But I'd a grand black eye and a split lip, and my injuries were more than enough to alert the hospital staff. They were ample to be photographed by the gardaí as evidence for an assault by my husband, too, if only I'd talk to them and make a statement. Which I was aware I should, as a good citizen if for no other reason.

By that time, however, I'd had time to think. I knew my injuries and a statement would mean a prosecution, and with any luck my bullying bastard of a husband would end up seeing the inside of a gaol on his own account. If he did, the last one to shed tears about it would be me.

But the other consequence would be that both of us would get sucked into the workings of the law, and those were painfully slow. All I wanted now was to get the hell away from him and forget he existed, not to be tied to him for as long as it took the court case or whatever to happen. So I stubbornly refused the gentle suggestions that the gardaí should be informed. I couldn't even think of going through all that. Not just yet, at any rate.

When I was finally let out, at first I wanted to go to Ciarán's. No way in hell was I going back to my house. But I had to think about what it would do to the children to see their granny in this state. In the end, I gratefully accepted the help offered by the Domestic Violence Services, and a room in a hostel.

Liam hadn't come to the hospital with me. I found out later he'd said he had to stay home because the grandkids were upstairs and couldn't be left unattended. Shortly after their parents collected them, he was gone. Pity knew where. Not that it mattered to me; I wasn't going back to that house. Not on my own, at any rate.

The news went off in the family like a bomb. At first the sympathy was all with me, but then Liam found out I hadn't told the gardaí on him and felt safe to come home and put out *his* version of the story. I could just imagine his sad, sanctimonious, self-righteous face as he broke the news that while I'd been away, I'd been whoring with some snotty English bastard at the cottage.

Of course, that changed everything. I'd been sure it would – he wouldn't keep quiet about anything that could turn *him* into the one to be pitied out of the two of us. I was saddened but not surprised when the calls from Brendan stopped altogether, and those from Fergal were short and tongue-tied. For them, it seemed, Mark's Englishness made my whoring even worse.

Ciarán met me in the park once or twice, and was appalled by what his father had done to me. The axe had finally fallen between the two of them, regardless of anything I could say to prevent it.

Though he was sympathetic to my reasons for having had an affair, and indifferent to my lover's nationality, I knew he was also shocked and disappointed in me. To be honest, I was glad he was still willing to talk to me, despite my fall from grace as a virtuous wife and mother.

It seemed he was no longer on speaking terms with Brendan, either, but he was still in touch with Fergal and kept me informed of events back home. I didn't know what they'd told the grandchildren. I hoped they'd not been too harsh on me. I could imagine Ciarán trying to be kind, but Aoife probably got told her granny was as bad as her mammy, and good riddance.

The estate agent Liam engaged thought we'd easily get €800,000 for our house. Naturally, he said, we'd put it on the market for a bit more than that and accept an offer if we had to. With a sense of utter unreality, I heard through Ciarán that Liam had signed the forms to put our home up for sale. I visited the agent and added my signature to my husband's as co-owner.

I should have been flattered and thrilled that the house sold in under a week, and for the price asked. My heart should have been beating inside me like the caged bird Liam had described, but at that point I was in mourning, in shock. I was having trouble functioning. I felt devastated with guilt, as if all this was *my* fault, the price everyone had to pay for my ten days in a stolen paradise. The ruin I'd wanted to prevent had fallen on the family after all.

The ones who'd done nothing to deserve it were going to get hurt the most: the grandkids. I'd be lucky if I was allowed to see Aoife again once the dust settled, especially if Brendan had anything to do with it. Deirdre probably wouldn't be all that surprised by my fall from grace, or keen on allowing the boys to see me again, though I thought Ciarán would be forgiving enough to put his foot down on that score; but if I followed up on my still-nebulous plans, I probably wouldn't be in Ireland all that often. Good, bad or indifferent, I'd been a part of their lives as they were growing up. True, if I'd meekly gone along with Liam's plans and returned to Donegal I'd have seen them far less, but at least I'd have still been part of the family. Now I was planning to forcibly wrench myself away, and must seem selfishly indifferent to their pain. I wasn't, I never could be, but what other choice did I have?

As for my own boys, I could only hope that one day they'd forgive me, even if they never understood. And, too, that if they took anything from this episode bar resentment, it would be the message that even the most placid of women can only be pushed so far. Brendan must already have found that out for himself, but it might stand Fergal in good stead one day.

There were no more calls from Mark. I wondered if he regretted that call, made on impulse when he was out of his head with the drink. A hundred times I went to delete the entry from the call log; a hundred times I stopped myself, hitting 'Cancel' at the very last second.

Finally, I decided to meet Liam. But not alone, and not in the house. I rang Fergal (who was still on speaking terms with his father) and asked him to arrange a meeting in a neutral, public place, and to be with us while we talked.

And to tell his daddy, if Liam proved reluctant, that there was still time for me to have that chat to the gardaí.

It wasn't until I saw him again that I realised I was finally free of him. As a matter of fact, I hardly recognised him. He just looked like some burly, ill-tempered stranger, a bull herded into the crush pen.

We were in a pub, one of the many on the High Street that was crowded for lunchtime. In a place like this, not even Liam would dare hit me again – not with a dozen potential witnesses to back me up.

He sat down with poor grace. Fergal, who looked as if he wished he were anywhere else, offered to buy us a drink. It was the first time he'd seen my face after his daddy had decorated it with his fists, and he kept glancing at it, wincing, even though a lot of the bruising had faded and the cut on my lip was healing nicely.

"No need," I said. "I've not got much to say."

"Well, say it then, and be damned to you!" growled Liam.

"Well, first and foremost, like I said before, I want half of the money for the house." I sat back in the chair. "But now I want a guarantee of the times you'll be out of the place so I can go in there and get what's mine.

"There won't be much. The last thing I want is to be reminded of living with you. But there's a few things that matter to me, and I want to get them without you being there to be tempted to have another go.

"I'll make sure there's someone with me, too, just in case. The Domestic Violence people help out with things like that, when a woman's safety's concerned."

I could tell he hated his attack on me being discussed in front of anyone else, particularly our son. I wondered bitterly how he'd look if I casually dropped it into the conversation was that the real reason I'd done a runner (and, by extension, taken to whoring) was that he'd raped me too.

"You can give Fergal here a list of the times and he'll send it to me. – You can do that, can't you?" I wasn't being all that fair to our youngest either, using him like this, but at that moment I couldn't afford to be choosy about what weapons I used.

Reluctantly, he nodded.

"And one other thing." I sat forward again. "When you were telling me you'd had enough of me, you said you'd be fair with the money if we split up. Now I'm not stupid, Liam. I deal with our finances, and I *know* how our affairs stand. I'm telling you now, you *will* be fair with the money, including what's in our savings an' all. Once the house is sold and the lawyers and that are paid off, you'll split the profits from that and everything else straight down the middle to the last penny. You'll send me copies of the receipts for the expenses and all, so I can check off what's been spent on what. Because if I find out you've tried to do me out of one bloody euro, I'll be into the nearest garda station before you can say 'divorce', and you can spend your half on legal fees trying to keep you out of a prison cell."

"You'd blackmail your own husband after I said off my own bat I'd be fair to you?" he spat.

"No, Liam. I'll blackmail my *ex*-husband after he put me in the hospital. And that's the last time I propose to insult myself with the sight of you, so I'll spare you the goodbyes.

"Fergal, I'll hear from you."

And with that, I stood up and walked out of the pub into freedom.

When I got the all-clear times from Fergal, I spent two afternoons going through the house like a whirlwind. I'd not been in my job long enough to be off probation, and I'd given in my notice as soon as I got out of the hospital; I was leaving Dublin for good. I took a couple of days off work so I could go into the house while it was empty, and a volunteer from the refuge stood guard to make sure no one came in to interfere. The charity shops for miles around benefited.

Jesus, I had an absolute beano with the stuff in Fergal's room. *Vengeance is mine*, I thought again and again as one piece of reusable junk after another was stuffed into black bags. Any rubbish I came across in the process, of course, was left for Liam to deal with, though I made an exception for a couple of pieces against which I held a particular grudge. The headrests were the first to go into the bag destined for the local tip, and the ceremonial tin of solidified tubes of glue rattled for the last time as it followed them.

At last I stood by the gateposts with a couple of suitcases containing everything that still mattered to me. Not much, for thirty-four years (clothes, mostly, with my legal documents, some photos and one or two bits and pieces including the box of 'coffee spoons'), but now I was looking towards the future. And soon I'd have my share of over €800,000 to make that future a hell of a lot more comfortable, as long as I used it wisely.

You could see the tops of the Poolbeg Towers from here. Behind them, the February wind was blowing the clouds offshore. Towards England, where Paul and Bid were already getting ready to welcome me. I'd been reluctant to turn to them again for help so soon, but their reaction had taken away any worries I'd had on that score.

We'd already talked on the phone. I wanted somewhere to rest for a while, but I also wanted someone to give me advice on plans I was putting together – plans about using the money to start a little business of my own somewhere. England or Ireland, I didn't know, that would depend on which side the coin fell that I'd yet to toss. But I was dreaming of opening my own art gallery, where I could showcase local artists as well as perhaps even selling some of my own work. I had contacts from my old jobs, good people I could get in touch with who'd be willing to let me sell their stuff, and I still got requests from the shop in Middleham now and again on my own account. I'd been doing my homework, and learned that having additional merchandise printed of my original works – keyrings, mugs, placemats, that kind of thing – could increase my income considerably. If I picked the right place, a craft centre maybe, and put the work in, I could make a go of it.

And I would. I was resolved about that. Alone if need be, I would survive and I'd succeed.

I turned to look at the house one more time. I'd been married thirty-four years, and lived here for most of them, but this was the end. Divorce in an Irish court took five years, but it didn't matter. No matter how the law dragged its feet, this was the end. After forcing myself to come back, with all the attendant anguish and heart-wrenching, it had all been for nothing.

I looked back towards the towers. The ferry left in about two hours.

"I'm coming, Lucifer."

Once again I was sitting in the queue to board the ferry. Once again my future was a blank page, but it was now one on which I could decide what got written – and who wrote it.

I took a deep breath and opened my phone. There was still a call record from New Year's Eve.

I clicked on it and went to 'Text'.

"Middleham Church hasn't been deconsecrated. Be there on Saturday if you can, Lucifer, three o'clock prompt. At your own risk." That would give him three days in which to decide how to react.

Then I hit 'Send', closed the phone, and started the engine.

# Chapter 39

Well so, here I was again. A couple of months older and wiser, with everything I'd tried to achieve lying ruined behind me. They said, truly enough, that 'Man proposes, God disposes', and the past four weeks had shown me the truth of that.

Even now, though, I couldn't be sorry for what I'd done. Fortified with the strength my love affair with Mark had given me, I'd given what was left of my marriage my best shot. I wasn't conceited enough to think its eventual failure was solely down to me, but I could honestly say I'd done everything I humanly could to save it. Now, I was finally free to think about my own happiness at last.

It wouldn't be unalloyed. Certainly not at first. My fall from grace had hurt others, and there was no escape from that and no cure for it either. But once you realise you've a lot fewer days in front of you than you have behind you, you start realising your responsibility to make the most of them – a responsibility I'd so nearly sidestepped under the excuse of 'I Do Not Quit'.

# A COTTAGE CALLED TRANQUILLITY 337

The three days had passed with agonising slowness. I'd had no reply to my text.

This in itself meant nothing. I knew it was the right number, and that it had been read. I'd received no apologetic message saying he couldn't make it.

That meant – unless I was completely wrong about Mark from start to finish – that he'd show up. What would happen then would at least partly dictate where I went from here.

I hadn't chosen the best weather to come back to Yorkshire. It had snowed recently, and though the roads were mostly clear, what was left of it was piled in dirty heaps against the hedges. The fields around the town were as pied as a lapwing, only one or two showing the first mist of green tips where an early crop was pushing through.

Still, there were signs of hope. In the border at the cottage, among the lavender that had been trimmed back to neat cushions, pale crowds of snowdrops were nodding. In between them, there were the first spears of daffodils, as well as the shoots of the early-flowering bulbs getting ready for their turn: crocus and grape hyacinth, miniature narcissus and iris, not a whit deterred by the cold.

I wasn't quite as impervious. As I turned into the church gateway, I was snuggled up in a woolly hat and scarf, my hands thrust into the pockets of my serviceable old duffel coat – a garment that might have been specifically designed to repel the most determined incubus. Still, even here it seemed Mother Earth was already about her business. It was too early for the flowers to emerge yet, but dense clumps of daffodil shoots under the trees showed that later on there'd be a tremendous display, and the ground in between was clotted with snowdrops. A blackbird perched briefly on a tilted gravestone, eyed me for a moment and then flew off with a chatter of warning.

I'd got here a few minutes early. Deliberately, I'd dawdled around the square until my watch said it was time to move. The nights were starting to draw out just a little now, and the empty sky above was the pale blue of a mistle thrush's egg.

The church porch was empty. For a horrified moment I thought the door was locked, but it gave and let me in, the squeak of the hinges and the rattle of the heavy metal latch sounding thunderous in the silent church behind it.

It felt as though it required an actual act of will to make my head turn to take in the rows of pews before the altar.

Mother of God, he was there. He didn't look around, but every line of him was familiar to me.

The church was very dim. The shadows were gathering fast, swallowing the altar at the far end of the nave. The colours in the tall, arched windows above it were muted almost out of existence by the dying light behind them. The air was still and cool, smelling faintly musty: the essence of old hymnbooks and even older sanctity.

Up beside the altar there was now a magnificent flower arrangement. More flowers adorned the top of the baptismal font, sitting defiantly under the ornate, carved cover suspended on chains above it.

Beside the lectern there was a fat white candle on a stand, circled by a wreath of lilies and carnations. The candle was burning, a point of brightness in the dusk. The light winked on the points of the brass eagle opposite that supported the Bible on braced wings.

In such a complete hush, it was impossible to take a step without it being audible from one end of the church to the other. He must have heard me come in, and now he must be able to hear it as I walked up the nave.

Old habits still died hard. As I stopped at the end of the pew he was sitting in, I bobbed a bit of a genuflection.

The wretch didn't even turn his head to look at me. He was sitting bolt upright, both hands thrust into his pockets. As I sat down beside him, he just went on staring at the altar, as though hypnotised by the two crowned coats of arms embroidered on the green damask frontal.

*'Love me, Lucifer.'*
*'With pleasure, Beautiful.'*

Neither of us said anything. Outside, the blackbird scolded again, but apart from that, there was silence.

This wasn't at all how I'd imagined our reunion. That said, it was hardly fair to hold it against him for not saying a word when it seemed the cat had got both our tongues.

Still, one of us had to start the conversation, if we weren't going to spend the whole evening sitting here like a pair of empty milk bottles. "I wasn't sure you'd come," I said at last.

"You summoned me, Mistress." His tone was so full of shadows I couldn't even start to decipher it, but you could have cut the tension in it with a pocket-knife.

After another pause, I spoke again. "I've got something to show you." I added, with a wobbly grin, "I hope it's not too late."

My hands were in my pockets too. I took them out and pulled the woolly mitten off the left one.

He stared at the bare, pale indentation where the gold bands had sat for thirty-four years. "Tell me those are gone for good."

"Yes. Am I too late?"

"You finally saw sense."

Another brief silence. "No, I didn't."

He drew out his right hand and placed it on his thigh alongside mine, not quite touching.

I fixed my gaze on the altar. The green and gold blurred as the tears welled up. "After all that. God and all His Angels, after all that. He dumped me."

He finally turned to stare at me. *"Your husband dumped you?"*

"After a manner of speaking. He told me I could either get my act together or get out. I decided to get out. I think he was surprised. He certainly wasn't very pleased." I looked back at him, drinking in the sight of him when I'd thought I'd never see him again. Even in the poor light, he'd probably be able to see the last, faint blue shadows of faded bruises on the left side of my face, where the worst had lingered. Lipstick might have gone some way towards hiding the small scar on my mouth, but I couldn't be having with that. He had to see what I was now, and take me or leave me.

His face had darkened with shock and fury. "Did *he*…?"

"Yes. I told him about you, and about how much better you were than him."

"Oh, my love. Oh, my poor, lovely girl." He touched my face gently. "*Whatever* possessed you to tell him? You should never have gone back to him in the first place."

"Hindsight's a grand thing, isn't it?" I said ruefully. "'It seemed like a good idea at the time,' as the bishop said to the actress. And at least my conscience is clear now. Clear*er*, anyhow."

I don't think he could help it. Even with the rage at what Liam had done to me, I could still make him laugh.

At last, tentatively, he put his arms around me. He could, now, even in church, because to all intents and purposes I wasn't a married woman any more. There would be legal processes and they'd take time, but I'd taken the first and most important step. And I'd done it all on my own.

I wasn't sure kissing me was entirely on, even in a Protestant church, even though he was unbelievably gentle. But the touch of his lips on mine and the feeling of being drawn against him began to thaw out the frozen lump inside me that had been there ever since that day in Richmond.

When he paused to let me draw breath, I looked up at him seriously. "On New Year... you said you loved me."

"I did. And I do." He kissed me again. "I love you, Frances McKenna."

"I think I loved you the minute I saw you, Mark."

"Then you must be very fond of mud."

"Not when you were all muddy, you eejit." I swatted him. "When you washed yourself."

"You mean when I revealed myself in all my demonic handsomeness."

"Well. Close." I snuggled up and sighed contentedly. He smoothed his hand across my hair and ignored the implied insult. "I wish I'd said before you left. I wanted to, so much, but I just ... couldn't. In case you didn't feel the way I did."

He sighed. "Christ. So we were both idiots, then." He dropped a kiss on my forehead. "Are you staying at the cottage again?"

"For a while. I've plans, you see. Liam's sold the house. When everything's done, he's going to send me my half. Then I'll be able to start out."

I felt him go still, listening. I had plans. Did they involve him?

"I'm going to stay here for a little while, till things settle down," I went on, rubbing idly at the place where my rings had been. I'd sold them in a jeweller's in Dublin and divided the amount I'd got from them between the grandkids. "I like it here, and I'm with Bridie and Paul. They want to help me get myself settled and make a good start over. There's official stuff to go through, but Paul's helping me with it. Then when I've looked around for a bit, I'm going to set up an art gallery. On my own. I've a bit of experience and some contacts, and if I rent a small place, maybe with its own living place attached, I should have enough to set up. I need to prove to myself that I can do it.

"And I can. I know I can."

Another silence. I listened to his breathing, just in case it stopped at any point, as my heart seemed likely to. On New Year's Eve he'd said he loved me, but anything could have happened in his life in the intervening weeks. At any rate, I'd hardly begun to emerge from the wreck of my marriage. The ice wasn't anywhere near thick enough yet to even think about bearing the weight of another relationship. The best I could hope for was a thread of hope to hold onto.

"Did you find anyone?" I asked at last, my voice very small in the silence.

*Love me, Lucifer.*

"No." He wrapped his hand around mine. "No. I did not find anyone. I tried a few times, but they all failed the one acid test."

I peeked up at him. "They all took one look at you and realised they'd forgotten an urgent appointment?"

He sighed, laughed and shook his head as if wondering why he'd come back. "I told each of them I'd hurt my ankle and not *one* of them mentioned getting a parrot from Amazon." He kissed my forehead again. "Which just went to prove there never *could* be anyone like you."

Smiling, I dropped my head back to his shoulder and nestled closer. "I've been painting, like I told you," I said, unable to cope with feelings of that intensity yet. "I got another little job, but I gave it up before I came over. I don't think I'll be going back to Dublin much, except to see the grandkids sometimes. When it all came out about me going off the straight and narrow, Brendan disowned me. Fergal might get over the shock one day, but it'll take time. Ciarán ... well." I sighed. "He tried to understand, God love him.

"How about you? I've wondered that much how you've been getting on."

"I changed jobs. Got tired of the old place. I'm based in Northallerton now. It's the same firm, but the job's different. I got a promotion, too."

"Aw, well done you! Northallerton? That's not far away, is it? At least I didn't have you racing all the way up from London."

There was another silence, but this one was peaceful. I shifted a bit, turning into him so that I could wrap my right arm around him. After a few minutes, though, he'd obviously been thinking things over and not found a satisfactory answer to all of them. "So how come your unpleasant husband decided enough was enough? I'd have thought he'd have been delighted to have his unpaid servant back again."

I said nothing for a minute. I knew he was blaming himself for me getting battered, the dear eejit, but I owed him the truth. "I couldn't get over you, Mark. I thought I'd be able to if I tried hard enough, but the heart for it wasn't in me. I suppose it was obvious enough, if you were looking. Some times more than others." I shuddered, and he tightened his arms around me even further.

"He must have been planning it for a while. On New Year's, right after you called, he said he wanted to talk. That was when he dropped it on me. He's going back to Donegal, to take over running his Daddy's firm. The only way he'd take me with him was if I went back to being his skivvy with a smile on my face, and agreed to help out with the business – probably doing the admin or something, to save costs. Otherwise, we were through."

He shook his head in wonderment. "And he expected you to go with him on those conditions?"

"He did. He was *most* put out when I didn't jump at the chance. Bejeezus, you'd have thought I was the most unnatural, ungrateful sod in Christendom.

"I told him I wanted the divorce, and I told him why. I told him a few other home truths as well, but I think it was telling him about you that put the tin lid on it."

"Frances McKenna, has anyone ever told you you have the survival instincts of a lemming?"

I admitted it wasn't the brightest thing I'd ever done. But there had been one good thing about it: he'd put me in hospital, and the staff guessed what had happened.

"He put you in hospital, and you think that's a *good* thing?"

"Well, not that exactly. But the thing is, you see, I could have reported him to the gardaí. I still can. And unless he plays fair and square with the money for the house, and gives me a fair half of our savings, I've told him I bloody well will, and damn the consequences."

"You would? Really?" He couldn't quite keep the doubt out of his voice.

"Yes, I would." Mine in reply was grim. "I didn't just give him thirty-four years of my life, I damn well near broke my heart going back to him because that was what I thought I ought to do. He took all of it and threw it in my face, so now he's going to pay for my future. As for the rest... well, 'Yesterday's history, tomorrow's a mystery.' But whatever comes, I'm planning to spend the rest of my life being a happy woman."

"I'm glad to hear it." He kissed my forehead and asked when we could meet up again.

*Love me, Lucifer.*

"You remember the Bolton Arms, in Leyburn?" We'd drunk there once or twice, and liked the place. And with him being based in Northallerton, it was well within driving range. I didn't know exactly how far away it was, but I'd seen it on the road atlas, so it couldn't be that far.

"I think I could find it again."

*With pleasure, Beautiful.*

"Tomorrow night. Eight. And don't be late." I looked up at him again, and I knew my face was alive with joy. "No excuses accepted, Lucifer."

"Come hell or high water. Bolton Arms, eight o'clock. I'll be there."

How was I supposed to turn away from that expression? I lifted my face to his. Resist temptation be damned. He was the Devil, after all. Temptation was what he was all about!

Our lips met, and that was all it took. Moments later, the two of us were clinging together like ivy on an oak tree, hands in each other's hair, bodies straining to make contact.

It probably wasn't appropriate in a church, but I still reckoned God was a lot more open-minded than the Church gave Him credit for. After all, He'd invented sexual attraction in the first place.

Maybe Mark would ask me to go back to his place after the meal. Maybe he wouldn't. To be honest, I wasn't sure I was ready for that just yet, but I knew that as long as I told him the truth, he'd be fine with me either way.

We had to take this slowly now, had to re-establish our relationship; had to work out whether there was something between us that could endure. I believed there was, but it would take time to be sure. Now, at last, there was time. And hope.

Christmas was long past. Mine had passed in a blur, the very essence of 'all sound and fury, signifying nothing.' But maybe even Lucifer qualified for a belated Christmas present, if he'd been good.

I'd been given something more wonderful than any Christmas present.

I'd been given back my future.

# Epilogue

"Your young man's just arrived, Fran!"

Bridie's shout up the spiral stairway set my heart thumping wildly with joy. I gave myself a last spray of perfume – the special perfume he'd bought me with the throw and the naughty lingerie – and almost threw myself bodily down the stairs in my hurry.

"He won't thank you for breaking your neck, *alannah!*" scolded my friend, catching me at the foot. "Eh, but you do look nice. He's just what you need to help you exorcise your demons."

The Tart reminded me that I had a lot of experience in exercising my particular demon and didn't need any help in that department. I was too happy to quibble. Besides, when Mark got going, the very *last* word I was likely to want to use was 'Exorcise'.

"That he is!" I said cheerfully.

Bridie and Paul had met Mark a few weeks ago when they came to look at the shop in Richmond I was negotiating to rent, and taken to him immediately. Bridie said afterwards there was no point in him driving from Northallerton and back to see me. Next time he'd a few days free, he could stay at the cottage overnight.

"He can always sleep on the sofa," she said breezily. And gave me a very large wink, unseen by Paul, who was reading *The Times*.

I'd a feeling Bridie and The Tart would get on like a house on fire if they ever met up.

My fingers were clumsy on the latch of the back door. Sharp was eager to come out, but I didn't want to share the moment, even with him. Paul called the dog to heel, letting me slip out alone.

The sun was still low in a sky blanched with cold. Its light sparkled on the hoar-frost on the lantern by the door. The bright freezing air struck me, so fresh it was almost joyful. But maybe that was just me.

Mark was just coming up the steps to the patio. For Paul's benefit, his expression was that of a first-time visitor, faintly apprehensive of having come to the wrong house. When the time came, he'd pretend he'd never met Sharp before. Luckily, the dog welcomed every visitor like a long-lost member of the family, so nobody should notice anyway.

My lover was wearing a dark blue coat I hadn't seen before, and smart trousers – a far cry from what he'd worn the last time he was here. Though on reflection, the last time he was here he'd rarely worn much at all while we were indoors.

*Better not let **that** slip out in the conversation,* said The Tart with a grin.

He was wearing the reflective sunglasses, too, necessary against the wintry glare over the open fields. At that moment, he caught sight of me waiting for him, and pushed them down his nose so that he could look at me over the top of them and smile.

God, he was gorgeous.

We'd met up quite a few times over the past couple of weeks. Gone for walks, when the weather permitted, or visited historic sites around Richmond. Once or twice we'd gone to a posh restaurant and had a meal, and on each occasion, he'd driven me home to the cottage and dropped me at the gate, not without a kiss that turned into quite a lot of kisses. Each time it had taken all of my self-command not to ask him to take me somewhere else, with The Tart yelling, *He's got a bloody flat twenty miles away, what the feck are you waiting for?*

I wasn't quite sure what I'd been waiting for. Some of it was apprehension, some of it was caution, but a lot of it was to do with showing him who I was now. I was my own person. I'd learned to stand on my own two feet at last. Maybe my progress would be wobbly now and then, but I was getting there. I didn't need anyone to lean on any longer, and could make my own decisions about what to do and when. Just as he'd prophesied, on that long-ago evening when we'd sat side by side on the grassy bank by the roadside: I had the right to say *this is what I want* or *this is not what I want.* Even when it applied to him.

Slowly, I was finding my confidence. Investing in my future, with all the risks that entailed. Becoming someone more than an unwanted ex-wife; becoming a woman who could offer him a love worth having. I wasn't fully there yet, but I was working on it. And, wonderfully, he was willing to wait; willing to bear with me, loving and wanting and tempting me, while understanding and respecting my reasons for keeping him – more or less – at arm's length.

Until now.

The red-gold throw had been folded up and put away carefully in the bottom of my wardrobe in the cottage when I first moved back in. But now it was back on my bed upstairs. Tonight, I was going to unwrap the best present life could ever offer me.

*I bet you'll get stuffed better than a turkey,* said The Tart gleefully. As I threw myself into his arms, his mouth on mine suggested that he was thinking along the very same lines.

God, I did like a man who was quick on the uptake.

We came up for air eventually, with Bridie crying at us through the window to come in before we froze to death, and Sharp yelping to be let out to greet the new arrival.

"Happy very belated Christmas, sweetheart," said Mark, smiling down at me. "I have a little present for you later."

"I was hoping you'd say that." I watched his face register what I meant. "Only, if it's what I hope it is, it's not so little. In fact, you could easily write 'A Present from Middleham' on it in capital letters."

His eyes darkened with desire, and my own flamed in answer to it. "I want you so much. If you're ready. And you're sure."

"Ready, willing and able. Tonight." I kissed him again. "Love me, Lucifer."

"With pleasure, Beautiful."

# Glossary

## GAELIC (IRISH) TERMS

Acushla - Darling

Alannah – My child

Amadán – Fool

Diabhal – Devil

Gossoon – Young boy, lad

# Author's Biography

Born and still living in Birmingham, but would follow her roots back to Ireland if only the Lottery would be obliging enough to come up with the right numbers.

In the meantime, being retired, she's finally got enough time to spend writing. Most of the effort goes into an epic fantasy series that probably won't be the next 'Game of Thrones', but hey, she has fun with it anyway!

# UpLitPress.co.uk

Publishing books that make you glad to be part of the human race.

Get a free anthology when you join our mailing list

Printed in Dunstable, United Kingdom